DRESSED FOR THE PART …

Judy stood up to fasten the suspenders to the stockings, the long, now taut, suspenders sexily emphasizing her firm thighs, pulling the stockings tightly upwards. The tiny black silk knickers, decorated with even tinier red rosebuds, were the last item of lingerie to be put on. These she stepped into, then bent over to pull them up. She twirled around briefly, asked if she now met my requirements, and when told that yes, she certainly did, she got back onto the bed, assuming once more her original kneeling position, her silk-covered rear well raised.

I began to warm to my task. I stroked her bottom again, the silk feeling crisp and cool beneath my hand, the material a caress between my fingers and her bare buttocks. I ran my hands down Judy's silk-covered legs, and back up again, slipping my fingers beneath the suspenders, enjoying the different textures, warm, soft flesh, warm, crisp, taut elastic. The only thing left to do with the knickers now was to remove them …

Also in paperback from New English Library

The Pearl: volume 1
The Pearl: volume 2
The Pearl: volume 3
The Pearl Omnibus
The Oyster: volume 1
The Oyster: volume 2
The Oyster: volume 3
The Oyster: volume 4
The Oyster: volume 5
The Oyster Omnibus
Rosie – Her Intimate Diaries: volume 1
Rosie – Her Intimate Diaries: volume 2
Rosie – Her Intimate Diaries: volume 3
Rosie – Her Intimate Diaries: volume 4
Rosie – Her Intimate Diaries: Omnibus
The Black Pearl: volume 1
The Black Pearl: volume 2
The Ruby: volume 1
The Ruby: volume 2
Arousal
House of Lust
The Uninhibited
Summer School 1: Warm Days, Hot Nights
Summer School 2: All-Night Girls
Summer School 3: Hot to Trot
Summer School 4: Up and Under

In the Pink: Stripped for Action

Tony Andrews

NEW ENGLISH LIBRARY
Hodder & Stoughton

First published in Great Britain in 1995 by Hodder & Stoughton
A division of Hodder Headline PLC

A New English Library paperback

10 9 8 7 6 5 4 3 2 1

A CIP catalogue record for this title is available from the British Library

ISBN 0340 63491 X

Typeset by Avocet Typeset, Brill, Bucks
Printed and bound in Great Britain by
Cox & Wyman Ltd, Reading, Berkshire

Hodder and Stoughton
A division of Hodder Headline PLC
338 Euston Road
London NW1 3BH

CONTENTS

CHAPTER ONE: THE ORIGINAL MODEL

I'd just got back to the office from Gerry's, and I was well boozed. Working in Soho had many advantages, including the fact that I could spend my lunchtimes at Gerry's if I felt like it. Most days I did. I'm talking about the old Gerry's, of course. After Gerry Campion's time (he started it, and that's when I first joined) but now I'm talking about while Dee and Brian were still there. While it was still in its original premises in a basement in Shaftesbury Avenue. It's never been the same since it moved around the corner. Well, not in my opinion.

It was always a haven away from the pressures of magazine publishing. A quiet place for a drink and a bite of decent food at reasonable prices, where one could be sure of meeting a friend or two, listening to Dee's gossip and banter, and just plain relaxation. It was what we used to call a drinking club, in that, as a member, you could buy alcohol throughout the afternoon, when the pubs were closed, before Britain's licensing laws were updated. In the evening you were unlucky if you couldn't find an attractive and willing fuck there. That's where I met my wife. You can't ask much more than that, can you?

I'd got back to the office early because I had to get together with Fred, the managing director, and interview applicants for the sub-editor's vacancy we had on one of the magazines. Someone had selected a short list of three, and Fred and I were going to make the final selection. They were all women. No reason for that especially, although, in my opinion, women make better subs than most men do. They're far more meticulous. And they're usually cheaper. So I'm a chauvinist. I'm also a businessman. Girlie magazines have to show a profit too, you know. One of the three applicants had been trained by *Reader's Digest*, and as far as I was concerned, she was the one. They don't come better trained than that. Not in the UK anyway. In the final analysis, the *Reader's Digest* girl had long legs, encased in laddered black tights, and Fred fancied her, so we were both keen to have her, albeit in different ways. She got the job. For the record, she didn't last long. Her idea of cutting an article that was too long by a couple of hundred words was to cut out the sexy bits. This because she disapproved of them. Her privilege, but not good subbing of an article for a men's-interest magazine. I guess *Reader's Digest* wouldn't have liked it. The copy, I mean. Fred didn't get to fuck her, either. She was a lesbian. Some you win …

I've worked in girlie magazines for over twenty years. I began as a humble freelance writer, specializing in writing about sex. When I started writing, I actually wanted to write about motor cars. I soon discovered that every newspaper, magazine, and radio and television programme in the country not only had a motoring correspondent, but there were also probably four people lined up waiting for him or her to die. So I had to find a different subject. One that wasn't quite so overcrowded. I'm talking about the Sixties. Sex was just coming in. You know, everyone remembers the Sixties. The Beatles. The Pill. The Swinging Sixties. The Establishment. Carnaby Street. The Ad Lib. The Trat. Grass. Miniskirts. It was a great time for girlie magazines. I rose from humble freelance to humble deputy editor. To arrogant editor. To arrogant (and rich) publisher. I ran girlie magazine empires in Britain and America. I had a ball. And a lot of sex.

Hence the title of this series. *In The Pink*. It doesn't mean –

as you quite reasonably may think – healthy. The pink refers to that pretty, pink-coloured, warm, wet flesh inside girls' vaginas. Are you with me? Good.

They do it differently now. All of the girlie magazines currently published in Britain are – in my opinion – tat. Produced by wankers, for wankers. In my day they had style. We made so much money, we could – and did – afford the best writers, illustrators, photographers and cartoonists in the world. And, of course, editors. Girlie magazines these days basically don't carry words. What words they do have are illiterate. The magazines are full of badly-photographed pictures of unattractive girls. The pages are laid out on computers by people who are key-strokers, using software layout packages. None of them have ever been to art school. They wouldn't know magazine design if they fell over it. It's still different, thank God, in America. But enough of that. This book is about the days when everyone but everyone – was having the time of their lives. There was full employment, girls dropped their knickers before you had even got around to suggesting it, and the girlie magazine business was a different way of saying heaven.

My offices were in Old Compton Street, not a million miles away from the old Marshall Cavendish offices. They've moved a street or two away now, of course. We were almost opposite the original Wheelers. Wheelers is still there, thank God. The old L'Etoile as it used to be has gone, though. As has the White Elephant. Not to mention the Trat and all its offspring. The first time I went to those Old Compton Street offices to see Fred, in my capacity as a freelance, and his then as editor-in-chief, the production editor – a delightful young lady called Carla – came into his office. I had dealt with her over the telephone for some time, but I'd never met her. Fred introduced me.

'Tony,' he said, 'this is Carla. Our production editor. She

loves your writing.' I mumbled something that I hoped was appropriate, looking at my shoes. 'And,' he continued, 'she's got great tits. Carla, show Tony your tits.' Carla turned towards me as ordered, and lifted up her sweater. She wasn't wearing anything underneath it. She did indeed have great tits. Beautiful, young, firm, pointed, brown-nipple-ended, suckable tits. 'What do you think?' asked Fred. 'Mmmmm,' I said, speechless with desire, lust, and filthy thoughts about what I would like to do to those tits. 'Thank you, Carla,' said Fred. Carla looked at me and smiled. 'My pleasure, Tony,' she said. 'Any time,' she said. She left. Suddenly I was speechless again.

I took a deep breath. 'Do you think she means it?' I asked Fred. He looked puzzled. 'Means what?' he asked. 'You know,' I said. 'I mean, when she said "any time," do you think she meant that, er, um...' 'Oh,' said Fred. 'I'm with you. You're asking if you can fuck her. The answer is yes. Of course. Everyone else does. And she was in love with you before you met her. She not only loves your writing, she says your voice makes her come in her knickers. She made me promise to call her into my office when she knew I had a meeting with you today. Just tell her where and when. She's not a bad fuck. And she gives terrific head. Are you ready for lunch?' We lunched at the Trat. Fred didn't eat much, but he drank enough to make up for it. He was a generous host, and I enjoyed my meal. As soon as I had finished my zabaglione, Fred ordered coffee and large brandies. If I remember correctly – and that became increasingly difficult – it was the first of eight rounds of large brandies, after which Fred was in no state to go back to the office. Nor, of course, was I, except that I didn't have an office to go back to. We went on to Muriel's, otherwise known as the Coronary Club. Or the Colony Club, if you prefer its real name.

I'd been pouring my brandies into the pot that one of the Trat's plants was growing in, so I was slightly more sober than Fred. Mostly because I wanted to get to a telephone, and call

Carla, and ask if she was free to have dinner with me. For dinner, read fuck. I made my excuses and left, as they used to say in *The News of the World*, claiming urgent copy deadlines. Fred was happy to stay where he was. I was happy to get away. I found a phonebox, and the right change. 'Tony,' she said, when I got through and propositioned her. 'What a delightful idea. Shall I come up to you in Hampstead?' She knew where I lived because of telephoning me there, and sending me proofs, and stuff like that. 'If you like,' I said. 'What's a good time for you?' 'Oooh. About seven?' she said. 'Great,' I said. 'I'll book us a table.'

Later that evening we had a decent meal at one of Hampstead's cheaper restaurants, and Carla accepted my invitation to come back for coffee and a liqueur. She professed an interest in playing backgammon when I suggested it, and she didn't play at all a bad game. After the second game, with the score standing at one game each, she looked at me and smiled and said, 'Are we going to play backgammon all night, Tony, or shall we go to bed and fuck?' The combination of her smile, her suggestion, and those fabulous tits falling out of the top of the little black dress that she had changed into from what she was wearing when I last saw her left no room for argument. I didn't want to argue anyway. I sat on the bed and watched her strip off. She didn't appear to notice. She wore minimal, black, lacy silk knickers, which she dropped on the floor. She was left in a tiny black lace suspender belt, and black silk stockings. She glanced over towards me. 'Shall I keep these on?' she asked. 'Please,' I said. My prick almost exploded.

As she turned back the bedclothes, and climbed into bed, she said 'I've been thinking about this ever since I read your first piece. It was so sexy, and in the middle of my reading it, you telephoned me, and we spoke together for the first time. I came in my knickers while we talked, just sitting there at my desk. I didn't touch myself, or anything.' She smiled at me as she slid under the bedclothes. 'Do you think that's awful?' I didn't think it was awful, I thought it was magic, and I told her so. I also thought that her tiny, almost pubescent, soft, silky, blonde pubic growth was magic. It made no attempt to hide her purplish-pink, swollen outer vaginal lips. I was aware of the strong scent of her arousal from across the other side of the bed, and it did marvellous things for my erection.

I had by now almost literally torn my clothes off, and I slid down in the bed beside her. She was like an animal. A gorgeous, lithe, slim, firmly fleshed, long-legged, sexy little animal. We kissed deeply, our arms entwined, as if kissing was going out of fashion. She tasted of mint. Her tongue invaded my mouth and made love to my tongue. Those fabulous tits pressed against me, her naked nipples hard against my flesh.

She took one arm away, and slid it down between my legs, grasping my rampant cock. 'Oooh,' she whispered. 'I just knew you'd have a huge cock. Fuck me with it. Fuck me now. I can't wait. Do it to me. Please, Tony. Please fuck me. Now. Please.' She was climbing on top of me as she spoke, and I was happy to lie back whilst she took my prick and guided it up into her cunt. She was wetter than any woman I'd ever known before. My cock slid up inside her and she pressed herself down hard onto me, forcing me deep inside her. She was hot, and wet, and she gripped me as I had never been gripped before. 'Oh, baby,' she sighed. 'Oh, sweetheart. Oh, that's good. That's soooh good. I'm going to come now. I'm coming. Can you feel me coming? Oh, Tony. You're making me come. I like it. I like it. Oooooh. Yeees. Oooooh.' Her cunt spasmed, its grip around my cock expanding and contracting, squeezing me, until, in just seconds, I was spurting my ejaculatory come up into her receptive pussy. 'Ooooh, yes,' she sighed. 'I can feel your spunk inside my cunt. Lovely. I like it. Can we do it again? Soon? Please?'

I promised her that we would. I couldn't wait myself. I was, of course, in love with the beautiful Carla. I hadn't had that many girls before her, and not a one who looked and behaved like she did, or spoke as frankly about sex. I'd started my sex life with a couple of furtive hand jobs in the woods behind my school, given by an enthusiastic, if spotty, high school girl called Margaret. Maggie to her friends. When I say enthusiastic, I mean about giving hand jobs. That was it. She'd let you look at her pussy. She'd squat down, pull her knickers down, and finger it while you watched. She'd spread it open while you looked, and put her fingers inside it, but you weren't allowed to touch. You could sniff her fingers (and we all did. I actually licked them!) and she'd give you a quick wank afterwards, but that was it. What Carla had just done to me was the total antithesis to those early, frustrating, exploratory fumblings. I'd just had the best fuck of my life. And this beautiful, sexy, gorgeous, exquisite young woman was asking me if we could do it again. It was my introduction to the girlie magazine business. I was – literally – in the pink.

Carla stayed the night, and I don't believe we slept at all. We fucked in every imaginable position. Carla sucked my cock, and I sucked Carla's pretty pink pussy. It tasted divine, and she loved what I was doing to her. She was very vocal about her sex. She used words like fuck, and cock, and cunt as if they were normal, everyday words. After I started to work within the same business as she, they became just that. They described objects or situations or pastimes that we all wrote about, drew pictures of, took photographs of, made jokes about, and indulged in ourselves. Frequently.

My work for Fred's magazine – *Tiptop* – increased, and I found myself working all day, every day, and playing all night, every night. My bank account improved beyond all recognition, and my bank manager started taking *me* out to lunch. I changed my MGB GT for a Porsche, and at the end of my first year of serious freelancing for *Tiptop* I took a month's holiday and flew off to Jamaica with one of Fred's favourite models. I'd rented a house on the beach at Port Antonio, which came complete with cook and houseboy, so we didn't need to think about anything but swimming, sunbathing, and fucking. Not necessarily in that order. The Jamaican cook produced fabulous food, once she had discovered that what we wanted to eat was the real Jamaican thing. Not pretend European food, as on offer at the resort hotels at Ocho Rios and Montego Bay. So we dined on curried fresh water langoustine, or curried chicken, lunched on salt fish and ackee, and enjoyed crab back and rice and peas, as well as some of the finest banana bread I've ever eaten. The houseboy did the house cleaning, and took the rental car off to the nearest market to do the shopping, and the cook cooked, and approved of our sexual preoccupation with each other's young bodies. Jamaican ladies are amongst the world's sexiest. Age has nothing to do with it.

The model was called Fran, and she loved everything about Jamaica. It was the first visit for both of us, and back in those days, not so long after independence, Jamaica was a great place to be. It still is, but back then, it was paradise. Fran fucked like a little stoat. She was lithe and fit and she loved to be on top, fucking me, whilst I lay lazily beneath her, enjoying her sexual attentions. Neither of us pretended that we were in love, but we liked each other. We were friends, and this was the first time that we had indulged in any kind of sexual relationship. I'd met her in Fred's office in London, and when I got her telephone number from Fred, and called her to invite her out to supper, she had accepted with alacrity.

I had something of a reputation in the men's magazine business by now, mostly due to Fred's help and encouragement. He started me off interviewing famous people – film stars, sports personalities, actors and actresses, politicians, people involved in the sex business – like Ann Summers, the woman whose name was over the door of Britain's first sex shops – that sort of thing. And the magazine's readers (and Fred) both liked what I wrote, happily for me. So when I met girls like Fran, and was introduced, they actually knew who I was. Now please don't misunderstand me. I don't mean that I was overwhelmed by people knowing my name. Absolutely not. The nice thing about it was that one never, ever, had to raise the subject of sex with women, because they knew immediately that one was in the sex business, and that almost always instantly became the topic of conversation. One spoke of sex as, in other circumstances, one might have spoken about science, or making films, or education, or whatever, depending upon the business one was in.

So when I asked Fran, after having taken her out a couple of times, if she'd like to spend a month with me in Jamaica – at my expense – she didn't think I was offering her a modelling job. Nor did she think we'd have separate bedrooms. She just smiled at me with that famous smile, which had adorned both the inside pages of *Tiptop* and the front covers of all of the better fashion magazines (a rare double for a model), and said 'Yes, Tony, thank you. I'd love to. I wondered how long it would be before you started wanting to get into my laundry.' She laughed, and patted my hand across the restaurant table. 'As far as I'm concerned,' she said, 'it's taken far too long. Let's work out dates.' And so we did.

In those days you couldn't fly direct to Jamaica, you had to fly via New York, going through both customs and immigration there, simply to change planes. Because of Fran's hectic work schedule, we flew out on Christmas Day. Which meant that we had Christmas lunch on the British Airways flight to New York, and – having gained five hours by flying westwards through time zones – we had another Christmas lunch flying down from New York to Kingston. I'd arranged to spend our first weekend in Kingston with an old friend, John Lane, and his wife Ann, and of course when we arrived, it was to discover that they'd held over their Christmas lunch in order to be able to have it with Fran and I. Such is life. That night Fran and I spent our first night in bed together. We were so shattered by the journey that all we did was to fall asleep in each other's arms.

But now, almost a week later, we had driven over the Blue

Mountains (where Jamaica's famous coffee grows) to Port Antonio, still for me the most beautiful of all Jamaica's beautiful places. The beach house (booked for us by John Lane) was out of this world. We'd spent the morning on the white sand beach, and in the aquamarine Caribbean sea, and we'd showered, and were reclining, naked, on sunbeds, on the first floor balcony. We were drinking Gold Star Rum and Pepsi in long, ice-filled, tinkling glasses. Fran's body had already become a pale coffee and-cream tan, and her skin looked almost translucent from its immersion in sun oil and sea water. Her breasts were firm and pointed, and her nipples stood out as a result of the cold water with which she had recently finished her shower. There wasn't a crease or a line to be seen on her skin anywhere. She was, thinking back, only twenty-three and she was probably physically at her peak. We had explored each other's bodies frequently, and with both enthusiasm and mutual pleasure, since our arrival up here at Port Antonio.

I had already discovered Fran's propensity for fucking on top, and I was getting a hard-on thinking about her fucking me before we went downstairs for lunch. There were times when I could have been persuaded that Fran was able to read my mind. She looked across at me and smiled. 'Why not, baby?' she asked. 'I'm all wet and ready for you. It would be a pity to waste it, wouldn't it?' She put down her glass, and sashayed into the bedroom, her taut buttocks swaying tantalizingly as she disappeared beyond the curtains that were blowing gently in the breeze, coming in over land from the sea. I finished my drink, my prick now standing to attention at the regulation 45 degrees. I could feel the blood engorging it as I anticipated the action that was about to begin.

Inside the bedroom, Fran was lying naked on the huge, oversized double bed, her legs spread, her right hand between her legs, playing with her pretty little pussy. She smiled up at me. 'I'm still wet, baby. What I need is a good fuck. I think this time I'll let you do the work. This Jamaican sunshine really takes it out of me, much as I love it. My get up and go has got up and gone. Do you mind?' I grinned down at her. 'Mind, sweetheart? The most beautiful girl in the world wants me to fuck her, and she asks if I mind. How could I possibly mind? I love every inch of your beautiful, young, desirable body. I love your wet pussy, your welcoming pussy muscles, your enthusiasm for the everyday business of sex. Just lie back and enjoy it. Think of England if you must.' Fran giggled, and lay back and spread her legs. I knelt down at the end of the bed and licked her pouting pussy lips from top to bottom. The clear, warm, lubricious liquid emanating from her tasted like honey, with slightly spicy overtones. She wriggled under my mouth. 'I love it when you suck my pussy, baby,' she said, her voice low and thick with passion. 'Don't stop, please. Do it to me. Do it some more. Suck my little pussy.'

I didn't need any encouragement. Whilst no way could I claim to be one of the world's great oral lovers, the gorgeous Carla had taught me, slowly and gently, the what, where and how of cunnilingus, encouraging me with the statement – new to me then – that women adored having their pussies sucked; or their cunnies lingussed, as she insisted on describing it. Earlier attempts to indulge in oral sex with the few girls that I had managed to persuade (for persuade, read plead with) to drop their knickers for me had mostly led to instant accusations of perversion, and of nasty, dirty habits. Fran supported the school of thought described to me by Carla, and she at least said that she enjoyed my tonguing attempts to bring her to orgasm. I say attempts, but it wasn't hard work. She was such a sexy little *coquette* that I believe she would orgasm if you simply blew gently on her pussy. One of the major attractions of these lovely girls whom I was beginning to get to know through my work in the men's magazine business was the fact that they all enjoyed sex so much, and indulged in it so frequently, that they became very practised at it. This experience meant that they were easily satisfied sexually or, alternatively, if you were causing any problems due to lack of experience, most of them would gently point you in the right direction. So to speak. This meant that after quite a short while, one began to feel modestly expert oneself, and the confidence that this bred in fact led to complete relaxation, and eventually to total pleasure. I thoroughly recommend it.

The converse was also true, of course. In all of my experience, I've never come across a girl in the sex publishing business, be she a model, a journalist, or working editorially, clerically, or in an advertising or production capacity, who didn't give great head. But back to Fran's pretty pussy. I licked its full length a number of times, savouring the taste and enjoying the feel of the warm, wet flesh on my lips, before I started to thrust my tongue between her outer labial lips and as deeply inside her pussy as my tongue would reach. She wriggled and squirmed, and moaned as she came for the first time. 'Oh, yes baby,' she whispered, 'that's good. I'm coming now. I'm coming. Please don't stop. I like it. Oh, yeeees. Feel me come. Nooow.'

I kept up my licking and sucking, starting to feel with my tongue for her clitoris for the first time. I found it quickly, thanks to Carla's detailed and oft-repeated earlier instruction, and it was semi-erect as I began to caress it with my tongue. I felt it stiffen as it became fully engorged, and this quickly brought on a whole series of orgasms, causing Fran to reach down and grasp my head, pressing it down, and thrusting her pubis up against my mouth, the better to enjoy my oral ministrations. She bucked and writhed as she orgasmed, and accompanied her physical reaction with a non-stop litany of verbal enjoyment. 'Oh, baby, baby. That's it. I'm coming all over again. I can feel your tongue up my cunt. I'm coming, darling, I'm coming again. You'll have to fuck me now. Oh, yes. Fuck me quickly. I want to feel your huge cock in my cunt. Fuck me. Fuck me. Now. Please. Oh, God. I'm coming again. Ooooh.' I wondered if the plump, happy Jamaican cook was listening to Fran's dissertation. I hoped so. She seemed to approve of the fact that Fran was getting well fucked out here in Port Antonio.

I kept going with the oral sex until Fran had enjoyed the

culmination of her series of climaxes, then happily stood up and got astride her, my rampant prick aching for insertion into her tight pussy. Fran drew her knees up somewhere around her ears, and reached down, first pulling her pussy lips apart, then grabbing my cock and inserting it into her waiting, wet hole. It felt fabulous. Tight, and wet, and moving around my prick like a small hand masturbating me. Fran had muscles where other girls just had pussies. I started to move in and out of her, pulling far back, until only a millimetre of my cock remained encompassed within her clinging cunt, then thrusting deeply back in, right up to the hilt, until my cock-head was banging against the entrance to her womb.

I looked down on the breasts that had first become famous in *Tiptop*, and revelled in thinking about every punter who ever bought the magazine and fancied doing unspeakable things to those tits, not to mention the pussy a few feet below them. Fran was certainly a fabulous fuck – and everything else – but she had a reputation for positively not putting it about. I don't suppose there were more than twenty men in the world who had looked down at Fran's tits while they fucked her, as I was doing now. The thought brought my ejaculation suddenly to the fore, and before I knew what I was doing, I was pumping spunk into Fran's pussy, while she worked her muscles until every last drop had been carefully milked away. She grinned up at me. 'Thank you, sweetheart,' she said. 'Even Stephen now, eh? We can start afresh next time. No-one owes anyone anything! Right?' 'Right,' I agreed. 'First come, first served, as ever.' She giggled. 'Come on, then, let's share a shower before we go down and see what delicacies the cook has prepared for our lunch today.' The shower was short, sharp, and refreshing. We ended with the cold water on full, until its stinging attack brought us firmly back down to earth.

Lunch was escovitch fish, a delicious local Jamaican white fish, served with fried plantain, and a hot, spicy sauce, and washed down with ice-cold cans of Red Stripe, the only beer brewed in Jamaica. It's good stuff. You can get wine at the tourist hotels, but it is usually of poor quality and very overpriced. There is no local wine as such, apart from a concoction made with imported dried grape powder, which no-one with any sense drinks. The locals drink either rum – preferably Gold Label – and mixers, or Red Stripe.

We ate lunch slowly on the downstairs balcony, overlooking the beach and the Caribbean sea, and looking out towards the small island that is in the middle of the bay at Port Antonio. As we ate, we watched the sting-rays swimming slowly up the channel that ran along the beach, about twenty yards out. Despite their frightening appearance – they had wing spans of up to about fifteen feet – they were quite harmless, and wouldn't come near you under normal circumstances. The only things to watch out for in Caribbean waters, generally speaking, are jellyfish, sea urchins, and coral. Coral cuts you to shreds in moments, if you are unfortunate enough – or stupid enough – to get washed against it by one or other of the many strong currents that surge around the island.

Fran and I spent an idyllic month in Port Antonio, with the weekdays spent swimming, sunbathing, and screwing, and with my old friend John Lane bringing up car loads of Jamaican friends at the weekends, filling up the house's other four double bedrooms, and adding backgammon, grass, and long nights of lazy conversation to the weekday attractions. We left at the end of the month, bronzed, fit, and happy. We spent a couple of days in New York staying on Park Avenue and 72nd Street with friends of Fran's. We ate in some fashionable restaurants, saw a couple of good movies, and plundered Bloomingdales, Saks, Macy's, and what seemed like most of Fifth Avenue. It was fun. I bought John Lane a backgammon doubling cube, which was quite normal in its 2, 4, 8, 16, and 32 sides. But when you went to turn it to 64, it didn't say 64. It said 'Oh shit.' He loved it, and still uses it, all these years later.

* * *

When I got back to London, I went into *Tiptop*'s offices to see what had been happening whilst I was away. Fred was there as usual, larger than life, and twice as amusing. I used to wonder where he got his energy from. He'd been talking about opening up an American edition of *Tiptop* for months now, and it suddenly seemed as if his efforts were coming to fruition. His chairman, Wally Singleton, now seemed prepared to put up the money, and Fred was scheduling a trip over to New York to set things up.

What had apparently decided Wally to invest the necessary cash was the fact that Paul Raymond's recently launched American magazine *Club* – edited by Tony Power – was apparently flourishing, and building circulation at a tremendous rate. In those days, *Penthouse* and *Playboy* in the States were selling literally millions of copies a month. Major business, compared with the comparatively small circulations of Britain's *Tiptop*, *Men Only*, *Mayfair*, and the rest. There was big money to be made for anyone who could find the magic formula. Fred was confident that he could.

But the significant thing in my life was the fact that Fred and Wally were offering me the job of deputy editor of *Tiptop* here in London, whilst Fred went off to the States to get things going there. Their offer was based on the material that I had been providing freelance for over a year now. Apparently the readers liked it, and circulation of the magazine had improved quite considerably.

'But I can't edit my way out of a paper bag, Fred,' I said. 'I've never edited anything in my life.' 'Don't worry about a thing, Tony,' he replied. 'Neither had I when I first came here. But you understand the market, and you know what the readers like. You're literate. Added together, that's more than half the battle. As to the rest, that's mostly administrative. There are good production and advertising people, and a good assistant editor, with a competent collection of subs, and an excellent art department. You can walk it. They all like you, and you get on with them. And just imagine, you'll have Carla working for you. What's the problem?' Put that way, I realised that there probably wasn't a problem. And if there was, Wally Singleton was there to keep an eye on things, and Fred would be on the end of a telephone. What had I possibly got to lose? 'O.K. then, Fred,' I said. 'How much is it worth?' It wasn't worth quite as much as I had hoped it would be, but after a while I managed to get Fred to agree that I could continue with my freelance contributions to the magazine, at freelance rates, in addition to my salary as editor. Fred remained on the masthead as editor-in-chief. If things went well, said Fred, I'd be promoted to editor within the year, with a suitable salary increase. He had it all put down in a contract, I had my solicitor look at it, and I signed it a week later. I would start in three weeks' time.

I felt the need to celebrate. I'd been writing recently for the White Elephant restaurant's magazine *Elephanta*, along with names like Len Deighton, Edna O'Brien, Johnny Speight, Barry Took, and Willis Hall. It amused my vanity to have my name on the masthead along with such illustrious contemporaries. Apart from all being members of the club restaurant, we were also all friends of Alec Hyams, who at that time was married to the restaurant's owner. The magazine was his idea, and it was sent quarterly to the restaurant club's members. The editor and art director was Arnold Schwartzman, and it was almost certainly the best designed and laid out, and undoubtedly the most expensively produced, magazine in Europe at that time.

I mention it because I was in love from afar at that time with a pretty girl called Pamela, who worked in a Mayfair art gallery. We knew each other by sight and by name, but we'd never been out together. She was a real Sixties blonde, with the haircut, the A-line, short-skirted dresses, a terrific body, and tremendous sex appeal. Tonight's the night, I thought, and I rang her up, told her of my new job, and asked her out to dinner with me to celebrate it. 'Darling, I'd love to,' she said. 'I just need to find a baby-sitter. It's not always easy at this short notice, but I'll do my best. Give me your number, and I'll call you back as soon as I can.' I did as she asked.

Baby-sitter, I thought. She never wears a wedding ring. Oh well. She must be one of those single mothers. Which means she'll want to get back home to let the baby-sitter go, rather than come back with me to Hampstead. She rang back quite quickly to say that everything was arranged. I met her in the bar at the White Elephant. Nino, the head barman there, was an old friend of mine. He poured my Black Label and water, no ice, before he greeted me. 'I hear you've been in Jamaica,' he announced. 'Lucky chap.' He looked cautiously from left to right, then leaned across the bar towards me, and whispered 'Who were you fucking there, then?' When I told him, he whistled. 'Wow,' he said. 'Can I have her when you've finished?'

At that moment Pamela came in. Nino knew her as well, of course. He greeted her, 'Good evening, Miss Pamela,' he said, pouring her a glass of champagne. 'Good evening, Nino,' she said, as she came up to me and kissed my cheek. 'Hi Tony. Good to see you.' 'Oh no,' said Nino, with a theatrical scowl. 'What's the matter?' Pamela asked him. 'You're surely not going out with this dreadful man here,' said Nino, indicating me. 'No, I'm not,' said Pamela. 'We're not going out. We're having dinner here.' Nino raised his eyebrows, and took himself off to attend to another customer.

We finished our drinks, and the head waiter came to tell me that our table was ready. Like most members of the White Elephant, I had 'my' table, which was a table for four with its back to that raised section of the restaurant known as Siberia – a place where people who didn't use the place very much used to get seated. We ate well, and drank some decent wine. It was difficult not to at the White Elephant, provided you could afford its prices. Pamela was an amusing companion, and we had a number of friends in common, which made for easy, relaxed conversation. We sat around over numerous brandies and cups of coffee, until Pamela said 'Much as I hate to, I really ought to go. If I'm too late, the baby-sitter gets uptight. Will you forgive me?' 'Of course,' I said, and I meant it. I had already conditioned myself to the realisation that bedding this lovely lady this particular evening was a no-no. A shame really, because we had got on together like a house on fire, and the physical attraction between us was strong.

We had of course discussed my new job with *Tiptop*, which had led naturally, as it always does, to the general subject of sex, and Pamela had said quite straightforwardly that it was something that she enjoyed enormously, whilst her body language and her facial expressions had all said 'I fancy you, darling.' Just as mine had said the same to her. The doorman fetched my Porsche, and I drove Pamela back to her little terraced house in Hammersmith. It was one of those streets that run parallel to the north side of the river, slightly west of Hammersmith Bridge.

As we drew up outside, the front door opened, and a delightful little girl of, I guessed, about six, ran out calling 'Mummy, mummy.' Someone who had to be the baby-sitter stood in the open doorway, the light behind her showing just her silhouette. Pamela got out of the car and bent down to give the little girl a big hug. 'Hello, sweetheart,' she said. 'Have you been a good girl? Of course you have. Say hello to Tony.' This as I got out of the car. 'Tony, this is Jenny.' Jenny came forward and, very properly, as if remembering carefully rehearsed lines, put out her hand to shake mine, and said 'Hello, Tony. How do you do?' I think that was the moment that I fell in love with her. I walked up to the door, and was introduced to the baby-sitter, whose name was Peggy. Peggy was a pleasant-looking young girl, who patently hailed from the Antipodes. Jenny went back into the house with Peggy, leaving Pamela and me on the doorstep.

I reached out to put my arm around her waist and kiss her lightly on the lips. 'Thank you, darling,' I said. 'I really enjoyed that.' Pamela kissed me back, and looked up at me. She was maybe six inches shorter than I was. 'Thank you,' she said. 'I enjoyed it too. But you don't have to go. You can stay the night if you want to.' I think my jaw must have dropped. Pamela laughed. 'It's all right,' she said. 'Jenny has her own room, and Peggy will be off home in a moment. Tomorrow's Saturday, and I don't know about you, but I don't have to be anywhere first thing.' She paused. And then, 'But of course if you don't want to…' I put my fingers gently over her lips. 'Of *course* I want to,' I said. 'I've been thinking of little else all evening. Thank you. I'd love to stay.' 'That's settled, then,' said Pamela, leading the way into the house. She took me into her sitting-room, sat me down in a comfortable chair, gave me a drink, and put on a Pink Floyd tape. 'I won't be long,' she said. 'Make yourself at home. I'll just get Jenny off to bed, and then I'm all yours.' She smiled, and shut the door behind her as she went out. Fifteen minutes later she was back. She took my glass out of my hand and put it down on a small table beside the chair I was sitting in, sat on my knee, put an arm around my neck, and kissed me fully on the mouth, her tongue invading, probing, exciting me as she so did. She tasted of good brandy, reasonably enough, and her scent was flowery and light. I kissed her back, and for a while we simply enjoyed one of the oldest and most pleasant occupations shared between men and women.

Eventually, she pulled back, looked at me and grinned. 'Well then, Tony,' she said. 'Are you going to sit here all night, or are you going to take me to bed and seriously fuck me?' I raised her up off my lap, took her by the hand, and said 'Lead on, MacDuff.' She took me upstairs, and we passed a bedroom with its door open, with a small nightlight burning beside a child's bed containing a tiny hump, which had to be Jenny. Pamela looked at me and smiled as we passed, but she didn't say anything. At the end of the passage we entered a largish bedroom with an oversized double bed as its main feature. The room was feminine and frothy, with pastel shades and flowery prints, and lots of white. 'Here we are, Tone,' said Pamela. 'Just don't turn into a frog. O.K?'

I undressed hurriedly, and took myself and my erection to bed. It was warm from an electric blanket, and I snuggled down and watched Pamela shed her clothes. She looked at me with that elfin grin again. 'Shall I put a record on?' she asked. 'You know, "The Stripper," something like that?' She hummed the old favourite whilst she peeled off her dress. This revealed her accoutred in a tiny, see-through bra and similarly tiny, matching knickers in some kind of transparent black and grey patterned material. She wore a suspender belt to hold up the black silk stockings, the long black suspenders running down her firm thighs in the most erotic fashion.

She kept on humming the song, and did a slow twirl before undoing the suspenders and rolling down the stockings in what I can only describe as a totally professional, and unbelievably sexy, manner. Next she removed the suspender belt which, after twirling it around her head in the approved stripper's manner, she threw into a corner. This left her in just the tiny bra and panties. I could see her dark brown pubic hair through the knickers, belying the blondeness of her fair hair. She saw where I was looking, and said 'Swear you'll never tell anyone I'm not a real blonde.' I swore, and crossed my heart and hoped to die. She next took off her bra, exposing pretty, firm young breasts, which showed no indication of her motherhood. They were small, prettily shaped, and pointed, with darkish-brown nipples – which I could see were fully erect – and eminently suckable. I licked my lips.

She fingered her nipples, one in each hand, pulling at them, until they stood out even more firmly. 'People say I've got pretty tits,' she said. 'What do you think?' I said that I thought that people were absolutely right, and that she could include me in people. This left her clad only in the briefest of knickers. I could see that there was a dark stain at her crotch. 'Shall I leave these on, Tone?' she asked. 'Are you one of those men who get a hard on tearing girls' knickers off?' 'No, I don't think so,' I replied. 'I think I get much more turned on by the sight of a girl taking them off voluntarily. Think about it.' She thought for a moment. 'I guess you're right,' she said. 'Psychologically, you have to be right.' 'I don't know about psychologically,' I said, 'but get them round your ankles.'

She turned towards me so that I might see her actions clearly, then started to pull her knickers down, very, very slowly. She had the waistband pulled down to just above her knees, when it became obvious that the crotch was stuck in her pussy. I felt my erection getting even harder. Pamela looked down. 'Oh, how embarrassing,' she said. 'Here I am trying to do a sophisticated strip routine, and the crotch of my knickers gets stuck in my cunt. Whatever next, I wonder?' She pulled the reluctant crotch out of her pussy, and stepped out of the briefs.

'Here I am, sweetheart,' she said, coming over to the bed and pulling down the covers on her side. She slid beneath the sheets, and snuggled up towards me. Her hand slid down between my legs, and settled on my erect cock. 'Mmmm,' she said. 'Not bad for starters.' I repaid the compliment by putting my hand between her legs. She was very wet. As my hand arrived, she spread her legs and pressed against my hand. My fingers slid inside her, willy nilly. 'Ooops,' she said, pressing hard again against my hand. 'Fuck me now, darling,' she said. 'There'll be plenty of time for foreplay later. Just fuck me. Now. Please.' I rolled her over gently onto her back, and climbed carefully on top of her. She was slim, and quite muscular. She obviously kept fit in some way, be it aerobics, gym, or dancing. Perhaps all three. She smiled up at me and spread her legs, feeling for, and finding once more, my cock. I expect all the girls tell you this, Tone,' she said, 'but I used to see you in the White Elephant bar from time to time, when I was in there with my gallery people, and you were always with some attractive woman, and I thought to myself, that Tone's got to have a very large cock to keep all those ladies happy. Because they always looked happy. And I was right, please

God. I was right.' She gave my cock a squeeze and inserted in into her waiting, wet, wanton pussy. She felt good.

I took her two tiny, perfect breasts in my hands as I fucked her, and she fucked me right back. We kissed, wetly, our tongues exploring each other's mouths, as our sexes explored each other's subtleties. I used the word wanton just now because that was the overall feeling that I got from this fervent liaison. She was hot. Sexy. And wanton. She wanted to fuck and be fucked. She held nothing back. Neither did I. There was nothing to hold back. She had all of me, right at that moment. I was totally dedicated. She grabbed me around my buttocks and thrust her tongue deeply into my mouth again.

At the same time she ground her pelvis hard against mine, her sex wetly sucking mine down deeply inside her. I felt the first trembling, anticipatory fluctuations of what was to be the first of a whole series of orgasms, each one gaining strength from the last, until she was shaking violently from head to foot as the sequence reached its peak. I began to ejaculate with her, my hot sperm pulsing into her receptive pussy, until we were just lying there, both of us spent, both of us breathless, both supremely satisfied with each other, clasping each other tightly as we waited for our souls to rejoin our bodies.

I must have fallen asleep almost immediately, for the next thing I remember was dreaming that I was being fucked by a large, heavy woman, who was shouting something at me, I couldn't tell what. I woke up to the reality of Jenny, bouncing about on the bed, crying 'Wake up, Tony. Wake up.' There was no sign of Pamela. When I opened my eyes, Jenny started bouncing all the harder. 'Wake up then, Tony. I've been trying to wake you for *ages*. Mummy says breakfast's ready.' I groaned. 'All right, sweetheart. Just give me a few moment to get myself together. I'll be down right away. I promise.'

Jenny departed, and I looked around for something to wear to breakfast. I didn't feel like dressing before I'd had a bath or a shower, and in any case, there probably wasn't time right now. In the end I settled for a large bath towel from the adjoining bathroom. Feeling somewhat embarrassed in the full light of day, I went downstairs slowly.

I found the kitchen by listening to Jenny's constant chatter, which I could hear over the clatter of dishes and pots and pans. Pamela raised a sympathetic eyebrow as I entered the kitchen. 'Good morning, Tony,' she said. 'Is it?' I said. 'No, I take that back. It's a lovely morning. Good morning, Pamela. Good morning, Jenny.' I sat down at the old-fashioned pine kitchen table, which had three places set at it. There was a high-chair at one of the places. I don't normally eat breakfast. Just a couple of cups of coffee whilst shaving and dressing. A couple of Alka-Seltzers if it was a heavy night. But sitting in that sunny kitchen, looking out over a tiny, well-kept garden, with the happy chatter of a six-year-old flowing over me like warm waves on a sandy beach, I demolished cereal, scrambled eggs and bacon, and toast and marmalade. It had to do with Pamela as well, of course. It all seemed so natural. So unlike my normal Saturday mornings. Radio Two was playing quietly in the background, and all was well with the world.

Pamela came and sat down beside me, having refilled both our coffee cups. 'Can I get down now, Mummy, please? Teddy hasn't had his breakfast yet,' asked Jenny. Pamela laughed. 'Yes, of course, sweetheart. Just see that Teddy doesn't eat more than is good for him.' She put a hand on my arm. 'I don't know what I'd do without her, really. She's my whole life. Do you like her? Do you like children?' 'I don't really know many children,' was my honest answer. 'I think she's adorable. Just like her mother.' Pamela gave me a very old-fashioned look indeed. 'No, really,' I said. 'I love you both. Truly.'

We finished breakfast, and I showered and shaved, and then got dressed, whilst Pamela looked on, and the two of us chattered quietly. We arranged to meet again the following evening – Sunday evening that was – subject to that being acceptable to the baby-sitter. Pamela would telephone me as soon as possible with the decision. She put her arms around me and gave me a big hug as I was leaving. 'Please don't be a frog, darling Tony. Please don't. I couldn't bear it,' she said. There were tears in her eyes as I kissed her goodbye. I left her house in Hammersmith full of the joys of spring, happily remembering the passion of the previous evening. As I unlocked the door of my Porsche 914, something about its rear end didn't look quite right. I went to have a look, to discover that whilst I'd been getting my end away with Pamela, some bastard had got the end away from my car. Literally. They had unbolted the combined rear section and bumper. Porsche spares are expensive enough, God knows, but I wouldn't have believed it was worth the time, effort and risk in removing that. I shrugged my shoulders and got into the car. It was only money. Money and irritation.

I was scheduled that morning to join Phil Gordon, one of *Tiptop*'s regular photographers, in a photographic shoot starting at ten o'clock, at *Tiptop*'s studio on the top floor of the office block. It was to be my job to write the words which accompanied the photographs when they finally appeared in the magazine. I drove back to Hampstead, showered and changed, dropped the car off at my local garage, and took a cab to Old Compton Street. I arrived on time, and was greeted by Phil, whom I knew well. He was opening a bottle of good burgundy, as was his habit. He always swore that it helped to relax the models, but I noticed that he drank far more of it than they did. Whatever. He certainly produced the goods, photographically, and was a thoroughly charming man, even if he did snort rather a lot of coke. There was no sign, as yet, of the model. Phil poured a glass of wine, and passed it to me. Oh well. I could tell that it was going to be one of those days. I raised my glass. 'Cheers, old friend,' I said. 'Happy days.' Just then the model arrived together with Phil's assistant, Mandy. 'Hi, Mandy,' I said. 'Hi, Tony,' she replied. 'What gives? This is Judy. Judy, say hello to Tony.' I said hello to Judy, who was a pretty, red-headed little thing of about, oh, twenty or so, I guessed. She had a great smile, and a terrific figure, as far as I could tell, beneath her dress. In any case Phil would have seen her naked before hiring her, so that was guaranteed.

This was to be a lingerie set, so it had been Mandy's job to obtain the underwear and accessories that Judy would wear for the photographs. These were already set out, hanging on a rail behind a screen that was there, rather ridiculously, I always thought, to save the models' blushes when they were stripping off. There was a plethora of bras, knickers, suspender belts, pairs of stockings (*Tiptop* models *never* wore tights!) garters, see-through blouses, petticoats, and so on. Far more than would ever be needed. Any used would be given a fashion credit in the magazine, unless, of course, they had been bought and paid for. Manufacturers were always given generous credits in these circumstances, for there isn't a lot you can do with underwear once it has been worn, if you think about it.

Phil greeted the model. 'Hi, Judy darling,' he said. 'Be a good girl and get out of your clothes, will you, please?' 'Sure, honey,' said Judy, who then retired behind the screen. She reappeared a few moments later, wearing a rather tatty dressing gown that was about three sizes too big for her. Phil looked up from his camera, which he was loading. 'We'll just wait for the elastic marks to disappear, and then we'll get going, darling,' he said. 'How about a glass of wine?' 'Ta,' said Judy, whose vocabulary wasn't of the same standard as her looks. 'That'd be nice.' Phil poured a glass of his burgundy for her.

You may wonder why he was waiting for what he called 'the elastic marks' to disappear. If you are a connoisseur of girlie sets in men's magazines, you will appreciate that these normally start with a young lady – or ladies – who is, or are, fully clothed, and who disrobe for your pleasure as the photographic sequence progresses. Now if this were the way that it really happened, the girl would strip down to her underwear which, when she then shed it, would leave the marks on her flesh of the elastic in her knickers, and from the band that kept her bra in place, assuming that she wore one.

These photographic sessions are therefore done in reverse, with the girl starting naked, having taken time out for the marks to disappear, and then slowly putting clothes back on, until she is finally fully dressed. It's logical if you understand the reason why. Phil selected a tape, inserted it into, and then switched on, his portable tape deck. It was all contemporary pop; Manfred Mann, Hermann's Hermits, The Stones, Picketywitch, The Bonzo Dog Doo Dah Band, Cilla Black, The Beatles. Good stuff. Relaxing.

Phil started to adjust his lighting around the set that had been built earlier in the week for this particular shoot. It was simply a luxurious bedroom set, built in a corner of the studio to give as broad a range of camera angles as possible. Good photographers of anything are few and far between. Good photographers of naked women are even fewer and farther. There's something about the colour values of flesh tones that eludes most of even the most professional of photographers. Skin is also very difficult to print. Vulgarity is difficult for the lesser photographer to avoid. Look at any contemporary girlie magazine. They don't avoid it.

Vulgarity is largely a matter of taste. Printing good flesh tones is a matter of skilled technology. If you are running a sixteen page sheet on press which includes, say, a whole-page advertisement for a cigarette brand with a bright red package (no names, no pack drill) and a number of pictures of an unclothed young lady, then unless you have one of Britain's absolutely top of the line printers, you are either going to get a dark red lady, or a pale pink cigarette pack. It's a balancing act, and one that needs a great deal of expertise to produce. Indisputably the best person in Britain at creating this balance is Barrie Hutton, an old friend, and one-time quality control and development manager for IPC, then Britain's largest magazine publishers. A print consultant for some years now, Barrie has, over the years, saved me a great deal of money, a considerable amount of embarrassment, and he has encouraged many a reluctant printer to actually provide value for the huge amounts of money that they get paid, something most printers, in my experience, do extremely reluctantly.

By this time, the model Judy's knicker elastic imprints had disappeared, and Phil and Mandy were getting themselves together to start shooting. As I have already explained, the shoot started with the totally naked shots with which the set would finish in the magazine. This meant that the total outfit needed to have been selected in readiness, in order that the relevant undies could be seen discarded in disarray around the naked culmination of the shoot. Judy was relaxed and confident, responding to Phil's directions with both humour and alacrity, two things often missing from some of the more famous models. Mandy had a cold container with the necessary cubes of ice with which to anoint Judy's nipples prior to each shot, ensuring that her nipples stayed firmly erect, registering sexual excitement for the magazine's punters. Most of these shoots involved either implied masturbation, or imagined lesbianism, the two most erotic situations enjoyed by purchasers of men's magazines.

I chatted idly to Judy as the shoot continued. The texts that accompany girlie photographs are almost always written to read as if they were the thoughts/ hopes/ ambitions/ fears/ sexual habits of the girl photographed. In fact they seldom have any relation at all to the real girl, whose pictures almost always appear behind a pseudonym. Judy was a pleasant change from this well-worn route, and she said that she was more than happy to appear with her real name and with some genuinely biographical notes, which made the exercise much more interesting for me.

It meant that instead of writing paragraphs about how Flossie (or Barbie, or Jane) enjoyed playing with herself, and really enjoyed, as a treat, getting fucked by someone with a giant-sized cock, I could write about Judy, who was nineteen in fact, and who had come up to London from Somerset to find fame and fortune in a modelling career. She spoke of her fascination with the big city, and of the excitements – and the disappointments – of trying to build a career in a highly competitive business. I knew that by the time I had got it home, and had worked at it, it would read really well. The shoot continued, with the time scale working backwards. Once Judy had got into the feeling of the shoot – beginning, as you will remember, completely naked – Phil started asking her to open up her outer labia just a tiny bit – 'You know, sweetheart,' he said. 'Just to give the punter that final bit of excitement that takes him over the top.'

Judy was quite amenable, and her efforts at arranging her labia to first of all please Phil, and then to remain within the restraints of the British obscenity laws, were a joy to watch. I had to sit down, lest my hard-on became visible to all and sundry. 'More wine, Tone. That's what we need,' said Phil. And while you're at it, perhaps you'll fill our glasses too?' 'No problem,' I said, pretending to drop my handkerchief on the floor, and adjusting my stiffened prick as I leaned down to pick it up. I filled up everyone's glass, including my own, and stood back, leaning against the studio wall, enjoying what was going on. By this time Judy's little-girl pussy was beginning to glisten from the exuding lubrication that the photographic session was bringing on. Her outer labial lips were quite wet, and some of the liquid was spilling over, trickling down onto her tightly curled red pubic hair.

'Good, sweetheart, good. Really good,' said Phil. 'Now let's get those knicks half-on and half-off. As if you were pulling them down, you know. Provocatively.' Mandy handed over a minimal pair of diaphanous panties, which Judy slipped up her legs, to just above her knee. 'That's good,' said Phil, raising his camera. 'Hang on a sec,' said Judy. As she spoke, she pulled the knicks up her legs slightly, then took the crotch (the double-lined gusset so loved of the lingerie ads) and tucked the very centre of it into her honeypot, so that it looked as if she was pulling the knicks down but that part of the crotch had got stuck in her tightly closed pussy. 'Oh yes,' said Phil. 'I like it. Hold it right there. Oh, yes, Terrific. Yes.' He fired off about twenty frames, bracketing each frame with a plus-one, minus-one exposure, leaving nothing to chance. A real professional. 'Thank you, darling. That was really good. Let's take a break for fifteen minutes,' he said. He put a new film-clip into his Nikon, and disconnected it from his lighting system. 'Good stuff there, Mandy,' he said to his assistant. 'What do you think?' 'Yeah, terrific,' said Mandy. 'That last shot was too much. It might just be too strong for Britain.' 'I guess you're right,' said Phil. 'But not to worry. We're only selling first British serial rights here. We can sell the set again in the States, with the stronger shots in. They'll like that. And they pay more,' he said, grinning at me. I must have looked surprised. 'Fact of life,' said Phil. 'Bigger circulations. More competition. Less really good material. Higher prices than here if you can make the grade.' He smiled again. 'I can make the grade. I'm already selling to Tony Power at *Club* in New York,' he said. 'There's so much demand for new material, you wouldn't believe.'

'Hey, I've seen *Club* with some of your stuff in,' I told Phil. 'It looks good. I like that new American photographer that Tony's using, too. What's his name? Fred Enke? Isn't that it?' 'Yes,' said Phil, slightly sourly, I thought. 'That's the guy.' Fred Enke was a Californian girlie photographer that Tony Power had found somewhere. He had tremendous style. His work was dead raunchy, but it brought a new, up-market dimension to a field that could so easily lack taste. It was terrific stuff. I loved it. As did everyone else. I'd heard that Tony was paying $1,500 a set for really good material over in New York, which was big money by English standards in those days.

Phil put down his camera and took out a small, round mirror that I'd seen him use before. He placed it flat upon a nearby table. He then took out a silver phial from a pocket, and tipped a small pile of white crystals onto the mirror's surface. He then found a razor-blade amongst his equipment – one of those in a sort of holder, with a blunt grip and a sharp single edge – and started slowly and carefully to chop the crystals into a fine white powder. This took about ten minutes, until the final product was to his satisfaction. Still using the razor-blade, Phil manoeuvred the small pile of powder into eight shortish, straight lines. He took a new five-pound note from his wallet, and rolled it into a tight cylinder. Putting one end of the cylinder up a nostril, and closing the other nostril by pressing it with a finger, he inhaled sharply, moving the cylinder along the line of powder until he had, as it were, hoovered it all up. He then changed the cylinder to the other nostril, and inhaled a second line. He took a few deep breaths, and then smiled, handing the cylindrically rolled note over to me, his eyebrows raised in question.

'Why not, Phil?' I said. 'Thank you.' I inhaled my two lines of cocaine, and passed the note to Mandy, who accepted it with a smile, and did her two lines, finally passing the paper cylinder to Judy, who accepted it with alacrity. She might not have been long up from Somerset, but she knew how to snort a line of coke. 'Oh, wow, Phil,' she said, breathing deeply, and handing back the rolled-up note. 'Thank you. That was terrific. Just what I needed.' The shoot went on. We all felt hyper as a result of the coke, which was good stuff. Obviously Phil had a good, regular supplier. We all talked too much, and waved our hands about too much, and were emphatic that each one of us was the only one talking real sense. When we came down from the high, Phil got the goodies out again, and we did a few more lines, hyping ourselves up again. When Phil announced around four in the afternoon that he was happy with what he'd got, we all helped to get the gear together and tidy up the studio.

I was helping Phil dismantle lights when Judy, now fully dressed again, came over to me and put a hand on my arm. 'I thought you might like to take me out to supper,' she said. 'In fact,' she said, putting her mouth close to my ear and speaking softly, 'having had a good opportunity today to see what's on offer, I thought you might like to take me home and fuck me.' She nibbled my ear. '*Before* supper, I mean. I think you'd enjoy it.' By God, I thought, I would that. But then I had a mental picture of Pamela's tears as I had left her that morning, and her plea that I didn't turn into a frog. I looked into Judy's dilated pupils and wondered how I could turn down such an offer. Then I thought of Jenny and her teddy bear, and I knew how I could.

I kissed Judy on the cheek. 'I'd love to, sweetheart,' I said. 'But can I take a rain-check? Please? I'd really like to do all the things you're suggesting, but I can't tonight. Or even this afternoon.' I knew if I took her home for a quick fuck, I'd surrender to those yellow eyes, with their dilated pupils beneath that auburn hair, and I'd still be there twenty-four hours later. 'Trust me, sweetheart,' I said. 'I'll call you. Soon. I promise.' Judy just managed not to pout. 'If that's what you want,' she said. 'It's your choice. See you.' I watched her tight little arse as she swayed through the studio door and out towards the lift, having said goodbye to Phil and Mandy. 'Made a bit of a conquest there, old boy,' said Phil, who'd probably fucked it for three weeks before condescending to book it for a photographic session. 'Nah,' I said. 'I don't think so. Just the coke speaking, probably.'

I didn't believe that, of course. But it didn't do to be arrogant about girls in this business in front of the other chaps. We all gave out a studied attitude of easy come, easy go. Mostly. Anyway, I liked Phil. I didn't need, or want, to impress him. 'Fancy a quick one downstairs with Fred if he's there?' I asked Phil. 'Why not?' said Phil. He finally got all his gear together, and Mandy and I helped him to hump it down in the lift to *Tiptop*'s reception. Fred was in, despite it being Saturday, and he came out to greet the three of us, shepherding us back into his office, where he opened up his drinks cupboard with obvious pleasure. Patently his lunch had been of limited duration. Or certainly of limited alcoholic content.

'Where's the model, then?' Fred asked us. Phil kept a

straight face. 'She seemed in a bit of a hurry to get away,' he said. 'I don't know what the problem was. She didn't say.' 'Damn,' said Fred. 'I wanted to fuck her.' As managing director and editor-in-chief of *Tiptop*, he took his *droit de seigneur* very seriously. It never occurred to him for a moment that any of the girls whom he regarded as fodder for his favourite sport might not fancy him. And in point of fact, most of them did find him irresistible. It was just as well. It's called charisma.

I sat back and sipped my whisky and water, and daydreamed about fucking Judy, imagining the gamey scent of her pretty, pouting little pussy, surrounded by her silky, auburn pubic hair. Redheads, in my experience, have a sexual scent all of their own. It is one that has always excited me, and young Judy had been giving it off in almost visible waves all day. And particularly after Phil had broached the cocaine. There had been one particular shot that Phil had set up, where Judy had been lying back on the bed, her back propped up by over-stuffed pillows, and she had been wearing just a black satin garter belt, black silk stockings, and a pair of diaphanous black silk knickers, which she had pulled down about her thighs, in order to give herself access to her pussy, which she was supposed to be playing with.

The knicks stretched taut between her thighs, the cotton gusset fully visible, and she had the middle finger of her right hand actually inserted into her wet pussy, doubtless massaging her clitoris to erection. Her outer labia glistened with her lubrication. 'That's very pretty, sweetheart,' said Phil, firing away shots at an alarming rate. 'But you know we can't show you with your finger in your cunt. At least, not in this country. Could you pull it out, darling, and just poise it over the top? You can get it as near as you can, but don't actually make contact.' At which point Judy had withdrawn her finger and, looking directly at me, she had put it in her mouth and sucked and licked it clean. I almost came in my trousers. She smiled at me, and then put the finger back exactly where Phil wanted it. A real professional.

I was feeling what I can only describe as philosophical. I had actually rejected a brand-new, exciting fuck, from an extremely attractive, exceedingly nubile young lady, who patently fancied me, in favour of the lovely Pamela, whose only real claim to fame was that she didn't want me to turn into a frog. Ah, well. I let the other three's conversation wash over me, adding a grunt here, or a nod there, if directly approached. Fred was discussing the attraction – or not – of including shots of ladies' anuses in the magazine. 'It's obviously a minority attraction,' he said. 'But I like a touch of anal sex from time to time. If I do, probably most chaps do.' Fred managed always to think of himself as the average man in the street. He was earning around £150,000 a year in those days, when it was an awful lot more money that it is now, and it's quite a reasonable income now. He ran an E-type Jag, and basically lived on his expenses. Average man in the street, bollocks. But he believed it.

'The question,' he was saying, 'is, if we include a couple of good arsehole shots to excite those who are into a bit of female buggery – and make no mistake, *Tiptop* is never, *never* going to pander to woofters – how many of the ordinary punters will we put off? How many subscriptions will we lose? How many readers will write to our lords and masters and complain that we've become a homosexual magazine?' I stopped thinking of Judy, and started thinking of Pamela. I called my garage, to discover that I could pick the Porsche up at six that evening. I didn't ask how much it would be. In any case it was all chargeable against tax. I refilled my glass, and began to take a more positive interest in the conversation.

Phil was a delightful chap. Girlie photographers vary enormously. There aren't any bad ones. Or perhaps it is more accurate to say that I hadn't met any incompetent ones. I suppose that it is such a competitive business that there's no room for failures. Or perhaps it is as simple as the fact that the failures don't get as far as magazines like *Tiptop*. Either way,

Phil was one of the more amusing ones. His first interest was photography. As a photographer of beautiful women in erotic poses, he had few peers. His second main interest was fucking women. You may think that's obvious, but I can give you the names of at least two photographers who earn good livings photographing female nudes, whose preference is for fucking *men*.

Phil also kept up with what was going on in the world. He didn't live in the exclusively artsy-fartsy world that some photographers live in, where they can tell you who the new editor of *Vogue* is but they don't know who is the Chancellor of the Exchequer. Phil worked almost exclusively for *Tiptop*, but he was, I knew, selling stronger versions of his material to Tony Power in New York for publication in Paul Raymond's magazine *Club*. The obscenity laws in the US were becoming much more lenient than those in Britain. Basically, the Americans had decided at that time that the photographic reproduction of male and female genitalia in magazines was not pornographic, however detailed the shots might be. Insertion of the one into the other was, however – and still is – forbidden. Since at the moment Fred bought only UK rights, this was totally acceptable to all concerned. No doubt young Judy's disappearing finger would feature in America, always depending upon whether Tony liked the set or not. I knew Fred was hoping to get all Phil's work back under the *Tiptop* roof once he started up *Tiptop*'s New York-based magazine. As to individual models, it was up to them and their agents to negotiate what they thought was an acceptable fee for their work. Strangely enough, few girlie magazines become involved in the hiring of models for girl sets. It has always been, traditionally, a matter between the photographer and the model.

Speaking of models, one aspect of the – to my mind – lesser girlie magazines that *Tiptop* had always, thus far, avoided, was the ever-popular 'readers' wives' section. Whilst the vast majority of the down-market magazines feature these usually appalling photographs of readers' wives and girlfriends in various unattractive poses of nudity, or near-nudity, *Tiptop* had, thank God, stayed away from the temptation. I say temptation, for the real reason that these awful pictures are used is that they provide however many pages the magazine's editor and/or owner wish to devote to them at absolutely minimal cost.

Readers are encouraged to sign release forms printed in every issue of the magazine, and send them in with their photographs, thus giving the magazine *carte blanche* to do what they like with the pictures, at ridiculously low costs. Around £5 for a selection of photographs used is not unusual in this field. Compare that with the cost of paying a first-class photographer for his work, and you'll see just how cheap these pages are to put together. The extraordinary thing is that, wanted or not, the photographs arrive at all mens' interest magazines in their thousands, and with monotonous regularity, proving, I suppose, that many readers actually do like to see their girlfriends/ wives in these tatty, amateurish poses. Not to mention tatty knickers. And worse. You wouldn't believe some of the pictures that come in. They are, for legal reasons, quite unreproducable. But I suppose flicking through an in-tray full of those first thing in the morning probably beats having to produce a spread sheet on the projected results of next year's marketing plan. Whatever turns you on. There are *some* pretty readers' wives.

Fred was pontificating about his forthcoming plans for the American magazine, and telling me how vital my own past contributions to UK *Tiptop* would be to its success. I wouldn't, of course, get any extra money for this extra-curricular (as far as I was concerned) use of my material, US rights of which still belonged to me. 'But,' said Fred, appealing to Phil as well as to me, 'the moment we can see that it's going to be a success, then you can start invoicing me for American use.'

Oh, yeah, I thought. That'll be the day.

The whisky I'd been drinking in Fred's office since we came downstairs from the studio had served one useful purpose at least: it had brought me down, and totally back to normal, from the highs induced by Phil's cocaine. When Phil brought out his little mirror and his silver phial and his razor-blade again in Fred's office, I realised that it was time for me to go. I had a date with the lovely Pamela. I'd received a message from *Tiptop*'s reception when I'd arrived, to say that the baby-sitter had been fixed up satisfactorily. I bade my goodbyes, and took a cab to the garage. They had done a really good job on the new end-section, and they had, they said, fitted a new alarm which would awaken my entire neighbourhood should anyone try such a tactic again. They demonstrated it for me, and I had to admit that they were right. I thanked them, and drove off to Hammersmith and *chez* Pamela. I was greeted by both Pamela and Jenny with such genuine affection that I couldn't imagine for a single moment why I had regretted turning down the invitation from sexy little Judy earlier in the day. Sex was sex, but love was love. And this was love, wasn't it?

CHAPTER TWO: HARD TO BEAT

I'd telephoned Pamela before leaving Fred's office to say that if she felt like it (and if the baby-sitter was on for it) I felt like a good dinner somewhere and then a touch of the Ad Lib, at that time London's trendiest disco. In fact, looking back, probably Britain's trendiest disco, bar none, before or since. So that when I arrived, Pamela was suitably dressed in the tiniest of black mini-skirts, grey stockings, and black patent leather, platform-soled, high-heeled shoes. The gear, as we used to say. I believe it was a Liverpool word.

We dined at the Trat, on the corner of Romilly Street and Dean Street, in Soho. I'd been going there since before it became *the* restaurant to eat in. When it still had plastic bunches of grapes, and a very poor oil painting of Mount Vesuvius, and they ran an afternoon bar called the Gatto Pardo – the Black Cat – downstairs in the basement, for Italian waiters who didn't want to go home between the break from after lunch to going back to work to get the evening restaurant session together. This meant that I got greeted personally by Mario, who was chief greeter, and loved leering all over everyone's girlfriends, and a lesser but nonetheless genuine greeting from Franco, who actually ran the restaurant. Mario ran a Ferrari in those days with the number-plate MAR 10. Well, he would, wouldn't he? It always saddened me that these two who, between them, built up probably the first-ever really successful restaurant empire in Britain, ended up not speaking to each other. That they had become millionaires in the process wasn't really the point. Wherever they are, I'd like them to know, after all these years, just how much pleasure it gave me spending my money in their many London restaurants.

We ate well that evening, as always, amidst the noisy pandemonium that was the Trat in the evenings. At the end of our meal, it was my opinion that my *zabaglione* either didn't have enough sugar in it, or that the sugar had been forgotten altogether. My waiter summoned Franco. 'I suppose, Tony, you think you can make it better yourself?' he said, jokingly. 'Certainly,' I said. 'Anybody can make better *zabaglione* than this.'

I was confident. There is no easier pudding to make in the whole of the world than *zabaglione*. As many eggs as people to feed, using only the yolks. Keep the whites for something else, or throw them away. One tablespoon of caster sugar per egg yolk. Marsala to taste. Say three-quarters of a cup for six people. Beat the ingredients together over a pan of boiling water. Eat immediately. In a restaurant they would beat the mixture in a copper pan over a direct gas flame, to save time. Time, in restaurants, is money. Ten minutes later I was down in the basement in the heat and clamour of the Trat's gleaming white tile-and-stainless-steel kitchen. The eggs, sugar and Marsala were laid out beside a gas stove. As I had thought, there was just a copper pan; no boiling water. I had reckoned without two things: that the entire kitchen would stop work and crowd around to watch this favoured customer make a fool of himself. Making *zabaglione* is one thing. Making it, watched by Franco, plus about twenty other professionals of one kind or another, is something else. Second, when making this Italian dessert in Hampstead, I would use an electric mixer. Here I was simply given a professional chef's egg-whisk. This didn't seem a problem initially, but as I continued to beat the mixture over the flame, using probably a slower flame than a chef would have used, since I was anxious not to burn the mixture, and wasn't accustomed to making it in this way, my wrist soon felt as if it would drop off. Masculine pride, however, was at stake. I managed eventually to complete the exercise to my satisfaction. Franco tasted it after I had pronounced it ready, and nodded his head in approval, bringing a resounding cheer from the kitchen staff. I was amused to note later, when the bill arrived, that both lots of *zabaglione* were charged for. I was more than happy to leave it at that.

We walked from the Trat around to the Ad Lib, which was just off the north of Leicester Square, where the Prince Charles cinema now stands. Earlier, it had briefly been a disco called Whips, with the walls hung with furs, but it hadn't succeeded, and had very quickly burnt down. Under totally new management it had become the Ad Lib, and it was the most popular disco ever to open in London. This was in the days before my old friend John Lane had opted for foreign parts, and he and I and a whole gang of people used to go around in a group, when we felt like it. John was probably the most assiduously committed night person amongst the lot of us, and it was he who had been to the new disco in its early days, and had strongly recommended it to the rest of us.

Consequently his membership was one of the first issued, and rather than all of us pay membership, we would simply ring up John any day we wanted to go to the Ad Lib, and get him to add us to his guest list that evening. This ensured the intense pleasure of ignoring the lengthy queue outside, going up to the doorman who controlled the crowd, and saying 'Mr Lane's table, please,' to be ushered instantly inside, and into the lift which carried members up to the first-floor premises.

The staff of the Ad Lib thought that John was one of London's rich playboys, an image he was happy to let ride. In fact, we always met up with him in the pub that we used to frequent in those days (the Elephant and Castle in Holland Street, off Kensington Church Street) the following early evening, and settled up with him before his cheque got as far as his bank. I'd called John that morning, and the request for Mr Lane's table brought the anticipated response, once the doorman had consulted his list, and up we went. John was there with a black model called Cherry, who had tremendous tits. You could tell she had tremendous tits, because you could see them. Her top was completely transparent. It was the fashion of the day, for girls who had both the nerve, and the tits, to wear them. Happily for us chaps, that was quite a lot of girls. The Ad Lib was its remarkable self. Some rock superstar tried to pull John's girl Cherry. Cherry didn't mind, but John did, so it didn't happen. John took her off before it became a problem. The place was full, basically, of people who simply enjoyed dancing to the intensely danceable music of the day, expertly mixed by the disco's DJs. The days of wanting to be seen hadn't really started back then.

Pamela and I worked ourselves up into sexual frenzy, a combination of alcohol and hot music. When Pamela whispered that the baby-sitter had volunteered to stay the night, which meant that she was free to come back to Hampstead with me, I simply grabbed her and hustled her down in the lift, and into the Porsche, garaged just around the corner. She gave me great head in the car on the way back to Hampstead, which encouraged me to think that we would probably have the most fantastic fuck when we got back there. It had, so to speak, released the tension.

We stripped off together in the bedroom, to the sounds of Neil Diamond's 'Hot August Night.' Pamela seemed a little preoccupied, but I took no notice. It had been a long day. I wished I had some of Phil's coke around, to revitalise things. Pamela was lying on the bed on her stomach, naked. Her beautiful arse was something else. The rest of her, from that angle, was slim and trim and attractive. Extremely sexy. She looked up at me. 'Do me a favour, Tony,' she asked, her eyes firmly fixed on mine. 'Surely, sweetheart,' I said. 'What can I do for you?' She paused for a moment. 'Beat me,' she said.

I thought I'd misheard. 'I'm sorry,' I said. 'What was that?' 'You heard,' she said. 'Beat me. Please. It excites me.' Nothing ventured, nothing gained, I thought. Beating girls was something that had never entered my mind. But there's always a first time. 'Er, what with?' I asked. 'Your leather belt will do,' she said. 'Beat me with that. Beat the fuck out of me. Please. Now.' My leather belt was typical of the fashion of the day, being about four inches in depth, and made from thick, strong leather. I picked it up from where I had abandoned it, and grasped it at the heavy, brass buckle end. I weighed it in my hand. It was a serious weapon. I took a trial swish through the air with it, looking all the while at Pamela's taut, white buttocks. 'Yes, baby,' she cried. 'Now, please. Now.'

I raised my arm and brought the belt down as gently as I could across her bottom. 'Harder,' she pleaded. 'Harder. Hurt me.' I tried to do what I was being asked to do. I swung the belt through the air, increasing the force with which it was landing across her bare flesh. But I knew I wasn't doing what was needed. She didn't say any more, and I kept up the pretence of thrashing her for as long as I possibly could, which wasn't actually very long. About five minutes at the most.

And then I threw the belt away, leapt upon Pamela, turned her over, spread her legs, and tried to fuck her. It wasn't a great success. Yes, I managed to come, much to my surprise. I've never felt so turned off in my life, before or since. I don't think Pamela achieved an orgasm, but that was the last thing I was worrying about at that particular moment. We both fell asleep immediately afterwards. I guess it was the food and the booze and the dancing, not to mention, for me, the cocaine of earlier in the day. I ran Pamela home the following morning. She was very quiet, as I was. Neither of us mentioned the débâcle of the previous evening, but we both knew that it was all over. We swore undying love as we kissed goodbye. That was the day I turned into a frog. I tried not to think about little Jenny. I really regretted the situation. It was also the beginning, and the end, of my only affair with a woman who got her kicks from being beaten.

* * *

I heard later that Pamela had recently emerged from a long, eventually unsatisfactory relationship with the drummer from a well-known rock band. Whether she picked up her – to me – bizarre needs from him, or whether they were something she had always been driven by, I shall never know. I rang Judy – you remember Judy? The little red-headed model who apparently had hot knickers for me at Phil's photographic session the previous day? She wasn't in, surprise, surprise. Crumpet of that quality doesn't spend too many evenings alone. But I left a message on her answerphone, and she called me the following morning. 'Hi, baby,' she said. 'It's me, your frustrated lover. When are you going to come and fuck me?' She giggled. 'Or should that be "when are you going to fuck me and come?" I'm easy, either way.'

That's a good start, I said to myself, hoping against hope that she didn't want to be spanked, or caned, or beaten, or anything other than just plain well fucked, something which I believed I was reasonably good at. 'I'd love to, darling,' I said, with genuine enthusiasm. 'You tell me when. I'll be there. Unless you'd rather come to my place.' 'Why waste time, baby,' she said. 'I'm already in bed here, since I haven't got up yet. To come to you, I'd have to get up, shower, dress, do my hair, my make-up, all that stuff. If you get in a cab, you can be here in fifteen minutes. It makes sense.' I had to agree. She gave me an address in Holland Park. 'I'll be there straight away, honey,' I said. 'Don't get cold.' 'Don't worry about a thing, baby,' she said. 'I'm waiting for you.'

I had a three-thousand-word interview with Tina Turner to put together from about an hour and a half of tape, with a deadline of the following day, but I felt so down that I couldn't think of anything better for my self-confidence and general well-being than going to fuck this delightful little dolly, who was doubtless lying in her pit in Holland Park, playing with her pussy and fantasizing about the size of my cock.

* * *

When God made the world, He was kind to me, and I've been around long enough, and am experienced enough, to know that when He was handing out cocks, He was downright benevolent to me. The world is full of nice girls who say 'Ooh, you've got such a big one, darling,' but mostly they'll say it to anyone, simply because they know that it is the one thing that all men want to hear. In my business, you see enough hard-core, pornographic photographs of rampant penises to know, beyond any doubt, and whatever the girls tell you, exactly where you stand. I have no problems regarding penis size. I also know that it's not clever to have a large cock. It's not anything to claim praise for. It's just the luck of the draw. But I also know that I couldn't have felt the same way, had God decided to give me a small one. Thank you, God.

Judy's place turned out to be a small, pleasantly furnished flat on the top floor of one of those big, five-storey blocks in Addison Road, just off Holland Park Avenue. She answered my ring at her door in what looked to me to be a case of carefully studied *dishabille*. She was wearing a shorty nightdress which was completely transparent, and with which she had noticeably neglected the matching knickers which these outfits traditionally include. I could see everything that was on offer, from her delightful, firm young breasts and her slim, flat, muscular stomach, to her curly, silken, auburn pubic bush. Her hair was a study in carefully arranged, casual tresses, intended to look as if she had just risen from her bed, but which simply looked as if she had spent some time trying to achieve that particular look. Her face was carefully made up to look un-made up, with very little makeup showing to the unpractised eye, other than lipstick.

Please don't misunderstand me. I'm not complaining. In fact, I was flattered that she had obviously spent time and trouble achieving a look which she patently thought I would find attractive. And she was right. I did. 'Hello, baby,' she said, opening the door, and reaching up to put her arms around my neck and kiss me, slipping her soft wet tongue between my lips as she did so. 'I thought you'd changed your mind. I thought you'd turned me down again.'

She continued to kiss me, shutting the door with one hand, which she then slipped between my legs, finding my burgeoning cock. 'Oh, that's nice, Tony,' she said. 'You're pleased to see me. I like that.' I returned the compliment, slipping my hand between her warm thighs, and feeling her half-open pussy beneath her silken bush. She was very wet. So wet, in fact, that I could feel the moisture running down her thighs. I've always thought that a seriously wet pussy is the greatest compliment any woman can ever pay to any man. Think about it. I'm right, aren't I?

Judy took me by the hand and led me down a sort of hallway and into her bedroom. It was dominated by a king-size bed. There was a stereo on a bedside table, softly playing Bette Midler singing 'Delta Dawn.' Apart from the fact that it should be played *fortissimo*, it's great music to fuck to, if you're in that sort of mood. I was. I tore my clothes off, threw them into a corner, and grabbed Judy. I kissed her deeply on and off as I eased the shortie nightdress off over her head and dispensed with that. This was the sort of body you wanted to be in close contact with. I kissed her hard-nippled breasts as I fingered her wet pussy, and I felt her cool hand grip my cock. I think I've mentioned before that I've always had a penchant for the particular odour given off by redheads, and particularly the scent of aroused red-headed pussy. I stopped sucking her erect nipples, and made my way down between her eagerly spread thighs to the source of my delight. She was so wet I was practically drinking her effluent. It was delicious, and the scent and taste and the sheer quantity of it had my cock absolutely rock hard in seconds.

Two can play at this game, I thought, and I carefully rearranged myself so that my cock was within both sight and reach of Judy' s eyes and mouth, should she feel so moved. She did, and I squirmed excitedly as her hand guided me into her warm, wet mouth. She ran my cock in and out between her soft lips before she actually started seriously sucking, and I felt himself jerk stiffly with the pleasure of the intensely erotic sensations that she was producing. We sucked and licked at each other for a delightful interval, and then I think we both decided at the same moment that actual fucking was what this first get-together was about, and thus it was with both enthusiasm and reluctance that my mouth relinquished her pussy lips, and I replaced tongue with cock. We kissed again as we thrust hard and deeply at each other, and I could taste her love-juice still upon my lips. She was an active participant in our love-making (as opposed to one of those girls – of which, sadly, there are quite a few – who simply lie there and let you do it) and she wrapped her legs around me, the better to grip me, and at the same time held me firmly by the buttocks.

She wasn't a shouter, in that she didn't have too much to say, but she had a whole vocabulary of grunts and moans and sighs that expressed exactly what she was feeling, and patently she was enjoying herself. Suddenly she gripped me even harder, and increased the rate with which she was thrusting up against me, and I felt her pussy muscles beginning to expand and contract as she started to reach her orgasm. I thrust harder with her, and felt myself come in a rush of semen jetting into her womb. It felt like a small fountain, spurting up inside her, and for a moment I prayed that she was on the Pill. And then I simply didn't care, as I reached the peak of my ejaculation, and I simply relaxed and enjoyed what was happening.

We ground slowly to a halt, but I stayed inside her for a long while afterwards. Neither of us said anything, but she stroked my forehead and cheeks with a gentleness that said more than any words could ever have done. I kissed her eyelids, then her breasts, then her lips, delicately, in an effort to return some of the warmth and affection and happiness that we both were feeling. I finally pulled out my by now totally limp cock. She seemed reluctant to let him go, and after he was gone she snuggled up to me, and we lay there for what must have been hours, sometimes chatting quietly, at other times just lying there, silent and content. Neither of us made a move towards a repeat sexual performance which, for me at least, would have been a more usual response than this relaxed, slightly contemplative companionship.

Finally, the interview with Tina Turner could be ignored no longer, and I took myself off reluctantly, promising to keep in touch, and in fact to be in touch as soon as I had completed my piece.

Interviews have always been one of my favourite forms of journalism. They are not at the most practical end of the market from a strictly financial point of view, simply because they take so much time to complete.

First of all you need to get someone to commission you to do the interview in the first place. Then you have to set it up. This, surprisingly, can sometimes take months. Then you have to do your homework, by which I mean you need to research the subject as thoroughly as possible. You won't get anywhere with an interview by turning up completely ignorant of the subject and their career. This is as true for some local councillor that no one has ever heard of as it is for a famous film star. Then you do the actual interview. I tape mine. Some people just take notes. Then I have to transcribe the tape. Then I have to edit it into shape and down to size – to the agreed number of words that you have been commissioned to write. In those days *Tiptop* ran interviews at 3,000 words. It's a good length for an interview. Not too many publications carry them at that length these days, with the exception of some of the 'heavy' Sunday newspaper magazines. And then there is always the possibility that you may need to go back to your subject, even if only by telephone, to clarify a particular point, or to ask a question that you didn't cover at the interview, and for which the almost finished article screams. All for the same sort of fee that you could get by writing a feature off the top of your head in an afternoon, simply because it was your topic, or speciality.

Having said that, interviews will always be my favourite form of expression. Yes, of course you depend upon the subject for the material that will make your interview more interesting than anyone else's. But it is the ability to get interviewees to relax and open up to you that is what interviewing is all about. The one thing that I have never done – and would never do – is to set up an interview with anyone on the basis that they could have sight of, and amend, if they so wished, the finished product. But then I've never interviewed any politicians.

At the time of the interview with Tina Turner, she was still with Ike Turner. Just. I was amused when I met them, because he was the one wearing the floor-length mink. She'd been over in Britain for a few days filming with Elton John, and it was a long time since anyone in this country had interviewed her. She was charming, and forthcoming, and I was more than happy with the outcome of the interview. So was she. She was kind enough to write and say so. I rang the lovely Carla, the production editor at *Tiptop*, at about six pm that evening, to tell her that I'd finished the piece, and she asked me to messenger it over soonest. It really *was* late. I said I'd do better than that, and I called a cab and took it along to *Tiptop*'s offices myself. Carla looked as ravishing as ever, and smiled sweetly at me when I took my manuscript up to her office. 'So when do you actually start work here, lover boy?' she asked. 'Maybe I'll get to see a little bit more of you then than I have of late?' 'It's just under two weeks now,' I said, nervously. 'The Monday after next. And you can see as much of me as you like,' I replied. 'Your wish is my command.'

'Knickers,' she said. 'Is this to length?' she asked of the interview. 'But exactly,' I said. 'Three thousand words to the very word.' 'Oh, great,' she said. 'How did it go?' 'Pretty well, I think,' I said. 'Tell me what you think when you've read it.' 'OK,' she said. 'I will.' She leaned over towards me and lowered her voice. 'Speaking of knickers,' she said, 'I haven't actually got any knickers on. Look.' She flipped up her short skirt, revealing the silky, brown, curly nest between her legs. 'I'm quite wet thinking about it,' she said. 'Would you like to fuck me? I mean now. We could lock the door.'

Carla's office was more like a cupboard than an office. If we were going to fuck there, it was going to have to be a knee-trembler. There simply wasn't room on the floor. And then I thought of her chair. 'What red-blooded man could refuse an offer like that?' I said. 'Go ahead and lock the door.' I sat on her desk, undid my zip, and pulled my rapidly stiffening cock out. Carla immediately knelt in front of me and took it in her mouth. I couldn't help but compare this act of fellatio with the one I had mutually indulged in with Judy earlier in the day. In the morning's indulgence, I had been too preoccupied with my own act of cunnilingus to fully appreciate the sensations that Judy's mouth had produced in me.

Here, now, with Carla, I was sitting down, my legs apart, whilst she knelt in front of me and took me in her mouth. I found it essentially erotic to watch my swollen cock distending her cheeks, and filling her mouth as she sucked and licked. I wondered if she could have any idea what I had been doing with my prick earlier that day, and, if she knew where it had been, whether it would concern her in any way. Somehow I didn't think so. Carla was, at heart, both totally amoral and completely incapable of jealousy. Sex was an animal act, to be enjoyed where it could be taken. It was like food and drink. It was something you did for pleasure, and also something you did to keep alive. I didn't believe that emotion, other than lust and satiation, ever really came into it for Carla. I watched my cock thrusting in and out of her mouth as her head bobbed up and down, and I began to feel the stirrings of my ejaculation down deep in my balls.

I took Carla's head in my hands, held it gently, and slowly withdrew my prick from her mouth. 'That's all very lovely, my darling,' I said, 'and thank you. But unless you want me to come in your mouth quite soon, I suggest we now leave that part of the proceedings, and get on with some fucking proper.'

'Kind of you to mention it, Tone,' she said. 'I did fancy a bit of the other myself, so if I may, I'll take your advice.' She stood up, crouched over my rampant cock, and slowly lowered herself down onto it, using a hand to guide me safely home. She was, as she had previously said, wet, and I rammed my cock hard into her. She clenched her pussy muscles tightly around my shaft, gripping me firmly, and then she started to ride me. I couldn't really do much more than sit back and enjoy myself, which is exactly what I did. 'This is fun,' said Carla. 'It sure as hell beats having to read your boring old interview.' 'Thanks a lot,' I said. 'Any time,' she said.

'But it's not the greatest position for clitoral stimulation,' added Carla. 'So if you've no objection, I'll help things along with a bit of a frig.' So saying, she put the middle finger of her right hand in her mouth, wetting it thoroughly with saliva, presumably to lubricate it, and then, slipping it down between our two bodies, I felt her insert it into her quim and start rubbing, providing the stimulation to her clitoris that this somewhat artificial position didn't allow from my cock.

She rode and frigged and frigged and rode for only a few, energetic moments, and then she suddenly said 'Here I come, sweetheart. I'm going to come any moment now. You can spurt your load up me any time you like. Oh yes'– this as I shot my load into her – 'oh, yes. Hot come in my cunt. That's lovely. Oooh, fuck, fuck, fuck.' She was finished quite quickly, and she climbed off, grinning at me as I tucked my cock away, and she went over to unlock the door. No-one, as far as I could tell, had tried it whilst we had been thus occupied, but it was, after all, quite late in the evening now. 'I'd better be careful where I sit for a while with no knickers on,' grinned Carla. 'Otherwise I'll be staining everything with your come. Oh, and I was only joking about your interview,' she said. 'I was just winding you up. You know I love everything you write.' I grinned back at her. 'Thank you, darling,' I said. 'You've made my day.' 'Now get out of here,' she said. 'I've got work to do.' She flung her arms around me and gave me a big, wet kiss, and then hustled me through the door. I could hear her giggling to herself as I walked down the corridor. What a lovely lady.

I was far more nervous than I would have admitted at the time about my now rapidly approaching new job as deputy editor of *Tiptop*. It was less than two weeks, and all I knew really was that Fred liked what I wrote, and the readers liked what I wrote, and nothing at all about editing. I rang up an old friend of mine, Allen Harbinson, who at that time was chief associate editor of *Men Only*. I'd written for *Men Only*, and had got to know Allen that way. He has for years now been a successful author and novelist. I explained my problem to him, and we got together that evening over a drink, during which he gave me some basic facts to help me on my way.

Editing, said Allen, was a matter of a combination of taste and knowing your readers. He pointed out that whilst Tony Power, his editor-in-chief, had started off *Men Only* for Paul Raymond, and probably did practically everything for the first few issues single-handed, he did little these days (until he went off to the States to start the American magazine) apart from provide ideas, and approve – or not – other people's work. There were plenty of staff to do the actual humdrum editing. Sub-editors corrected grammar, incorporated house-style, and cut or filled to length. Art and picture editors initially selected the all important girl sets, and commissioned their photography, as well as commissioning illustrations. Production editors looked after everything once it left the magazine's art department in pasted-up form, ready for the originators (the people who produced the film from which the magazine was printed) and the printers, themselves. He made it sound simple. I know now, of course, that it is rather more complicated than that. But Allen had the intelligence to see that the best thing he could do to help me at that particular time was to get me to relax. There would certainly be enough people about me to make sure I didn't make any serious mistakes.

I knew, of course, through my writing, and my editorial

schedules provided to me as a freelance by Carla, that all monthly magazines work three months ahead. It took me a while to get used to it at first, but eventually you get into a frame of mind where you're planning Christmas material in August, and writing it in September. And of course Fred kept emphasizing that there was enough editorial material available in the office at any one time – features, fiction, girl sets, cartoons, competitions, interviews, fashion, film and book reviews, food and drink columns, humour, and the rest, to put together at least three editions of the magazine if necessary.

This was true in essence, but I quickly discovered that the majority of this material was there because it had been shelved at one time or another as not being up to standard. This meant that much of it was unusable because it was very out of date, or shouldn't ever be used because it was not worthy of the pages of *Tiptop*. It was regarded, technically, as usable because it had been bought and paid for, and was therefore part of the company's assets. In fact, this accumulation of a number of years aside, Fred ran a very lean ship indeed, and there was many a night when I'd knock out the odd two or three thousand words to fill what would otherwise have been a gap in the magazine. But I'm getting ahead of myself.

I felt much better equipped to start my new job after Allen Harbinson's comprehensive briefing. 'Don't worry, old lad,' he'd said at the end of it. 'If the worst comes to the worst, remember that I'm always at the end of a telephone.' I have always remembered his kindness.

I spent a happy couple of weeks bedding Judy, whilst during the days I caught up with a backlog of writing. I had cut back on the number of commissions that I accepted in the month before I started work full-time for *Tiptop*, since I was committed to producing quite a quantity of editorial material for them, which I patently couldn't expect to write during my office hours with them, so I was basically clearing the decks for action. I heard not a word from Pamela during this time, and I didn't make any effort to contact her. I've thought a lot about her over the years, and have often regretted letting such a delightful young woman slip through my fingers. But come the end of the day, I believe that her need to be beaten precluded any possibility of our enjoying life together for very long. She was unlikely to give up something which was obviously an integral part of her sex life, and I was equally as unlikely to work at making it part of mine. I discussed it with Judy one evening. We'd been out to dinner at Julie's Restaurant, in Portland Road, off Holland Park. A delightful restaurant in the converted basement of an old bakery. It's still there, in fact, although Julie herself has long gone from the restaurant that she started.

We'd gone back to Judy's place, and slaked our sexual appetites, and we were lying naked on her bed when I brought up the question of pain and sex, and told Judy about Pamela's request to me. She didn't seem to find it unusual. 'It's whatever turns you on really, isn't it?' she said. 'There's no place for pain of any kind in *my* sex life, but I've met people to whom it's vital. They just need to meet someone who feels the same way.' She laughed. 'But there's pain, and pain, isn't there? There's real, sado-masochistic pain, and there's fun, playing-at-it pain. For example, I've never been spanked,' she said. 'Give me a little spank now, just so I can see what it feels like.' I must have looked as hesitant as I felt, because she turned over and stuck her naked bottom up in the air, and turned and looked at me. 'Come on,' she said. 'I'm not serious. It's just for fun. And there's one very important proviso. If I say stop, that means stop. Immediately. OK?'

Looking at it that way, it didn't seem quite so bad as I had at first thought. She had a beautiful bottom. Taut, smallish, firm globes. Not an inch of fat, but delightful handfuls. You know the sort of thing? A narrow cleft separated the two halves, and her silky, auburn bush curled up around her tiny pink anus which, from this particular viewpoint, was entirely visible. I wondered for a moment if she liked getting fucked in the arse. I thought I'd lead up to the spanking slowly, rather than go straight in, so I started stroking her buttocks. Stroking and squeezing and feeling her bottom, a part of the female body which for me has always – with all women – been totally concupiscent. I slipped my hand between her legs and stroked her puckered little bottom hole, which caused her to wriggle her bum for a second, but which brought forth neither acquiescence nor complaint. I filed that fact away for future reference. I was beginning to get into the mood of what I was doing, although I suspect that it was the preoccupation with the area, rather than any desire to indulge in spanking as such, that brought on this change of attitude.

It did occur to me very strongly indeed that a bottom covered in tight silky – or satin – knickers, preferably in black, the soft, shiny material pulled tightly over the proffered buttocks, would be sexually far more attractive than naked flesh. At least to begin with. And the added attraction of black silk stockings, held up by a garter belt and real suspenders, would again add sexual attraction to what I was being asked to do. I am given to understand that the *thwack* of naked palm on naked buttock has much to do with the attractions of administering a spanking. But for me, the feel of firm flesh through silky materials is far more exciting. And in any case, such pretty accoutrements can be taken – nay, torn – off, if necessary!

I mentioned these desires to Judy, who was extremely understanding, and who got off the bed and immediately began to put on the requested underwear. 'I do believe,' she said, 'that you are making history. It is absolutely the very first time in my entire life that any man had asked me to put my knickers *on*.' Watching her put on first the suspender belt – a black satin one, with long, thin black elastic suspenders – was a truly erotic sight. She had a trim waist, which served seemingly to exaggerate the curves of her hips and thighs. Her small prettily shaped breasts hung forward as she bent to fasten the underwear around her waist, like small, beautifully-shaped pears. She then took a pair of new, unworn, black silk stockings from their packet, and, sitting on the edge of the bed, she first rolled each stocking, in order to make easier the drawing of them up her pretty legs, then unrolled each in turn, pulling them up the long, slim length of her calves, and up to her thighs. Somewhat reminiscent of unrolling a condom.

She stood up to fasten the suspenders to the stockings, the long, now taut, suspenders sexily emphasizing her firm thighs, pulling the stockings tightly upwards. The tiny black silk knickers, decorated with even tinier red rosebuds, were the last item of lingerie to be put on. These she stepped into, then bent over to pull them up, pulling them well into her crotch, then adjusting them for comfort, pulling the crotch of the knickers down slightly. She twirled around briefly, asked if she now met my requirements, and when told that yes, she certainly did, she got back onto the bed, assuming once more her original kneeling position, her silk-covered rear well raised. I simply looked at her for a while, taking in the added attractions, for me, of the underwear. I loved the way the material of her knickers was pulled tightly over her buttocks by the kneeling position that she had adopted. The thin, black suspenders against her thighs, running down to the deeper black stocking tops, were intensely erotic. I felt my cock burgeoning with blood as my heart rate increased, pumping blood to all my extremities. Hard-ons didn't come harder than this. I began to warm to my task. I stroked her bottom again, a so much more tactile pleasure than before, the silk feeling crisp and cool beneath my hand, the material a caress between my fingers and her bare buttocks. A tangible, essentially sensual contact.

I met a Sunday newspaper fashion editor once on a press trip to Germany, who told me that her husband couldn't fuck her without the black-knickers-and-suspenders routine. He actually couldn't get it up without the undies. She got to the stage, she said, where she wondered whether he was fucking her or the knickers. I know what she meant, but, much as I delight in sexy underwear, it is not a prerequisite. I can get my end away without it. Any time. I fucked the lady in question a good few times in the flesh, so to speak, perhaps to prove the point. I like champagne with my caviar, but I wouldn't refuse the caviar if I could only drink white wine with it.

I ran my hands down Judy's silk-covered legs, and back up again, slipping my fingers beneath the suspenders, enjoying the different textures, warm, soft flesh, warm, crisp, taut elastic. The only thing left to do with the knickers now was to remove them. Or at least pull them down to reveal her bare skin once more. I pulled them down, oh, so slowly, exposing her bare bottom inch by tantalizing inch. I pulled them down until the waistband of the knickers was just below the curve of the underneath of her bottom, where I left them. In sight, but out of touch. I placed my hand across her two buttocks, and without more ado, I gave her a firm slap. The noise surprised even me. It was more like a pistol shot than a slap on a girl's buttocks. Judy said 'Ow,' and wriggled her bum about a bit, but I think it was more of a nervous reaction than a genuine cry of pain. I slapped her again, at about the same intensity, and then twice more, in quick succession. Each slap brought either an 'Ow,' or a sharp intake of breath, or both. I suddenly began to feel for what I was doing, and began to slap her harder. What I was doing probably now qualified as genuine spanking, even if not over-generously applied.

Judy moved aside. Quickly. 'That's enough,' she said. 'Stop. Now.' A pause. 'Thank you.' 'My pleasure,' I said. 'Will you do me a favour?' she said. 'What's that?' I asked. 'Fuck me,' she said. 'Now. Quickly. Please.' 'I thought you'd never ask,' I said. She rolled over on to her back and pulled the knickers off. She left the stockings and suspenders in place. Terrific, I thought. She spread her legs. Wide. I put a hand between them for just a moment. As I anticipated, she was running with lubricating moisture.

I swung a leg over her and she grabbed my rampant prick and guided it into her waiting cunt. 'Oh, yes,' she said. 'That's what pussy needs. Now fuck me stupid.' I did my best. She pulled her knees up around her ears (the only place, Fred always used to say, for a woman's legs) the better to let me fuck her as deeply as possible. Her pussy actively gripped me, and massaged my cock as I thrust in and out of her. She was, for Judy, quite vocal about it. Grunts and moans of pleasure were interspersed with 'Oh, yes,' and 'I like it,' and 'More. Harder. Fuck me harder. Please.' There was no doubt in my mind that we had both, in our different ways, been sexually excited by the 'spanking' in which we had indulged. Judy's reaction was manifesting itself right now. Certainly the addition of the sexy lingerie had improved my approach to the whole thing, added to which the submissiveness of a woman bending over, voluntarily, to be spanked, or punished, was mildly erotic, whilst the act of pulling down her knickers, immediately prior to the spanking, was truly sexual.

Judy began what was to become a whole series of orgasms, each one seemingly increasing in duration and intensity, until, reaching her peak, I finally let myself go, and ejaculated my semen into her, jetting it in spurts which brought moans of pleasure as she felt them, warm and wet, in her pussy.

She said afterwards, when we had got our breath back – for the second time that evening – that she had found the spanking as such tremendously stimulating. Sexually exciting. She couldn't really explain why. It turned her on to the point where, as she had evinced at the time, she just had to get fucked. There was, she said, no question of pain. She could have taken a much harder spanking than the one I had administered that evening without feeling serious pain. Or so she said. Yes, she agreed, she'd be happy to try it again another day, and go for a much harder seeing to, always provided that I promised to stop when she said stop. Which sort of brought the conversation full circle, and back, at least in my mind, to Pamela. There was, of course, no comparison to the 'spanking' I'd given Judy, and the beating that I had tried, albeit half-heartedly, to give to Pamela. My belt had brought up raised, reddened weals on Pamela's buttocks, which were still there the following morning. In one or two small places, the skin was actually broken. And that was without trying. Judy's pretty little bum wasn't even any longer the blush-pink it had been for a few minutes after my 'spanking.' Perhaps what we had learned was that Judy and I were turned on – in slightly different ways – by *playing* at S&M, while Pamela was sexually excited by *real* pain. Quite an important difference. One never knows about other people's sexual preferences.

I always remember introducing an ex-girlfriend of mine, with whom I had remained friends (and still do), to a man friend who was visiting London from abroad. The next time we met, Jenny said 'Hey, Tony, you never told me your friend was a spanker ...' Nor had I — because I didn't know. Strange how you can know people for years, and know nothing of their sexual proclivities. All I knew of this man's sexual mores was that, whilst truly British in matters of etiquette, honour, manners, and all those nice, old fashioned things that separate us from our Euro-partners, he had one totally blank moral spot. He would – if he could – fuck your girlfriend, your wife, your fiancée, your lover. In fact, *any* woman with whom you were having a relationship, however serious, however unimportant. In terms of sexual morality, he simply didn't have any. But God forbid that he should ever wear a club or regimental or school tie to which he wasn't entitled. But at least I know where I am with him. Once bitten, as they say.

I bade Judy farewell, and took myself back to Hampstead. The following Monday was my first day as deputy editor of *Tiptop*, and I wanted to spend a lazy weekend recharging my mental and physical batteries in readiness for the fray. Battle it wouldn't be. That I knew. But I needed to be on my mettle. Fred had held his farewell party before leaving last week for New York at the Golf Club, at the back of the bottom end of Fleet street. The entire staff of Tiptop Publications Ltd had attended, and it had been one of the better parties, ending finally somewhere around four am. It had helped me, because although I had met most of the editorial staff during my time as a freelance, there were a lot of people I hadn't met, and it was good to be introduced to them in an informal atmosphere.

There was the advertisement director, for example, Eileen Grey, and her staff. She was carrying on a tradition started by Kathy Keeton, back in the early *Penthouse* days, when Kathy had been the magazine's first advertisement director. And a very successful one. Kathy became Mrs Bob Guccione, and now lives with her husband in one of New York's grandest townhouses. It includes, amongst other excitements, a full-size Olympic swimming pool, a gymnasium, and a small herd of Rhodesian Ridgebacks, the reason, in my opinion, why it is the only house in the street that hasn't been burgled. I also met the administrative staff—accountants and so on. Fred was helpful in making it obvious that I was there at his choice, and with his blessing.

The lovely Carla took time out to take me around and meet the people whom I hadn't met before, after which she sat me down in a quiet corner and whispered to me the details of what she was going to do to me when she got me back to Hampstead. It was such a good party that I couldn't tell you, to this day, whether she did it or not, but she was still there the following morning, and what we did then certainly made up, as far as I was concerned, for anything I may have missed the previous evening. Fred was apparently carried from his home, still unconscious, and put on his morning flight to New York.

CHAPTER THREE: MONARCH OF THE GLEN

The Monday dawned, and I drove to Old Compton Street, parking the Porsche in that garage just off the bottom of Windmill Street, all of five minutes' walk from the office. I knew Freda, the glamorous *Tiptop* receptionist, of old, of course, and she gave me a particularly warm welcome that morning. 'Oh, and Mr Singleton asked me to get you to go to his office when you arrived, Tony,' she said. 'You know the way, don't you?' I nodded.

Wally Singleton was the owner of Tiptop Publications, as well as being chairman. A pleasant, straightforward, honest, tough businessman, who had started out in life as a printer. He'd done well, concentrating on high-quality colour printing, and investing enormous amounts of money in new machinery in the late Fifties, long before most other printers had caught on that good quality colour was the way printing was going for the next decade or so. He'd had a head start, and had made a fortune. He'd decided to go into the girlie magazine business when he'd started printing one of what was now his competitor's products, and had seen the vast circulation, the enormous advertising revenue, and the heavy cover price. Now he was the market leader, thanks to his capital, and Fred's undoubted position as the best editor in the business, here or anywhere in the world. Fred *was* one of his magazine's punters, which gave him a distinct advantage over the rest of the editors in the so-called men's-interest field, who were either all Eton and Cambridge and pomposity, and really believed that the readers bought the magazines to read the features, or else they went to the other extreme, and were street-wise, ill-educated morons who would be more at home in a Soho dirty bookshop.

Wally's office was guarded by his secretary, Anthea, through whose office you had to pass to reach Wally. Her door was always open. Wally's wasn't. She looked up as I tapped on the door and stepped through. 'Hello, Tony,' she said. 'Welcome. I hope you have a long and happy stay.' I smiled back at her. 'Thanks, Anthea,' I said. 'I hope so too.' 'Wally's waiting for you,' she said. 'Just go through, will you?' I did as I was asked. Wally got up from behind his desk and came round and shook my hand. 'Good morning, Tony,' he said. 'I just wanted to catch you before you started and say good luck. I want you to know that you have Fred's complete confidence, which means that you have my full confidence too. Any problems, come and see me. Don't hesitate. Off you go, then. Have a good day.'

I thanked him, and took myself off. I had to laugh at the 'have a good day' routine. Wally wasn't greatly travelled, and he'd been over to the States recently for the first time ever with Fred quite reluctantly, except for the fact that he really did believe that he could make serious money there, which was what Wally's life was all about. The 'have a good day' bit was to impress all of us lesser folk with his worldliness, bless him. I went back to reception and asked Freda where my office was. 'Oh, didn't anyone tell you?' she asked. 'I'll get Carla to come down and take you up to it. It's really rather nice. I had a peep at the end of the day last Friday. They've done you proud,' she said. I looked at her slightly askance. 'No, seriously, Tony,' she said. 'For Tiptop Publications, they've done you proud. Honestly.' She smiled at me and picked up her telephone and asked Carla to come down to reception.

'Hi, honey,' said Carla, coming out of the lift. 'Welcome.

I guess this makes you one of us now.' She grinned at me. 'Let me show you to your office. Follow me.' We got into the lift, and Carla pressed the button for the third floor – the editorial floor. When we got out we walked through the main editorial department, through the art department, and down a passageway to one of a row of small, individual offices at the rear of the building. 'As you can see,' said Carla, 'you're next to me.' She put an arm around me and gave me a big squeeze. 'It's so I can keep an eye on you,' she said, 'and keep you out of the clutches of those dirty model girls.' She lowered her voice. 'I don't want you fucking them when you could be fucking me,' she said. She took a look at my face. 'Just joking,' she said. 'Where's your sense of humour?' She opened the door of my office. Someone had certainly made an effort. It had been freshly painted, and the desk and chairs looked new. There were some pictures on the walls, mostly out-takes from girl sets shot for the magazine. There was an electric typewriter, a telephone, a filing cabinet and an ashtray. 'Anything else you need, just ask,' said Carla. 'I'll be back in a minute with some work.' She closed the door behind her.

The phone rang. I picked it up. 'Tony Andrews,' I said into it. 'Hello, sweetheart,' said Judy's breathy voice. 'I just wanted to wish you well on your first day. How's it going?' 'Great,' I said. 'Just great.' 'That's good,' she said. We chattered on for a bit. Then 'I must go now, darling,' she said. 'You'll probably be tied up for a few days, what with one thing and another, and I understand that. But don't forget, I'm here waiting for you. Good luck again. Goodbye, sweetheart.' And she rang off. Almost immediately there was a knock on the door, and Carla came in, carrying an armful of papers. She put them down on my desk. 'There's a pagination meeting for the August issue tomorrow at ten,' she said. 'This is the editorial material that you'll be discussing. It would be helpful if you could read it before that meeting.' I thanked her, and she left.

Pagination meetings are meetings, held usually between the editorial staff – including the art editor – the advertising director, and the production editor, to plan the way the contents of a particular issue of the magazine will be put together. Which will be the lead (main) feature. Where the fiction piece or pieces will go. What is planned for the girl sets – at the pagination stage these won't have been decided, but the pages that they will grace will be put aside. The main girl set in those days – traditionally placed in the middle of the magazine – would get a minimum of seven pages. More if the photographic shoot had provided sufficient useable shots. Lesser sets usually warranted between three and five pages. The editor would discuss with the art editor at this meeting what kind of illustrations the art editor had in mind for the various pieces that required illustrations, and the art editor would normally produce roughs of the illustrations that he had already discussed with the various artists that he was about to commission. The right of veto remained with the editor. Different magazines work in different ways, but at Tiptop Publications, when I joined them, the editor was the boss, and it is a system I have always retained, wherever I have worked. There is only room for one boss on a magazine. He takes the can back if anything goes wrong, and he accepts the kudos when things go well. You can't, for my money, split the responsibility for a magazine between an editor and an art editor. Whilst my official title was that of deputy editor, I was replacing Fred in his absence, and both Fred and Wally had made it clear that my word was law.

The advertisement director is at the meeting to agree with the editor the specific pages upon which his most favoured clients' advertisements will appear. Some of them pay extra to be on specific pages. The inside front cover, for example is always a favourite position for an advertisement, as is the outside back cover, and both cost considerably more than an advertisement which is purchased on a 'run of paper' basis, which means that the publisher can put it anywhere in the magazine he or she so wishes. Deals are often done over advertising pages. An editor or a publisher will decide that he is prepared to give away an agreed amount of advertising space in return for product, rather than cash. The product, for an airline, might be an agreed amount of air fares, redeemable over an agreed period of time, which of course doesn't cost the airline what it would cost the magazine, were the magazine paying the going rate for the tickets.

The magazine is happy, because it is saving money on airfares. The airline is happy because it is saving money on advertising. It is all done on a totally above-board basis, with the airline invoicing the magazine, and the magazine invoicing the airline.

We used to take motorcars, exotic holidays, meals in restaurants, anything we could barter. Why not? It's all money at the end of the day. Once the general shape of the magazine has been agreed at the pagination meeting, it is up to the production editor, in my case the lovely Carla, to do the fine tuning. I always used to think of paginations as making a kind of pattern. The magazine needs to be balanced, in terms of words and pictures. The features need to be presented in a way which puts the more important ones up front, and those of lesser interest at the back. Certain features always appear in specific places. Like, for example, film and theatre reviews, book reviews, restaurant reviews, and the like. One changes those about at one's peril. Move any of those, and letters from 'Disgusted, Tunbridge Wells,' will come in by the sackful. The whole thing needs to be visually appealing, pleasing to the eye as well as to the mind. It's not a difficult job, given a little experience, but it is surprising how many editors do it badly.

I read through the manuscripts, and decided to abandon the humour piece. Humour is a very personal thing, and I simply didn't like it. If I didn't like it, then I wasn't going to run it. The author would get paid. It just wouldn't appear. It would join the pile of rejected manuscripts to which I referred a while ago. Being, until this day, a freelance writer myself, I can tell you with feeling that the worst thing that can happen to a freelance is a change of editor. All editors are different, and the one who has moved on, who loved everything you wrote, will probably be replaced by a man or woman who has either never heard of you and doesn't want to – or who hated everything of yours that they ever saw in the magazine before they took over. Believe me. As a freelance, a change of editor can mean that a feature that has actually started to go through the production process can be pulled, and never appear.

The piece can have been paginated for a specific issue, edited, cut or filled to fit, an illustration or photographic illustration commissioned, type can have been set and proof-read, and then a change of editor – for whatever reason – and the new person simply doesn't like your piece, and out it comes. Like it says with the competitions, the editor's decision is final. Yes, you usually get paid, although not always the originally agreed amount, for full fees are often payable only upon publication. And yes, you normally get the right to sell the piece elsewhere, if you can. But if you think about it, the chances of any other publication wanting to publish something written specifically to order for someone else are pretty remote.

So I was fully conscious of the angst I was causing the author when I decide to pull the humour piece from the next issue scheduled for pagination. After tomorrow's pagination meeting I would write a letter to the person concerned, telling them exactly why I had taken my decision, and asking them to come and see me to discover whether we might perhaps agree on something else for them to write for *Tiptop*. The rest of the material looked fine, and I wrote out a rough pagination as a basis for discussion at the meeting. I looked at my watch. Suddenly it was lunchtime. I took myself off to Gerry's for a scotch or two, and some of Dee's home-cooked food, only to find Allen Harbinson already ensconced there. 'So how's our new editor after his first morning?' he enquired, grinning like an idiot. 'Thirsty,' I replied. 'A large scotch for our new editor, please, Dee,' said Allen. 'Don't you come in here with your bloody airs and graces,' said Dee, putting a glass to an optic. 'It's bad enough having you in here at all without any of that old nonsense.' She smiled and handed me the glass and passed the water jug along the bar. She then filled Allen's glass, and finally one for herself. 'Cheers,' she said. 'This one's on the house. So how's it all going?' The three of us chattered on for a while, until the bar began to fill up, and then Allen and I ordered our lunch from the menu, and went to sit at one of the tables.

'I suppose you're all fixed up with something new to fuck tonight,' said Allen. I told him that, quite to the contrary, I hadn't even thought about it. 'What?' he said. 'No new crumpet? A whole morning at Tiptop Publications, and you're crumpetless?' At any other time I would have taken Allen's banter in good faith, but on this particular day I suppose I felt rather more seriously about my new job than about the latent possibilities for new sexual adventures. I changed the subject as tactfully as I could. 'There's an invitation on my desk for a press reception this evening to meet some sexy new film actress,' I said. 'What's her name, now? Ah, yes; Jane Watson. Are you going? It's at the Savoy. The River Room, I think.'

'I've got the invitation,' said Allen. 'I hadn't decided whether to go or not. I can't think it's going to produce a story, and if we want to interview, well, we don't need to go to the press reception. But if you're going, I might just toddle along. We can always tell each other dirty stories. It'll be cheaper than buying our own drinks here in Gerry's.' One of Dee's waitresses brought our first course, and we settled down to enjoy our lunch. As we parted company later, we agreed to meet at the Jane Watson press reception, which was scheduled for six that evening.

I'd attended many a press reception for Fred in my capacity as a freelance. Fred hated them on principle and would regularly send me along to see if there was anything in the event for

Tiptop. If there was, he would commission me to write it. If not, tough. He trusted my decisions, and we had never actually fallen out over a difference of opinion on these matters. As a freelance, press receptions were also useful as places to meet other journalists. I might well meet someone who would commission me to write something for them. A freelance just can't have too many contacts. I was soon to discover that professional journalists (professional in the sense of full-time) took a rather different view of both press receptions and the people who organize them, the public relations men and women who either work in-house for an organization, or for a consultancy which handles a number of different clients. There are some good people in both categories. But not many.

Be that as it may, I met Allen that evening at the Savoy Hotel, where Ms Watson was holding forth on the subject of her new film. She was something to be seen, and with the dress that she was almost wearing, you could see a lot of her. 'I'd give that a length,' I said, chauvinistically, to Allen, 'given half a chance.' 'Who wouldn't?' said Allen. 'But I don't fancy your chances. Do you want a bet? I'll give you ten to one.' 'Thanks, friend,' I said. 'And no, thanks.' Ms Watson wasn't just out of my class, she was out of every normal person's class. She would almost certainly drop her panties for the likes of Tom Jones, but you and I would stand no chance. I've always been a realist. Ms Watson wasn't going to drop her knickers for me, any more than she was going to strip for nude photographs for *Tiptop*. She wasn't yet well known enough to warrant a serious interview, and that really precluded her from the columns of the magazine. No doubt when she became famous, we'd be happy to do the full interview bit. By that time, she probably wouldn't want to.

But there were other attractions. Ms Watson's PR people were being generous with their bar. You could have anything you wanted, whenever you wanted. Some of these events offered just red and white wine – and bad wine at that. And the Savoy's canapés (along with those from the Connaught) are the best in London. No question.

A pretty brunette came up and stared at my name badge, pinned on by the girl at the door when I arrived. 'Hello, Tony,' she said. 'We haven't met, have we? I'm Glen Rosemore, from Jane Watson's film company. How d'you do?' I shook her hand. It was firm and cool. She wasn't pretty, she was beautiful. Her dress revealed cleavage to rival Ms Watson's. I tried not to stare at it, but I didn't succeed. 'I suppose I should expect an editor from *Tiptop* to stare at my tits,' she said. 'But I got to be managing director of Jane Watson's film company's PR subsidiary by sheer hard work. And not on my back. You can't see it, admittedly, but I do have a brain as well.' She could see my discomfiture, and she took my arm in the friendliest of ways, and laughed out loud. 'Now, don't be cross with me, Tony,' she said. 'Come on, sweetheart. Don't be like that. If I can't take the piss out of *Tiptop*'s new editor, who can I take the piss out of. Let's go and find ourselves a drink.' She led me over to the bar, where she ordered scotch and water, no ice, for me, and champagne for herself. We moved away from the bar, found ourselves a reasonably quiet corner, and toasted each other silently. She turned to look at Jane Watson, still the centre of attraction.

'So what do you think of our Jane?' she asked. 'Terrific,' I said, and followed that up with a slightly more polite version of my conversation with Allen. 'I have to agree with you,' said Glen. 'That's pretty spot on. She's basically here hoping to set up radio and television interviews, and interviews with the heavies. You know, the *Sunday Times* and *The Observer* colour magazines. That sort of thing. But if you want a quote, I'll write one for you, and send you a colour transparency which actually shows more tit than she's showing today. Now you can't ask much more than that, can you?' She looked at me and grinned.

'Yes, I can,' I said. 'I can ask you to join me for dinner. This evening, I mean. After this is over. Since we're here, we may as well eat here. What do you say?' She didn't hesitate. 'I say yes, please, and thank you,' she said. 'I'd like that. I don't think this will last much longer.' She looked at her watch. 'It's seven-thirty now, and madam is due at the Mirabelle at eight for dinner. What say I meet you in the American Bar, back upstairs, at eight-thirty?' 'Done,' I said. 'I'll be waiting.' She smiled, squeezed my arm, and went off to talk to madam. I wandered back and found Allen, who was telling an attractive blonde journalist the story of his life. She was patently riveted, interspersing his monologue with appropriate 'ooohs' and 'ahs.' He'd got to the place where his Elvis Presley book had become a bestseller. I wouldn't detract for a moment from his ability, his success, or his story-telling, but I had heard it a couple of times before, so I wandered off and amused myself chatting up a real blue-stocking of a reporter from one of the movie trade press publications. I wanted to shock her, and I did. She'd just walked away from me in disgust when Glen went up to the dais and announced that Ms Watson was leaving us. Ms Watson waved, we all applauded politely, and I made my way up the back stairs, through to the front of the hotel, and up the flight of stairs to the American Bar.

I'd had far too much whisky to change to anything else, so I decided to stay with it, despite being tempted by the fact that the Savoy's American Bar makes a seriously good dry martini. They're almost in the Connaught's category for this delightful, but wicked cocktail. One of those, and I'd probably be on my ear. I wasn't sure what I was saving myself for, but I had a premonition about Glen Rosemore. I could be very wrong, but it was certainly worth staying reasonably sober for.

She arrived on time, and sat beside me, giving me an unexpected peck on the cheek. 'Hey,' she said. 'Did you miss me?' 'I most certainly did,' I said. 'Champagne?' 'Thank you,' she said. 'That would be nice.' I waved at the waiter, who was in any case already on his way over. That's the nice thing about good hotels, and bars, and restaurants. They know what you want before you do. It costs money, but if you can afford it, it's fun. I soundly recommend it. The waiter brought the champagne, and me a new whisky and water. No ice. We raised our glasses, and drank. She looked at me. 'You're not married, are you?' she asked. 'No,' I said. I wasn't at the time. 'Look,' she said. 'I'm a pretty up-front person. I like you.' She smiled at me. 'Perhaps more importantly from your point of view,' she said, 'I fancy you.' I smiled back at her. 'I fancy you, too,' I said. 'Isn't that nice?'

'Don't be clever with me,' she said. 'I was just thinking that, since we're having dinner here together, and since I'm staying here tonight, courtesy of Ms Watson's film company, it seems sensible to ask you now if you'd care to stay here with me? That means that, whatever your reply, we can relax and enjoy ourselves, instead of spending the whole evening wondering who's going to do what to whom? What do you say?' I leaned over and kissed her on the cheek. 'I say I'm extremely flattered, and yes, I'd love to stay the night here with you. In fact, I'd like to spend the rest of my life here with you. But I'll settle for tonight, for starters. And thank you.' I raised my glass again, and silently toasted her again. What a very switched-on lady.

I'd got the barman earlier to ring through to the restaurant and book us a table for nine o'clock, and just then he came over to tell us that they were ready for us when we were ready for them. I've always believed that the Savoy Grill Room is for serious eating, and the Savoy Restaurant is for serious flirting, so, naturally enough, I'd booked us into the restaurant. Apart from anything else, the restaurant offers cabaret, an orchestra, and a group that fills in while the orchestra is taking a rest. We finished our drinks, and made our way through to the restaurant. We'd been given a pleasant table for two in a quiet corner. I wasn't exactly well known at the Savoy. I didn't have that sort of money. But a year or two earlier I'd written a piece about their head chef, and a particular recipe he'd evolved for duck, and my piece had been well used in newspapers all around the nation.

That brought me a thank-you letter from the chef, with the

request that I always let him know when I am in the restaurant. His speciality was a langoustine soufflé, and when I asked the waiter if he was on duty this evening, and the waiter said yes, I suggested to Glen that we started with this mouth-watering first course. She agreed, and we sat back and waited, knowing that it would take a little while to arrive. The head chef was not only a charming fellow, but he was the only person I have ever met with a false nose. Apparently as a young lad, serving his apprenticeship in some hotel kitchen, he had slipped on a wet floor, and cut off his nose on the edge of a bucket that was standing on the floor in front of him.

I asked Glen if she would like to dance, and she said yes, she'd love to. She danced well, and we had a lot of fun, holding each other tightly, whispering sweet nothings into each other's ears, and enjoying the closeness of our bodies. I began to get a hard on. 'That's very naughty,' she said. 'I haven't even ground my crotch into yours yet. That comes later.' I laughed. This was some girl. I was delighted that I had decided to come to the press reception earlier. Just think what I might have missed! This was a positive improvement on sitting around drinking with Allen Harbinson.

Glen's scent was strong, but subtle, and very sexy. I didn't recognize it, but that doesn't mean anything. I don't recognize most scents. This one was growing on me. 'If you don't mind, sweetheart,' I said to Glen, 'I think we'd better sit down.' 'Oh, honey,' she said, 'I'm enjoying myself.' 'So am I,' I said. 'But if we stay out here doing what we're doing, you'll very shortly be performing an up-dated version of ride-a-cock-horse.' She giggled, and led me off the floor, staying tactfully closely in front of me, to hide my embarrassment. Spelt 'erection.'

In fact it was well timed, for we had just seated ourselves when the head chef himself appeared, carrying two plates bearing his renowned langoustine soufflé. 'For-a Signor Andrews,' he said. 'With-a the compliments of-a the Savoy Hotel.' I thanked him profusely, introduced him to Glen, and we tucked into the soufflé. It was mouth-wateringly exquisite, as always. For our main course I'd chosen lamb chops, Glen had chosen some exotic form of chicken, and I'd ordered a decent bottle of claret to accompany the food. It was all served as competently as everything always is at the Savoy, and we enjoyed our food as we chattered away nineteen to the dozen, beginning to learn a little bit about each other's lives. I can never go to the Savoy without remembering the very first time I was taken there. I had been working abroad, and whilst I had been away, my mother had married for the second time. On my return to London, I had been summoned to lunch at the Savoy Restaurant to meet my stepfather for the first time.

He was a pleasant man, who had spent most of his life in government service in the Far East, and had recently retired with the then obligatory knighthood. We met in the hotel foyer, and he led us through to the restaurant. 'I'm Sir Charlie Farnsbarn,' he said (I won't tell you his real name.) 'I've booked a table for three.' 'Yes, of course, Sir Charles,' said the head waiter of the day. 'We are expecting you, sir. This way, please.' And he led us to our table. Everything went as you might expect, and at the end of the meal, Sir Charles called over the head waiter, and asked for the bill. I didn't see it, but it must have been quite high, for the old boy hadn't spared on anything. He paid it with what looked like about £40, as far as I could see without staring, and then threw a ten-shilling note on the table. 'Thank you, my good man,' said Sir Charles. 'Share that amongst you.' Not only mean, but ungrammatical. The head waiter didn't turn a hair. He bowed politely, and said 'Thank you, very much, Sir Charles. It has been a pleasure to serve you, sir.' A great head waiter.

Discussing it with my mother later, she said that she could only think that my stepfather had been out in the Far East for so long that he was still tipping at the rate that he had as a young man, all those years ago. A nice little story, I think, that tells you a lot about the Savoy Hotel. We will all rue the day some dreadful mass catering organization finally gets its hands on it.

Glen and I lingered on long after we had finished our meal, dancing closely, anticipating what we knew we were going to do upstairs. The fact that we knew it was going to happen seemed in a way to soften the urgency that might otherwise have been there. We didn't even have to drive anywhere, or take a cab. Just the lift. The crowd that had filled the restaurant earlier dwindled slowly as parties and couples made their way home, until there were only three couples left on the dance floor. Glen and I finally took pity on the group, which had replaced the band when it retired for the night some time ago. We bade them a happy goodnight, and made our way slowly through to the lobby, into the lift, and up to the third floor, where Glen had a small suite, courtesy of Jane Watson's film company.

We simply took off our clothes and leapt at each other. I noticed that Glen was wearing a pretty line in lavender-coloured Ann Summers' own-label Janet Reger-designed knickers, and that she was wearing stockings and a suspender belt which, had I been more sober, I would probably have asked her to keep on. Despite her large, well-shaped bosom, she wasn't wearing a bra. Nor did she appear to need one. There wasn't a great deal of subtlety about what happened next. I had been discovering all evening that Glen was pretty much an up-front lady. She didn't waste too much time on niceties. She lay on her back on the bed, spread her legs, and said 'Come and fuck me, lover. I've been waiting all evening for this.' 'So have I, sweetheart,' I said as I went over to the bed, my cock preceding me in arrogant fashion. 'Here I come.' One of the things I had been thinking about from time to time throughout the evening had been sucking this young lady's pussy. Now, seemingly suddenly, there it was in front of me, waiting for me.

Her pubic hair was soft and silken, and curly, and the same dark, shiny brown as her other hair. I could see a pink line nestling in the middle of that hair, and as I lowered my face down towards it, I could see moisture seeping through the line, like tiny, crystal tear-drops. The skin of her thighs was smooth and soft as I placed my hands on them, and I leaned forward and ran my tongue down the pink line, savouring the taste and scent of highly aroused woman. Glen shuddered, and said 'Ooh, that's nice. I like that. Don't stop.' So I didn't. (I wasn't going to anyway.) I kissed the closed lips of her sex, pressing down on them until they popped open under the pressure, lazily, stickily, and I was able to insert my tongue deeply into her.

She tasted good. Young, healthy, clean, fresh, all those nice things. I used to go to a dentist who always claimed that the tongue was the mirror of one's bodily health. He may well have been right, but for me, a woman's vagina is the mirror of her bodily health. It tells you everything about her. And the way that she reacts to cunnilingus tells you a great deal about her attitude to sex, and whether that is healthy. You will want to know that Glen's reaction was everything that any man could want. She loved it, telling me so in a deep, husky, sexy voice, that very soon demanded that I rearrange my position in order that she could suck my cock. I only needed to be asked once, and I rearranged myself forthwith. I felt her soft, hot, wet mouth on me almost immediately, taking my whole stiff length between her lips and into her mouth, and then slowly withdrawing it, almost to the very tip, then completely immersing it again, wetly, gently, erotically. She started sucking and licking very slowly, and began, after a while, to build both her rhythm and her intensity, sucking harder, using one hand to squeeze the base of my cock, the other to cup my balls.

I knew that I couldn't resist what she was doing to me for too long, and I wanted my first ejaculation with her to be in her pussy, rather than in her mouth. Don't ask me why. It just seemed right and proper. So I speeded up my own oral attentions, feeling for, and finding, her engorged clitoris with my tongue. I started to concentrate all my attentions on her lovenub, and before long I felt her coming. Slowly at first, and quite gently, then more quickly, and more deeply. She began to accompany this series of orgasms verbally, taking my cock out of her mouth from time to time to say 'Oh, yes, sweetheart. I'm coming now. Can you feel me coming? Oh, that's good. So good. Oh, yeeeeees.' She built up to a crescendo, which proved to be the final – for the moment – big one, at which point I stopped, and slowly withdrew my burgeoning cock from her mouth.

'Oh, that was good, baby,' she said. 'Now fuck me. Please?' I fucked her. It was memorable. She used her cunt muscles in a way that I'd never come across before, almost as if she were masturbating me with them. With the build-up from her fellating me moments before, it was no time at all before I was spurting my sperm into her in great warm jets. 'Oh, yes, honey,' she said. 'I can feel your spunk. It feels, oh, so good. Oh, yes. You're fucking me now. Really fucking me. I like it. Oh, God, I like it. Don't stop. Please don't stop.'

Inevitably, I had to stop. When a man has ejaculated, that, for the moment, is it. I had, and it was. Different men take differing amounts of time to be ready and capable of ejaculating again, having performed for the first time. With a new girl, that time is usually minimal. With Glen, it was very minimal indeed, and we spent a happy night fucking ourselves stupid. It was terrific. One of the better nights. We fucked and sucked, and fucked again. She gave me the first French necklace I had ever received, where she masturbated my cock between her soft, generous breasts. It was a delightful sensation, and I came all over her tits with both pleasure and enthusiasm. I don't know where she learned that particular trick, and I don't want to, but it was an unforgettable occasion.

We finally fell asleep at I know not what hour, and I was awoken by the sound of Big Ben striking nine o'clock the following morning in Parliament Square, down in Whitehall. Glen heard it too, and reached out a hand for my cock, which had also decided that it was time to get up. 'Oh, good,' she said, as she pulled me on top of her. 'I'm ready, too.' And so she was. We fucked lazily and pleasantly, all passion spent, but with a great deal of affection. We came together, and I very nearly fell asleep again when I remembered that I had a pagination meeting in the office at ten o'clock. I showered and dressed hurriedly, kissed a sleepy Glen goodbye, and just made it to the office in time. Freda took one look at me as I walked through reception, and asked 'Alka-Seltzer?' I nodded, and minutes later she arrived in my office with a glass of water and the tablets. 'You probably won't believe me,' she said, 'but these *will* help. I'll bring you a couple more in a little while.' I thanked her, and dropped the tablets into the water. Carla was the next into the office as I waited for the Alka-Seltzer to dissolve. She was carrying a tray of coffee, milk and sugar, cups and saucers, and biscuits, for the pagination meeting. She took one look at me. 'Oh, dear,' she said. 'I hope it was worth it.'

'I don't know what you mean,' I said. 'What I mean,' she said, 'is that you look as if you've been up all night, with no sleep whatsoever, fucking and boozing, and all that sort of thing.' 'Oh, that,' I said. 'You could be right.' She came over to me and gave me a soft, sweet kiss on my fevered brow. 'Poor Tony,' she said. 'It'll all be better soon.'

At that point the rest of the meeting arrived in a body, and when Carla had dispensed the coffee and biscuits, she – as production editor – chaired the meeting. It was all pretty straightforward stuff. Everyone present had seen all the material that we were discussing before. I had a little trouble with Harry Warner, the associate editor, who had commissioned the humour piece that I had decided to pull. I wasn't heavy with him, but I was to the point. 'I'm sorry, Harry,' I said. 'I just don't like it. It's as simple as that. No offence meant.' I think he was probably just seeing how far he could go on this, my first formal meeting with members of the staff. He was a cocky little sod, and my least favourite of all the people who were employed by Tiptop Publications. He backed down quite quickly, albeit reluctantly. He didn't have much option, really. What I didn't like about him was that he knew as much about journalism, writing, editing, and girlie magazines as I did about brain surgery, which was nothing. How he ever got the job I'll never know. Fred must have been drunk. It had been known to happen, although the incumbents of these unfortunate hirings didn't usually last as long as Harry Warner had. He produced very little for the magazine. The manuscript I had pulled was something of a rarity.

But he did produce a never-ending plethora of goodies and freebies for Harry Warner, from free holidays at home and abroad, to records, cars on loan, tickets for first nights, and meals at restaurants. All these things were offered, of course, on the understanding that Harry was going to write about them in the magazine. Which he never did. After I'd been there for a while, I spent so much time, as the senior editorial person, trying to calm down angry manufacturers who had misguidedly loaned or given something to Harry that I fired him. But that's another story.

Freda brought the promised Alka-Seltzers in at about eleven o'clock, and Carla pronounced the meeting over at twelve-thirty. I did feel a little better, and I crawled down to Gerry's for a hair or two of the dog, to be greeted once more by Allen Harbinson. He looked at me, and looked away. 'Good morning, Allen,' I said, trying to sound cheerful. 'Oh,' he said. 'We are speaking, then?' 'Why would we not?' I asked, signalling to Dee for a refill for Allen and her, and a drink for me. 'Well, seeing as you abandoned me last night at the Savoy for some cheap tart, without so much as a thank-you and goodbye,' he said, 'I thought perhaps I'd done something to offend you.' 'Don't be so bloody silly, Allen,' I admonished. 'Sometimes you're just plain stupid.' 'Oh, I am, am I?' he said. 'Well, screw you for a start.' 'And not so much of the cheap tart,' I said. 'I'll have you know that the young lady in question is the managing director of a public relations company, and was staying last night in a suite at the Savoy Hotel.' Allen turned to me and grinned. 'Where, no doubt, you stayed with her,' he said. 'And looking more closely, I can see that a good time was had by all. Well done, lad.' He laughed at me and raised his glass.

CHAPTER FOUR: GOING TO ANNABEL'S

That first week at Tiptop Publications seemed to herald a new beginning to my sex life. Or a beginning to a new sex life, one or the other, I'm not sure which. It had started with Glen, whom I saw again, of course. No man in his right mind would leave that delightful situation as a one-night stand. And I continued to see Judy, reasonably enough. And the lovely Carla was always available. But let me tell you about the kind of thing that started happening to me.

Having found such an enchanting partner at my first press reception as deputy editor, I began to accept far more of that kind of invitation than I ever imagined I would. Later that week I accepted an invitation from one of Soho's better-known night clubs to preview their latest cabaret. It was a good show. Pretty showgirls, good choreography, excellent band, first-class singer. If you wanted to spend the kind of money that it costs to go to a place like that, this one was undoubtedly good value. Like most clubs of its kind, there were young ladies sitting around who would join you at your table if you wished. In some places you have to fight them off. Here, they only joined you if you told the waiter that you'd like a little company. It cost you, of course. Apart from the champagne that the girl would inevitably order, there was usually a hostess fee on top. If you wanted to go all the way and take the girl home, most establishments didn't object, provided that they had made a bob or two out of you on drinks before you left. The cost of the girl was just between the two of you.

These transactions were never undertaken blatantly, and if you didn't know that they were available you could probably sit in the club all evening without having the slightest notion of what was going on. This particular club had a manageress, rather than a manager, whom I'd met when I arrived, and up to now, my evening – drinks and entertainment – had been on the house. Thinking that it might make an amusing piece for the magazine to include a review of one of the girls, rather than just the straight review of the cabaret, I got up from my table and went over and told the manageress that I fancied taking one of her young ladies home if she had no objection, and which one did she recommend? I added that I naturally expected to pay for the privilege, and said that if I was going to pay for it, I wanted value for money. She smiled at me, and didn't reply for a moment, and I wondered if she was actually going to tell me that none of her girls were on the game. But I was wrong.

Her only objection, she said, smiling at me, was that I was considering paying for a fuck – and expensively at that – when I could fuck her for nothing. I looked at her rather more closely. She was in fact considerably prettier than any of her young ladies, if a little less overtly made-up. I would put her age at around the late twenties, and she was wearing a little black dress that displayed a delightful amount of cleavage. Her skin looked smooth and velvety.

She spoke softly. 'I can guarantee you a good fuck,' she said. 'You certainly won't have any complaints on that score. The only disadvantage is that I can't leave until three, which is when we stop serving drinks. Any of my girls can leave whenever they want to. It's entirely up to you. And to answer your original question, while I can't vouch for it personally, a lot of my customers speak highly of Veronica over there.' She smiled at me. 'But then none of them have been to bed with *me*.' She pointed out a pert-looking little brunette with a Mary

Quant haircut and a very short dress that revealed long, lissome legs. She looked like a little painted doll. A very fuckable little painted doll. But it was no contest. A bought and paid-for fuck from a professional is never going to be as good as a free fuck offered willingly from a girl who, first of all, has to fancy me. That's arrogant, but it has to be true. Next, she has to like fucking. And on a straight comparison basis, she was a lot prettier – and sexier – than any of the others. Like I said, it was no contest.

'I'm very flattered,' I said. 'Thank you.' I looked at my watch. 'It's nearly two now anyway. I can wait an awful lot longer than an hour for a pretty girl like you. But forgive me,' I said. 'I know you as Miss Ford, but I don't know your Christian name.' 'What fun,' she said. 'An hour might not seem long to you, but it seems like an eternity to me. My name's Annabel. One other thing,' she said. 'Did you come by car, or should I order a cab to be here for us at three?' 'I brought my car,' I said. 'No problem.' The drink/driving laws had come in by then, but those were still the days when we all thought that it couldn't possibly catch up with us. Only stupid people got caught. Ah well. These days, I know who the stupid people really were.

I went back to my table and ordered another scotch and water. After a few minutes I was delighted when Annabel came and joined me. She ordered a glass of champagne, which she raised to me. 'Here's to a new friendship,' she said. 'Long may it last.' 'I'll drink to that,' I said. 'Cheers.' We chatted on for a while about our respective jobs.

Annabel had been an accountant, she told me, working for the Inland Revenue. One day she had dealt with the annual tax return of a Soho club manager, and that was the day she had decided that she was in the wrong business. She worked out her notice, at the same time investigating the various Soho clubs, until she had decided that the one we were sitting in was both the most successful and the most respectable, comparatively speaking. She had written to the owner on

Inland Revenue paper, asking to set up a meeting. When she had arrived, she told him that she was looking for a job as a club manager, and that, subject to sight of his books – both sets – she believed that she could not only manage the club successfully, but that she could save him around £50,000 a year in tax. He took her on that day. She had done everything that she had promised, and more, she said. She was now a partner in the business, and earning more than the club manager whose tax return had persuaded her that she was in the wrong business. There were some disadvantages, she said, but nothing that bothered her too much. The hours she kept tended to exclude her from other, more normal people's lives. More normal, that is only in the hours they kept. This had a roll-on effect on her love life. Or lack of love life, as she put it. Not too many men wanted to start their evenings when Annabel finished work at three-thirty, four in the morning. But she wasn't planning to do it for ever. It wouldn't be too long, she said, before she had enough tucked away to keep her comfortably for the rest of her life.

'And then you came in,' she said, putting a hand on my arm. 'Most of my customers, if you look around you, are elderly men who only come here to pick up the girls. Or, occasionally, I'll get a group of young men who come here to celebrate something, anything. A birthday. A new job. Leaving an old job. Getting engaged. Getting divorced. That sort of thing. They're looking to get drunk, not laid. So when I saw you come through the door this evening, I thought, that's for me! I was only half serious, of course. And then when you came over and asked me which of the girls was the best fuck, well... I simply had to say my piece. I do hope you don't mind. I mean, you must think it's very forward of me. But if I see something I like, I do my best to get it.' 'Mind?' I said. 'I'm absolutely delighted. I came here to look at your cabaret, and go away to write a piece about it for the magazine, and I get the loveliest lady in the whole place propositioning me. What more could any red-blooded man want?' She giggled, and took hold of my hand. 'Come and dance,' she said. 'It'll help to pass the time. And it will give the girls something to gossip about. They've never seen me dance here in all the time I've been running the club.' Like Glen, she was magic on her feet. It was like dancing with a feather. We held each other close, and she whispered naughty things in my ear. 'I can feel your cock pressing against me,' she said, leaning her pubis into mine as we turned a corner on the dance floor. 'It feels good. It's only about half-erect, so that augurs well for later. Us girls never believe all that "size doesn't matter, it's not how big it is, it's what you do with it that counts" rubbish that they write in the women's magazines. Big is beautiful in my book.' There's no answer to that, really, is there? I mean, not on a dance floor in the middle of a crowd of other people.

Suddenly, thank God, it was three o'clock, and the waiters started dishing out bills to all and sundry. Except to me, I was pleased to see. Annabel got up from our table and said 'I'll see you outside in about ten minutes, if that's all right.' It was, of course. I found the Porsche where I had parked it, in a side street five minutes away from the club. I drove back and waited outside. True to her words, Annabel appeared exactly ten minutes later. I gave a soft beep on the horn to attract her attention, and she came over and got in.

The nice thing about those old 914s is that the front seat (their only seat) is a bench seat, so she was able to snuggle up against me. Mine was a left-hand drive model. The 914 had never officially been sold in Britain, and whilst there were a few about that had been converted to right-hand drive, mine hadn't. But it did have a three-litre Porsche engine that a previous owner had put in it, instead of the standard one-point-six. Quite pokey it was. And that lovely Sportamatic gearbox. Did you ever come across one? A Porsche speciality of the day. Forerunner of the press-button gearboxes they're using in Formula One nowadays. You put your hand on the gear lever, and the box electronically disengaged. You changed to whatever gear you selected, let go of the lever, and it electronically re-engaged. No clutch. Magic.

'This is very flash,' said Annabel. 'Is it part of your ill gotten gains as editor of *Tiptop*?' 'No, actually,' I said. 'It's part of my ill-gotten gains as a freelance journalist for the last three years, writing about sex. Along with month-long holidays in the Caribbean, eating in expensive restaurants, and generally living high on the hog. But I work my guts out earning it. The deputy editor bit is very new indeed. Like this is my first week.' 'You're kidding,' she said.

'More to the point,' I said, 'is where are we going?' 'Oh, sorry,' she said. 'Aim for Marble Arch.' I drove north to Oxford Street and turned left, keeping well within the speed limit. Orange Porsches attract a lot of unwanted police attention late at night. I didn't want to get breathalyzed. We came up to the end of Oxford Street. 'Go around the Arch to the Edgeware Road,' said Annabel, 'and then take the second left. It's called Connaught Street.' She lived in a modern block off Hyde Park Square which made my Hampstead flat look like a squat. We parked in her underground garage and took the lift. She pressed the button marked 'Penthouse.' It was on the fourteenth floor, with a balcony running around two sides of the entire apartment, with fantastic views over south and west London. 'If you describe my car as flash,' I asked, 'what would you call this?' She came over to me and put an arm around my waist. 'Never mind about that,' she said. 'We can talk later. Do you want a drink?' she asked. 'Or shall we go to bed?' I turned around until I was facing her, and took her in my arms and kissed her. She slid her tongue into my mouth, exploring mine lewdly, excitingly.

Then I felt her disentangle an arm, and I next felt a hand unzip my fly and reach inside my trousers, finding my cock through the gap in my boxer shorts. She clasped it firmly, and squeezed it, gently but so erotically. '*That*'s what I'm after,' she said. 'I can show you a place to put it that I think you'll find quite interesting.' She took me by the hand, just as she had earlier that night to take me onto the dance floor at her club.

'Follow me,' she said. I did as I was told. I wasn't taking too much notice of her penthouse at this stage, but I was aware of a lot of good, contemporary art everywhere. Paintings and sculptures. The furniture was modern, and expensive. The occasional antique piece of furniture made an effective contrast against what might otherwise have been overwhelming modernity.

I followed her into a bedroom into which I guessed you could probably have fitted my entire flat. It featured a huge, modern, stainless steel and chromium four-poster bed. There were white upholstered armchairs, and a pretty Victorian sewing chair done up in the same material. Everything whispered money. But tastefully. It didn't say 'designer.' It said 'This is my home, and this is how I like it to look.' Everything on the bed – pillows, coverlet, sheets, the lot – was white. 'If you think it all looks a bit virginal,' said Annabel, 'you'd be right. I haven't had a fuck for over a year. Come and fuck me, darling. Now. Please?' She was undressing as she spoke. Underneath the black dress she wore expensive silk lingerie. Bra and knickers in plain white, but with little embroidered rosebuds here and there. The sort you buy in Harvey Nichols's lingerie department. I looked, but couldn't see her pubic hair, which I would have thought would have shown as a darker patch through the almost transparent silk of her panties.

In the semi-dark of the night-club I had taken her hair as dark brown. Here, in the better light of her bedroom, I could see that it was a darkish auburn. She took off her bra, in itself simply a titillation, if you'll forgive the bad pun. Something to draw attention. Support she didn't need. Her breasts were of good size, and perfect shape. She had the tiniest growth of silky, wispy, pale auburn hair around her aureola. I could see from where I was standing, divesting myself of my clothes, that her nipples were large and hard, standing up with sexual excitement. So was my prick.

Then she bent down and pulled down her knickers, stepping out of them with a small flourish, and I could see why I hadn't been able to see her pubes through them. She was shaven. Down there, as they say. A completely bald pudenda. Among the many things that turn me on, shaven pubes is probably singly the biggest turn on of them all. My cock was hurting, it was so hard. Annabel was patently amused at my reaction. She came over and took hold of my cock, and put an arm around me and whispered 'Of course you can suck it first, darling. I'd like that. Now you know why I said to you, when we were dancing, and I could feel your cock pressing against me, that I could find you somewhere interesting to put it.' She took hold of my right hand, and placed it on her bald pussy. 'Is that interesting enough?' she asked. I could feel the heat of her.

I nearly came right then. And in any case, how did she know, without my mentioning it, that sucking a bald pussy was, for me, almost – only almost – better than fucking one? Perhaps we chaps are all the same, with the same nasty, boring sexual habits. But I don't believe that. Not really. She was wet between her legs. I could feel the exudation trickling down her thighs. 'Come on, sweetheart,' I said, taking her hand and leading her over to the bed. 'Let's not waste any more time.' I ought to have carried her really, I suppose. There was definitely something cave-mannish about the way I felt. She lay on her back, and opened her legs. Wide. I looked at that gorgeous, hairless pussy, drinking in its beauty, its sexual significance, its sensuality, its sheer, unadulterated depravity. Nice girls don't shave their pubes. Naughty girls do.

I pressed my lips against her unprotected labia, licking their full, fleshy length, feeling the baldness of the surrounding skin, as against the more usual, hairy surround. My libido was inflamed. I wanted to rape her. My carnality was all-consuming. I drank in her genital nectar, probing her cunt with my tongue, running my mouth all over her entire shaven genital area, licking, sucking, slurping, drinking, inhaling her strong, feminine scent. I was pleased that whilst I was devouring her sex, she left mine totally alone. Any manual or oral stimulation of my cock right then would simply have brought on my ejaculation instantly. She just lay there, moaning slightly, whispering odd words, which sometimes I could hear, sometimes not. There was the occasional 'Oh, yes,' and I heard 'Yes, I like it,' once or twice, but mostly it was an incomprehensible, if appreciative, background noise. I remembered that she had said that it was a year since she had been fucked. That was tantamount to saying that it was a year since she'd had sex, unless, of course, she was bisexual. I would, I thought, reserve any opinion on that.

After a while she began to move her hips slowly, pressing them up gently against my face and mouth, getting a rhythm together, and then she put her hands down and held my head in them, moving her shaven groin more strongly up against my mouth. I delved deep inside her with my tongue and found her clitoris, and started to orally massage it. It was fat and engorged and hard.

Her movements became much quicker, and she started off her murmured litany again. And then she was coming. Noisily, shouting out 'Oh, fuck, yes. I'm coming. Oh God, I'm coming. Oh, Jesus. Oh God. Oh fuck.' A little sacrilegious, perhaps, but I think I knew what she meant. I kept up my oral ministrations as she worked her way through a myriad of slowly diminishing orgasms, until, finally, she lay there, breathing heavily, her spasms, for the moment, complete. After a little while she reached up and pulled my head down to hers and kissed my mouth, so softly, so lovingly, so gently. 'Oh, Tony, my darling,' she said. 'That was heaven. Pure heaven. Will you marry me?' 'Of course I will,' I said, immediately. 'Of course I will.' 'Now fuck me,' she said. 'Please.'

She drew her legs up and spread them, and I thrust my rampant, engorged prick toward that lovely, shaven pussy, with its waiting, wet, open pink lips. She saw it coming, and took hold of it, guiding it in, thrusting herself up towards it, swallowing it within herself. She was so wet now that it slid deeply into her without the slightest hesitation, and I started to pump it in and out of her, needing to come quickly. This could well be the world's shortest fuck, as far as I was concerned. We could always do it again more slowly later on. I just needed release from the agonizing sexual tensions that I had been building up in my cock during my session sucking her lovely pussy. She must have understood my need, for she then grasped the base of my prick, and masturbated it rapidly as I thrust in and out of her. I came within seconds, spurting my jism deeply into her. She kept on masturbating me until every last drop was milked, and I then withdrew, slipping down beside her, our arms about each other, and falling asleep almost instantly.

The next thing I knew, I was dreaming a lovely dream, where I was just lying back, doing absolutely nothing, except enjoying to the full the fact that this delightful woman was on top of me as I lay there, fucking the sweet Jesus out of me. I awoke, I know not how much later, to find the dream sweet reality. Annabel was astride me, her eyes closed, riding my cock for all she was worth, her breasts brushing my chest as she bent forward, giving it her all. I took hold of her buttocks and started pushing up against her. Her eyes opened wide in surprise, and then she smiled and said, 'Good morning, lover. I thought you might like to be woken up this way. I do hope you don't mind.' 'I can't think of anything nicer,' I said, entering into the spirit of the situation. We reached a joint culmination quickly, and Annabel climbed off me, giving me a big kiss as she so did.

'Breakfast?' she asked. 'I've got various cereals, bacon, eggs, bread, sausages, tomatoes, potatoes, orange juice, toast, marmalade, tea, coffee. Whatever. Can I tempt you?' I got up out of the bed and took hold of her and kissed her again. 'You can tempt me any time you like, my darling,' I said. 'But no breakfast, thank you. Just some coffee would be nice. Black with two lumps, please.' She looked at me in my nakedness. 'You can't walk around like that,' she said. 'You might get assaulted. By me. And I haven't got a dressing gown that will go anywhere near you. Why don't you have a shave and a shower and get dressed while I get the coffee going? You'll find my leg razor in the cupboard over the wash-basin. There are fresh blades there with it. Is there anything else that you need?' 'Just another kiss, thank you,' I said, helping myself.

Her bathroom was the kind you see in *House Beautiful*. All chrome and mirrors and pretty tiles. The bath was let into the floor, rather like a small swimming pool, and the shower was a glassed-in cabinet in its own corner. Not like mine, which is screwed onto the wall over my bath. It was all very expensive. And also very pleasant. Some expensively done-up places are often quite offensively expensively done-up, if you know what I mean. I could have lived happily in the surroundings of Annabel's luxury. I wondered what she meant when she had said would I marry her. I hoped she wasn't serious. Much as I liked her, I hardly knew her yet. Well, not really. And marriage wasn't on my current list of objectives. Not to anyone.

Annabel's leg razor was rather better than most of the other girls' leg razors I've been fortunate enough to have to suffer over the years. Usually they hadn't had a new blade for what felt like a year, and had never been washed. Have you ever shaved with a blunt, rusty leg razor? Annabel's was clean. There were, as she had said, new blades available, and it was a rather better model than any I had seen before. Thinking about it, this was probably the razor she shaved her pussy with. No wonder it was clean, and sharp, and efficient. Pussies are tender things to shave. I know. I've shaved them. But that's another story. Shaving my face was no problem. I shaved, showered, enjoyed playing with the adjustable shower-head on Annabel's power shower, and got myself dressed. I could smell the coffee from the bedroom. It said freshly ground, proper coffee.

'There you are,' she said, as I walked into the kitchen. I had noticed since I'd been up and about that there was a large, formal dining room, with a beautiful Georgian mahogany dining table, and twelve matching mahogany chairs. Quite a contrast to the furnishings in the rest of the penthouse. But the kitchen had a table large enough to seat six, and this was where we were having our coffee. 'Here I am indeed,' I said. 'I don't know how serious your asking me to marry you was last night, but looking around this morning, I'm seriously considering marrying you for your money.' She laughed. 'When I asked you,' she said, 'it was completely serious. Looking back, I think it was entirely appropriate at that time. This morning? Well, I still think it's a good idea. But perhaps we should get to know each other a little better before we finally commit ourselves. What do you think? Marrying me for my money wasn't especially what I had in mind. But there are probably worse things in life. This past year hasn't been particularly amusing. But last night has made up for a great deal. I do hope I shall see you again.' She poured my coffee, and passed me the sugar bowl.

'Of course you will, if you want to,' I said. 'I'm keen to see you. I had a delightful evening, a wonderful night, and an excellent start to the day this morning. What more could a person possibly want? The only thing I would say, if you will forgive me, is that I have the sort of job which often takes up quite a bit of my evenings, and at the weekends I spend most of my time writing things that I haven't got the time to write in the office. It leaves a few gaps. But if that doesn't faze you, I can't think that we'll have too many problems. You work yourself until late anyway. Do you work Saturday evenings, by the way?' It wasn't something I'd thought about before now.

'Usually not,' she replied. 'Strangely enough, most of our customers are Londoners, and they don't tend to go to night-clubs on Saturdays. The club is open, of course, but it's not often very full, and the customers are usually out-of-towners. The only exception to my not working on a Saturday is if a regular customer wants to put on a party, or a special celebration. Then I would expect to be there.' She came over to me and sat on my knee. She kissed me, long and hard. 'I do hope that we'll stay friends,' she said. 'Last night and this morning have been the two happiest days in my life for longer than I care to remember.' I kissed her back, remembering at that moment, I'm not sure why, Pamela saying 'Please don't turn into a frog.' It rather took the wind out of my sails. I wondered where Pamela was, and what she and the delightful Jenny were doing at this particular moment. I had heard that Pamela had given up her job, and gone to stay with friends in Italy, but I didn't know for sure.

'That's the nicest thing that anyone has said to me for a very long time,' I said to Annabel. 'I thank you. And yes, I think I do love you. It's just that I've never really been in love before. Not for more than a day or so, anyway. So I'm a little wary of my feelings. May I say I think I love you? Will that suffice for today?' Annabel laughed. 'Yes, of course it will,' she said. 'As to this evening,' I said, 'this being a Saturday, are you working?' 'No,' she said. 'Terrific,' I said. 'I'll think of somewhere nice to go for supper. How about if I pick you up about eight?' 'Thank you,' she said. 'I'd like that. Shall I dress up, or down?' 'Comfortable,' I said. 'Relaxed. Is there anything you don't like to eat?'

'No,' she said. 'I love it all. Except, if you're being serious, tripe. I've never eaten it, and I don't think I could.' 'That makes two of us,' I said. 'Although I've got an old friend who was born in Leeds, and who used to work on the *Yorkshire Post*, who swears by it. And he's something of a serious foodie. "You'll love it, Tony," he always says. "Forget all that *Tripe à la mode* nonsense. Just plain boiled, in milk, with mashed potatoes and onions. That's the only way to eat tripe."' Annabel laughed. 'I still think I can manage without it,' she said. 'Drive carefully now. The lift will take you down to the garage. See you this evening.'

The telephone was ringing as I got back to Hampstead. It was Carla. I think she was hoping that I would ask her over for the day/ night/ weekend, but I said, as nicely as I knew how, that I was pretty tied up for the weekend. She seemed cheerful enough when she rang off. An indomitable young lady. I spent a while catching up on everything from writing my freelance material to the usual weekend domestic trivia. I turned over the question of where to go for dinner that evening with Annabel, and decided that the Chelsea Rendezvous was as good a place as any.

Always one of my favourite restaurants from the day that it opened its doors, it was, I believe, the first restaurant in London to combine first-class Chinese food with Italian waiters and service. It very quickly became fashionable, and it was a fun place to eat, especially later in the evening. Cheap it wasn't. It was run by a delightful man called Sandro Tobi, an Italian restaurateur of great charm and enormous experience, who turned a rather plain basement almost on the corner of Sydney Street and the Fulham Road into one of London's chicest restaurants. He was small, good-looking in a very Italian way, and – according to any woman I ever took to any of his restaurants – very sexy. He later left the Chelsea Rendezvous and opened up his own Italian restaurant, Sal E Pepe, just off the Sloane Street end of Basil Street, in Knightsbridge. It's still there, and it's still some of the best Italian food in London. I picked Annabel up at eight, as arranged, and we drove down to the Chelsea Rendezvous, where I had booked a table for eight thirty. We had a drink in the upstairs bar, and Sandro came up to say hello. I introduced Annabel, and there were a lot of ornate Italian compliments, accompanied by much hand kissing and rolling of eyes. Annabel loved every moment of it, as all women did. Sandro showed us down to our table, and left us with the menus, having told us of the evening's specialities.

I waved at a few people I knew. It was that sort of restaurant. There was Evel Knievel, who was in London to do his Harley Davidson motorcycle jump across thirteen London buses. I had interviewed him for *Tiptop* the previous week, and had tickets for the press box at the event the following week. (It was his 301st such jump. When he finally did it, he cleared the buses, but crash landed, and suffered a crushed spinal vertebra, and an injured right arm). He raised a languid hand from the other side of the room, where he was sitting with his retinue.

I saw Margie McClean, who was the public relations officer for Macey's in New York, sitting with Ann Summers, Britain's first sex shop owner, together with her boyfriend and publicist, David Jones. What no-one knew at that time was that the shops didn't belong to that gorgeous lady at all. She was fronting them for Dandy Kim – Michael George Caborn Kimberly Waterfield. That company went into liquidation, and was bought from the official receiver by the present owners, who have made it the success it is today. I'd met Ann Summers when I interviewed her for *Tiptop*, and had been struck by, first her beauty – the hackneyed and much-used press description of her was as a 'typical English rose' – but it did describe her accurately. I don't mind admitting after all these years that I fancied her very strongly indeed. She literally oozed sex appeal. I was impressed too by her intelligence. And I was an admirer, professionally, of her monthly sexual advice column in *Men Only* magazine.

Sandro came to take our order, and the food came quickly, enticingly, and deliciously. As was often the case, Sandro came and sat with us and bought us a liqueur or two on the house, and gossiped with us about London, and life, and love, and other vitally important matters.

As we left, Annabel asked if we could go back to my place at Hampstead, rather than home to her place off Hyde Park Square. She was, she said, curious to see how I lived. Reasonably enough. I wondered if my sheets were clean, and then, remembering that it was Saturday, I knew that they were, for that was one of Saturday's little domestic chores. If I was expecting – or hoping – that the lady of any particular evening would join me back in Hampstead for the night, I always made sure that I had changed the sheets, even if they had only previously accommodated me. Crisp, newly laundered, clean sheets are vital to early early sexual encounters. But Saturday morning was clean sheet day anyway. I breathed a mental sigh of relief.

Annabel spent her time exploring my flat whilst I put on some music – some very early Presley – made coffee, and poured drinks. My flat is not big. At least, it's certainly not big by the standards of Annabel's penthouse. But it's not small either. It's a reasonable size of flat for two people to live in without feeling too crowded. Inevitably, it bears witness to the business by which I earn my living. There are specially drawn, mostly rude, cartoons, by cartoonists I've bought work from over the years. There are paintings and illustrations that are rather more specifically detailed in their sexual content that the kind of pictures that you see on most people's walls. There are the inevitable pictures of me with people that I have interviewed, taken at the time of the interview to illustrate them in whatever magazine or newspapers they were written for.

There are nudes, simply because I like nudes. I've got one by Stephen Ward that I particularly like. It's gentle, like he was. I've got an original piece of 'Wicked Wanda' artwork done by Ron Embleton for the *Penthouse* feature that he used to do with Fred Mullally. He's dead now, sadly. Ron, that is. Not Fred. Not too many people in the girlie magazine business know that Ron was Britain's best-known, and most respected, Dickensian illustrator. There's a photograph of a teddy bear, autographed for my teddy bear Henry. And so on. Annabel was enjoying looking at everything.

The Sixties, of course, were the days before we all had personal computers. In those days I used an Olympia portable typewriter that I had bought in the Fifties. I've written literally millions of words on it, and it had been around most of the world with me in its time. I can't believe, these days, how I used to work, but all journalists did it the same way back then. You wrote a draft, corrected and edited it, and then retyped the final version. I'm writing this on screen, and will edit it page by page as I write it, spell check it through the PC's facility, and print it off. It takes a fraction of the time that it used to take. Magic. Soon we'll simply be dictating to PCs, which will do everything else necessary. Don't laugh. You can dictate letters to PCs now.

'That was a lovely meal,' said Annabel, settling herself down in an easy chair. 'And I loved the restaurant, and your friend Sandro. And Chinese food doesn't come any better than that. Is he married?' 'Yes,' I said. 'Mmmm,' she said. 'Have you met his wife?' 'No,' I said. 'I haven't had that pleasure. People tell me that she lives back in Italy, but I don't know whether that's true or not.' 'I wonder,' said Annabel, 'if he's faithful to her?' 'I think that's something you would have to ask him yourself,' I said. 'He and I don't have those sort of conversations.' Nor did we. 'You just want him to fuck you,' I said. 'One look at those seductive brown Italian eyes, and you're his slave for ever. What you don't understand is that it's his business. Now that you've met him, leave aside going back to the Chelsea Rendezvous with me, you'll take your friends there, you'll recommend it to everyone you know, and you'll probably increase his business profits by two per cent annually entirely on your own. Fifty ladies like you in a year, and he's doubled his profits. Think about it.'

'Mmmm,' said Annabel again. 'I'm enjoying thinking about it. In fact, I've been thinking about it all evening. But not with Sandro. With you, lover. I've been thinking about it so much that my pussy is all wet. What can we do about that?' she asked, fluttering her eyelashes exaggeratedly. 'Do you think we should go to bed and, er, fuck? Otherwise I'm going to make a nasty stain on your lovely chair here. My knickers are sopping wet, and my skirt is getting wet, and if I don't move soon, there's going to be a problem. Of course, I could always go home and have a hot bath. If you'd rather?' Her eyes were so full of fun, I had to laugh. 'Come on, sweetheart,' I said. 'Get them round your ankles. Failing Sandro, I promise to do my best.'

My bedroom is functional rather than exotic or luxurious. The bed is modern – Maples's best – and king-size. The bedroom lights are soft and low, the carpet is thick and deep, and the music, piped through from the sitting-room, can be soft and sexy, or loud and raunchy. I can choose. *You* can choose. The pictures are, frankly, rude. They are all of women, and they are very detailed. There are no men. The pictures are not there for effect, but because I like them. Over the years, I've spent a lot of time in there. I feel relaxed there. Not threatened. I'm at home. Annabel had included the bedroom in her earlier tour of inspection. 'It's a pretty bedroom,' she said now, starting to undress. I didn't really want to start a conversation at that particular moment. I simply wanted to watch her undress. 'Thank you,' I said. 'But it's not at all masculine,' she said, undoing the waistband of her skirt and letting it drop on the floor. 'No,' I agreed. 'But it certainly isn't feminine. As far as I'm concerned, it's just comfortable.'

She was standing there in lavender-coloured satin bra and knickers, both minimal in concept. The bra only just held her firm breasts, and as I watched she undid the catch behind her back and let her breasts free from the bra's restraint. They were as beautiful as I remembered them. Her knickers were of the kind described as briefs, and brief they were. I could see the damp stain at her crotch, of which she had complained but minutes earlier, but even more intensely erotic, I could see that the actual crotch of her knickers had caught in her pussy lips. It has always been for me one of the sexiest sights on God's earth. Particularly when the knickers are pulled down towards the girl's knees, and the knicker crotch is still caught in her cunt. Instant pornography. Even as I thought of it, that was exactly what Annabel did. She looked down. 'Oh, dear,' she said. 'I seem to have got my knicks caught up somewhere.' She even blushed as she pulled the disobliging crotch out. I could smell the scent of aroused pussy from across the bedroom. My cock started to get seriously hard.

Having at last removed the offending (her, not me) knickers, Annabel was left in just a pair of black, very small mesh, fishnet stockings, held up by a tiny, satin, lavender suspender belt, with over-long suspenders. I looked at her. She looked back, quizzically, and smiled. 'May I ask a small favour please, love?' I asked. 'Yes, of course you can,' she said. 'What is it?' 'Will you keep the stockings and suspenders on for me? Like with all reasonably normal men, it's a tremendous turn-on. Please?' 'Of course, darling,' she said. 'Whatever you would like me to do, you only have to ask. Don't you know that? Or if there is anything that you want me to do to you, you only have to tell me. All right? It takes time to get to know people, but whatever you want, just tell me. OK?'

Jesus, I thought to myself. I could tell that she meant it. 'Thank you, my sweetheart,' I said. 'The stockings and suspenders will do nicely for now. I'll tell you about the serious perversions later.' She laughed. 'There's just one thing perhaps I ought to tell you,' she said, just a mite nervously, I thought. 'I'm not into pain. I don't think pain has anything to do with sex. Or love. At least not for me. Is that likely to be a problem?' It was my turn to laugh. 'Not with me, sweetheart,' I said. 'I'm with you. I'm not a pain freak.' I took her in my arms, and kissed her, my tongue delving deeply into her mouth. She tongued me back, her hand reaching down and encompassing my rigid cock. I put a hand down between her legs and found her wet, throbbing pussy. 'Let's do it now,' she whispered. 'Let's fuck. Please?'

She lay on the bed and drew her legs up. She had terrific legs. The stockings and suspenders looked sensational. I entered her, perhaps a little roughly. It wasn't intentional, I was just in a hurry to get my prick inside her. It slipped in as if it had been greased. She was so wet, there was no friction at all. Just all-involving, slippery, total suction. It was fantastic. We thrust and bucked and fucked at each other, both of us anxious to get our oats, both heedful of the other's needs, but more intent, individually, in getting our purely selfish rocks off.

Sex is like that sometimes, I don't have to tell you. What is good is when both partners have the same kind of sex in mind at the same time. That's when the bells start to ring, and the world starts to turn a little faster, and that was exactly what was happening to Annabel and me right then. 'Oh, yes, baby,' she said. 'You're fucking me so well. So hard. I like it. Your great stiff cock is deep inside my cunt, and I can feel it pushing against my womb. Soon now you're going to come, and I'm going to feel your spunk spurting up inside me, and that will make *me* come. Do it now, baby. Come now, sweetheart. Fuck me now.' I did as I was told. I couldn't have held on any longer anyway. Gentle it wasn't. Rough it was. I'd heard about girls who liked a bit of rough, but I'd never thought of myself in that category. Oh, well. Live and learn. Annabel's orgasm joined my ejaculation, and we writhed together in each other's arms, spasming and panting and groaning aloud. The sounds of sexual climax are strangely similar to the sounds of pain when you think about it. And then, suddenly, it was all over, at least for the moment, and we just lay there holding each other.

After a while, Annabel let go of me and turned over onto her tummy, resting her head on her folded arms. She had a pretty back. She had a pretty everything, let's face it, but I hadn't studied her back at close quarters before. Her shoulders were well shaped but narrow, and led down to her slim waist. Her flesh was firm, but you could see the muscles beneath the skin. There was no fat. Below her waist the lavender satin suspender belt topped off her taut, firm, also well-muscled buttocks, and the long, thin, elastic suspenders themselves ran down to her black stocking tops, the three contrasting materials framing her bottom in the most exciting way.

I put out a hand and lazily stroked her buttocks. She wriggled her bottom appreciatively, and murmured, 'That's nice.' I began to pay rather more serious attention to her, and I turned over onto my side, the better to see what I was doing. Her pudenda might be shaven, but her anal area was covered with fine, silken, dark auburn hair. The nearer to her anus that it grew, the thicker it got. Just as shaved pussy drives me wild with sexual desire, so do hairy female armpits and hairy female sphincters. Perverse, I know, but there you go. I felt my cock stiffening at the thought of anal sex, as I slid an exploratory finger down into her anal cleft, finding and feeling the puckered object of my desire. Annabel pushed up against the pressure of my finger. 'Mmmm,' she said. 'Have you got any cold cream? Something like that?' I had. I'd got some sexual lubricant. 'Yes, sweetheart,' I said. 'Hang on while I go and get it.' It was in the bathroom. Don't ask me why. I don't fuck in the bath. Well, not very often.

I found the necessary tube, and went back into the bedroom, where Annabel was still lying on the bed in the same position. I squeezed out an inch of the lubricant, and began to massage it into her anus. I then took another inch, and thrust my finger as deeply as it would go down inside her rectum, lubricating as much as I could, whilst she wriggled and pressed hard against my finger. 'You're going to bugger me, aren't you?' she said. 'I like that. Do all girls like that? I've often wondered.' 'I can't speak for all girls, darling,' I said. 'But from my limited experience, some do and some don't.' For good measure, I rubbed my cock all over with the lubricant, and then wiped my now greasy hand on a tissue from a box on the bedside table.

I took hold of Annabel's hips, and pulled her back towards me and up, until she was kneeling in front of me, and I began to ease my stiff cock into her anus. I was as gentle as I could possibly be, and the lubricant worked well. Even so, Annabel said 'Slowly, please, sweetheart. It's been a long time.' I slowed down as requested, stifling my desire for anal rape, wanting to thrust deeply, strongly, immediately. I eased my cock in, inch by slow inch. Her rectum was tight. Gloriously tight. I felt my cock becoming even more engorged as I fed it slowly up her anus. And then, finally, it was in all the way. Up to the hilt. Annabel let out a sigh – perhaps of relief, who knows? – and started to move her hips back against me. I began to fuck her, anally, holding on to her hips, thrusting deep, drawing almost out, only to thrust in again my full length.

I felt Annabel moving her right arm, and looking down, I could see that she had started playing with herself, manipulating her clitoris as I buggered her. Having a girlish wank. She glanced over her shoulder, and looked up at me, smiling. 'Would you like some pussy juice?' she asked, holding her right hand back over her right shoulder, her fingers wet from where they had been. I didn't reply, I simply put my head down and took her fingers in my mouth, sucking and licking off the scented mucus from her cunt. It tasted good. 'More, please,' I said, and she put her hand between her legs again, and brought it back up, once more charged with her delicately flavoured feminine nectar.

'Do you like buggering me?' she asked, her voice a low, throaty whisper. 'Yes,' I answered back, my own voice husky with satiated desire. 'Yes, I do.' 'Do you like it better than fucking me?' she asked next. 'No, sweetheart,' I answered, truthfully. 'Not better than. Not worse than. As well as. I love it all. I love all of your body. I love all of you. I'm going to come now,' I said, feeling my ejaculation forcing its way up from somewhere deep down in my balls. And I did. 'Oooh,' said Annabel. 'That feels nice. It's all hot. I can feel it spurting up me.' And she began to move her fingers faster, playing a staccato, carefully orchestrated, sexual sequence on her no doubt burgeoning clitoris. And then she started to come too, groaning with pleasure as she did so, bucking her hips against me, pressing back hard, ensuring that my still rampant prick stayed deeply inside her. I waited for her to complete what seemed to be a fairly short, but quite intense, series of orgasms, and then, certain finally that she had finished I carefully withdrew, collapsing all of a heap, as they say, beside her on the bed.

Annabel put an arm across my shoulders, and leaned across and kissed me, licking and tonguing me lasciviously as she did. 'I'm so glad you're not inhibited,' she said. 'It makes sex so much more fun.' 'I do agree with you, sweetheart,' I said. 'But I do have *some* inhibitions. One man's meat, as the saying goes.' She looked at me. 'What inhibitions?' she asked. 'Well,' I said, 'there's the question of pain, which I think you and I both agreed upon. Didn't we?' I asked, nervously. 'Oh, that,' she said. 'Yes, of course. That's not an inhibition. That's just common sense. What else?' I thought for a moment. 'Well, not a lot,' I said. 'But, for example, whilst I'll happily fuck whilst a woman is having her period, I'm not into cunnilingus under those conditions.' 'Good God,' she said. 'Is anyone?' 'Surely,' I replied. 'Like I just said. One man's meat.' 'But that's disgusting,' she said. 'Well,' I said, 'I have to admit that it doesn't do anything for me. But for some men, it is the biggest turn-on in their otherwise sexually dissatisfied lives. *Hustler* magazine, in the states, regularly features cartoons in full colour – on the subject. If I think about it, I'm not into fucking animals or children and I'm not into that other aspect of S&M, bondage. The idea of sex with women who are tied up doesn't appeal. Although I think bondage is more of a fetish than most people realize. Have you ever seen any of those Japanese pornographic bondage magazines?'

'No, I haven't,' she said. 'Are they interesting?' 'Not to me,' I said. 'Not sexually, anyway. Professionally, yes. It's all part of my job. But they're cruel. Brutal. The women aren't just tied up. They're tied so tightly that their bodily parts are deformed. Their breasts and nipples, that sort of thing, excruciatingly, painfully bound. I don't think sex is part of that kind of bondage, other than masturbatory sex, while looking at the results of the bondage. I don't think insertion of the penis anywhere is part of it. But I don't actually know. All the magazines show are the unbelievably complicated knots that the women are forced to submit to. In every other kind of pornography, the actual act of sex, one way or another, is normally compulsory. The culmination of the activity depicted. It might be straight sex, oral sex, anal sex, what have you, but it is what the perversion concludes with. Even with bestiality, they're either fucking, or getting fucked by, the animals, unattractive as that might be.'

'Go on,' Annabel said. 'What else?' I thought long and hard. I find I tend to concentrate, sexually, on the things that I like, rather than on the things that I don't like. 'The only other area that truly leaves me cold,' I said, 'is that of water sports. You know. Having girls piss in your mouth. Pissing in girl's mouths. The giving and receiving of enemas.' 'I've heard of people who like enemas,' said Annabel, 'but pissing down people's throats is a new one on me. What's that all about?' 'Don't ask,' I replied. 'But it doesn't stop at piss.'

'What an extraordinary thing,' said Annabel. 'Do you think we're missing something?' 'I don't really think so, darling,' I said. 'I mean, I'm more than happy to admit my own particular sexual fetishes. I'm a tremendous knicker fetishist. Knickers, suspender belts, stockings. Sexy lingerie. Silk. Satin. Soft, shiny, sexy material. All that kind of thing. I love it. Oral sex of any kind. Giving, receiving. Either. Both. Shaven pussies. Magic. I could come at the thought of it, never mind looking at yours,' I said. I leaned down and kissed her shaven pudenda, giving her slit a long, deep lick as I did. 'Mmmm,' I said. 'Too much.' My cock started to stiffen once more. 'Anal sex, in the right circumstances, as you've just discovered,' I said. 'What do you mean by the right circumstances?' she asked. 'Where the girl genuinely enjoys it too,' I said. 'It's not half as good if she doesn't really enjoy it, but is just letting you do it because you want to, and she likes you. Or even loves you.' 'I guess that's understandable,' said Annabel. 'Aren't you the lucky one …' 'Yes, sweetheart,' I said. 'I am. And don't think that I don't appreciate it, because I do.'

I don't usually spend a great deal of time thinking about obscure perversions, other than when my writing or editing requires me to. Then again the description, sight, sound, or thought of participation in sex with two lesbian women is always intensely erotic to me. I had no embarrassment in telling Annabel this. I have, in my day, fucked lesbians. Not in an effort to convert them, but because I have liked them, and they have liked me. There is nothing exclusive about lesbian sex. Most (although not all) lesbians enjoy heterosexual sex at some period in their lives. I have shared a bed with two lesbian lovers, for three weeks. They made long, relaxed, erotic oral love with each other, before one of them fucked me whilst the other played with herself. The stuff of dreams? It certainly was for me. It was the slightly older of the two who fucked me, and I was not permitted, under any circumstances, to touch the younger one. Watch, yes. Touch, no. Had she been on her own, I do believe I could have persuaded the younger one to give straight sex a whirl.

I do not truly understand why there is this attraction to lesbian sex, or why – along with a lot of other men – I have it so deeply ingrained in my libido. But then I've only got to look at two girls doing all those naughty things together, and my cock stands to immediate attention. I guess it is as simple as one instantly wants to join in. Not just one naughty, raunchy, half-naked, fuckable beauty, but two! The other strange thing about minority sex in general, is that whatever you want, however unpleasant, painful, disgusting or unacceptable your wife, girl-friend, lover or partner may find it, it is always available for money. That might be quite a lot of money, but whatever you want, it's for sale. Having discussed this fairly extensive catalogue of my sexual likes and dislikes, of fetishes, perversions, call them what you like, I asked Annabel to tell me about hers.

'Oh, I don't know, sweetheart,' she said. 'I haven't got that many, really. I like anal sex, as you now know. I think I like it because I always thought it was so naughty. It excites me to think I'm doing something that I was always brought up to believe was for serious sexual perverts. I love oral sex. Both giving and receiving. Although I must admit that I have a preference for either on their own. You know, if I'm sucking your cock, I like to be able to concentrate on what I'm doing. Really work at it. I don't like the distraction of you sucking my pussy at the same time. And vice-versa. When you suck my pussy, I like best to be able to lie back and enjoy it. Think of England. All that. Doing both at the same time, for me, detracts from both of them.' She paused. 'I have to agree with you, my darling,' I said. 'You're right.' I hadn't actually thought about it before, but now that I did, she *was* right. Always assuming, of course, that the person who was doing it to you knew what they were doing.

'What else?' I asked. 'What else turns you on? Or off?' 'Well, off is easy,' she replied. 'As you know, anything to do with pain. I *do* have rape fantasies, and I enjoy those, but they actually have nothing to do with pain. They're usually sheiks with huge cocks who fuck me and fuck me, and I come and come. There's absolutely no pain at all.' 'When do you have those fantasies?' I asked, curiously. 'When we fuck?' 'No,' she said, looking faintly embarrassed. 'When I'm alone. When I'm playing with myself. You know. Masturbating. Don't you masturbate?'

'Well, yes,' I said. 'Of course I do. Doesn't everybody? It's just that most people don't talk about it. I only ever met two women, for example, who admitted to owning vibrators. The great sex toy of the age we live in. And I think the two of them only brought the subject up because they both loved me to do it to them. They found that a big turn-on. So did I, thinking about it.' Annabel laughed. 'Well, *I*'ve got a vibrator, and you can use it on me any time you like,' she said. 'But frankly, I'd rather be fucked. I only bought it as a rather more efficient way of achieving an orgasm on my own. Now that I've got you...' She hesitated for a moment, and suddenly her face looked quite disconsolate. But only for a moment. Then she smiled again, lighting her face up from within. It was a heart-rending few seconds. She corrected herself. 'Whilst I've got you,' she said, 'I don't feel the need for it. But as I said, if you think it would be fun, feel free.' I grinned back at her. 'Well, thank you. I'll bear that in mind. But tell me more about your fantasies. About what turns you on sexually.'

She laughed, and I could see that the moment of desolation

had passed. 'You know, Tony,' she said, 'you're going to grow into a dirty old man. Right now, you' re a dirty young man.' She paused. 'Thank goodness.' It was my turn to laugh. This was quite a lady. 'I'm particularly glad that you like the sexy knickers, and black stockings and suspenders bit,' she went on, 'because I do too. I love wearing things like that. I love wearing what I have on now, and I was excited when you said keep them on. They heighten my sexuality by an enormous amount. And then there are lots of dressing-up kinds of things that I've often thought about, and wondered if they would be fun, but I've never found anyone before whom I've felt relaxed enough about to discuss them with, never mind try them out.' 'What sort of things?' I asked. 'Oh, quite a variety, really,' she replied. 'You know, like rubber knickers, for example. Black latex. And bras, of course. I'm just plain curious to find out what they might do for me. Or you. If anything at all.'

I didn't say anything. Frankly, the idea didn't do a lot for me, but it was something I'd never experienced, and I remembered surprising myself by getting quite turned on by my pretend spanking session with Judy. Annabel continued, 'And, in rather a similar context, there's a lot of sexy patent leather gear about, isn't there? Black patent leather bras, corsets, high heeled shoes. I don't know, really. It's just a thought. Maybe those are too specialized fetishes to do anything for either of us, but it might be fun to find out. But perhaps nearer home,' she went on, looking directly at me, 'I've always wanted to really dress up in all the classic erotic outfits. Like a schoolgirl, for example. You know, a short little navy blue gymslip, with black woolly stockings, and little white knickers. Does that turn you on, my sweet ?'

I had to admit that the idea of it most certainly did. 'Yes,' I said. 'I could happily fuck an Annabel schoolgirl. Any time.' 'And then of course there's the basic French maid's outfit,' she continued. 'Short black skirt, with frilly black knickers showing off the black suspenders. Little white apron, and one of those little white cap things on my head. What do you think of that?' 'Sounds good to me,' I said. She slipped a hand down to her shaven cunt. 'My pussy's getting wet just at the very thought of all these kinky ideas,' she breathed.

I looked down at her bald quim, into which she had slid her forefinger, and I watched as she started working it away, framed by the lavender suspender belt, with its long, thin suspenders, and the black, fine mesh stockings, with their shiny, solid black tops, and I wondered, just how kinky can one get? But don't misunderstand me. I wasn't complaining. Absolutely not. She continued gently frigging as she went on.

'Not forgetting, of course, the nurse's uniform. Although that isn't all that sexy, unless it's a parody of the real thing. But I read that it turns some men on. I think it's got more to do with the unavailability of sex in hospitals, and the fact that the nurses are mostly the only women around. Hence the male fantasies. And then there's your actual tart. I mean, serious tart. More than my present outfit, even if I had the knickers on. You know the kind of thing. Peep-hole satin bras that your nipples poke through. Crotchless knickers, showing off your pussy. Ooooh,' she said suddenly. 'What is it?' I asked. 'I've just remembered,' said Annabel. 'When I was talking about rubber knickers, I should have mentioned that version of rubber knickers that come with a built-in dildo. Now that's *got* to be good news for any girl. Imagine walking around all day wearing those. Or how about riding a bicycle?' She laughed uproariously at the idea, and I had to join in with her. Meanwhile her right hand had picked up speed, and her fingers were moving rather faster. I felt my cock rising to the occasion at the sight of her wanking herself. But it didn't stop her talking. At least, not for the moment. I leaned over her and, first putting a finger on her lips to put an end to this conversation about sexual preferences, fantasies, perversions, and the like, I then kissed her. 'Shall I fuck you now, my dearest?' I asked. 'I see you're busily bringing yourself off, and if you would prefer it, I'll happily take over and do the job properly for you.'

'That's kind of you, sweetheart,' she said. 'But, despite my earlier protestations, I'm actually enjoying what I'm doing to myself. It probably has a lot to do with the fact that you are here beside me, and I know that you're available, should I so wish. I'm not in the sadly solitary situation that is normal for me when I masturbate. But what you can continue to do, if you will, is kiss me whilst I finish myself off. I'd like that.'

That, of course, was no problem, and I kissed her, wantonly, appreciatively, excitedly, as she continued to finger herself to orgasm. We tongued each other, slurping and licking and sucking, and then she started to moan and writhe about as she started to come. She was a noisy girl, given her head, and it was a pleasure to listen to her enjoying herself. 'That was nice,' she said, when she'd finished. 'I enjoyed that.' She put her fingers up to my lips. 'Would you like some pussy juice to suck?' she asked. There is only one answer to that question in my book. As I began to suck and lick her fingers clean, tasting the sticky, tantalizing, delicious effluent from her now satiated cunt, I felt for and found her other hand, and I put it on my burgeoning prick. 'Now wank *me* please, darling,' I said. 'I'd enjoy that.' 'Oooh, you naughty boy,' she said. 'How lovely.' And so saying, she stuck her tongue down my throat, and started to pull my foreskin slowly, oh, so slowly, up and down my glans. Then she took her other hand and placed it firmly around the base of my cock, squeezing gently. 'Do you like girls wanking you, darling?' she asked. 'Mmm,' I said. 'Have you had lots of girls wank you?' she asked. 'Mmm,' I said. 'A few.' 'Tell me about it,' she requested. 'Not now, darling,' I replied. 'Later.' 'Shall I talk dirty to you?' she asked. 'Would you like that?' 'Mmm,' I said. 'Please.'

'While I was playing with my naughty pussy just now,' she said, 'I was thinking about getting fucked by three men. I don't know who they were, but they all had giant pricks. Just like yours.' She giggled as she said it, slightly increasing the rhythm with which she was masturbating me. 'One of them was fucking my cunt. That's a lovely, dirty, explicit, exciting word, isn't it? Cunt. Fucking my dirty cunt. His cock was stretching my cunt wide, really wide, and he was deep, deep inside it. I was so wet from him fucking me that my cunt was running with juice. It was running all down my thighs, and down my legs. I could feel it dripping all down me.

'And then the second man started fucking my arse. He forced his swollen prick right up my tight little arsehole. It didn't hurt. It was lovely. He must have greased his prick before he started pushing it up me. And then this third man came and knelt in front of my face, with his rigid cock in his hand, and he said "You know what you're going to do with this, don't you?" And I looked at this third huge, rampant penis. He had been circumcised, and his cock-head was all purple and swollen with engorged blood, and I could see the blue veins running down his shaft, and I said yes. And he said, "What are you going to do with it?" And I said, "I'm going to suck it. I'm going to suck your cock until you spurt your hot come down my throat." And then he deep-throated me. You know, pushed his prick so far into my mouth that he was actually fucking my throat. In real life, I'm sure I'd choke, or vomit, or something awful. But in my fantasy, he fucks my throat, and just as he starts to spurt his hot come down my throat, the man who is anally fucking me starts to pump his come up me, and the man in my cunt shoots his load too. So all three men are spurting their come into my three orifices at the same time. It's a tremendously exciting, erotic feeling.'

While Annabel is talking dirty to me, she's moved her other hand away from the base of my prick, and she's stroking the cleft between my buttocks. Then her finger is over my anus, and whilst she's wanking me with one hand, she's massaging my anus with the other.

It turns me on, to my surprise, and I press my anus hard backwards, against her hand, and her finger slips inside me. She starts to push it in and out, quite slowly and deliberately, and suddenly I am ejaculating all over her other, hard-working hand. I come in great gouts, my cock pumping, and Annabel keeps up her masturbatory motions until the very last of my ejaculate has been milked. I feel satiated, gratified, fulfilled, content. As I watch, Annabel licks my come off her fingers, sucking and licking, rather like a child with an ice-cream cornet. 'Mmm,' she said. 'Nice.' I sighed. 'Yes,' I said. 'For me, too. Thank you.' I gave her a big kiss. 'Don't be cross, but I think I'm falling asleep.' I looked at the bedside clock. It was after three. 'Sleep well,' I said. 'And you,' she said. 'Goodnight, my darling.' We fell asleep in each other's arms.

Sunday dawned just after ten for me. Annabel was still asleep, snoring very gently, curled up like a little cat. A happy little cat. I smiled. She was still wearing her stockings and suspender belt. I felt pretty good, surprisingly, but I wasn't in any kind of a state to contemplate cooking a meal. I rang the White Elephant on the River, an offshoot of the White Elephant restaurant, situated on that part of the embankment called Grosvenor Road, just east of Chelsea Bridge, and made reservations for Sunday lunch. They did a marvellous American-style brunch in those days, which was both delicious and excellent value. In the evenings they were a late-night supper club, with an excellent group that played just the sort of mixture of gentle jazz, moody swing, and the kind of romantic music that gets girls into a knicker-dropping mood. Marvellous place. There was also, for a short time, the Pink Elephant, in Jermyn Street. There was an awful lot of competition in those days, and it didn't last too long, sadly. Its premises are better known these days as Tramp.

I put some coffee on, showered and shaved, and checked through my freelance schedule. My editorial work was, surprisingly, reasonably up to date. I saw that I had a batch of readers' letters to write for *Tiptop*. Yes, I do mean 'write'. All the girlie magazines that I have ever been involved with do it. So do most of their competitors. Someone who understands the business writes the readers' letters. The reason is that, if you were to read all the letters that arrive intended for publication in a men's magazine's correspondence column, you would find that they almost all fell into a fairly limited number of well-worn categories. Let me give you a few examples: does penis size really matter? (Letters for and against). I like black crumpet/ white crumpet/ green crumpet. My wife/ girlfriend/ lover won't suck my cock/ let me take dirty pictures of her/ wear sexy lingerie. I'm shagging my best friend's wife: should we tell him? Is it all right to fuck my sister, since we both enjoy this? And so on.

There *are* genuine letters printed, of course. Anything that arrives that is different, interesting, and reasonably well written, will almost certainly get published. But since these columns are always one of the most popular features in the magazine, the editor cannot afford to be repetitive, or he would simply lose sales. 'I'm not going to buy X magazine again,' the punters would say. 'Its readers' letters column is always full of the same kind of letters.' Hence my task that Sunday.

It's not actually as easy as you might think. Each letter has to be a complete little story, with a beginning, a middle, and an end, even if it is only posing a question. Each one must, of course, be totally different. All of them should, ideally, be sexy, and stimulate a response. I remember one from years ago that appeared in a specialist magazine, long before I knew that most of these letters were a figment of someone's imagination, where the writer allegedly obtained pleasure from inserting his cock into the hose of a vacuum machine, and then switching it on. I often wondered if there was a run of out-patients in hospital casualty departments of people foolish enough to try out this feat, which I realize now was almost certainly the result of an over-enthusiastic letter writer of the kind I am describing to you. I decided to postpone that particular chore until later that afternoon. The thought of lunch with Annabel was far more enticing, added to which, it was probably about time that I woke her up, or we wouldn't make the restaurant on time, the more so if, as was likely, she would want to change her clothes on the way. And, being practical, I could come home alone after dropping Annabel off at her penthouse, the better to concentrate on what I had to do.

I went through to the bedroom. Annabel was still sound asleep, sleeping the sleep of the innocent. I half-drew the curtains, letting through a shaft of sunlight, and went through to the living room and put on Neil Diamond's 'Hot August Night.' Not *too* loudly. I always think that's the greatest eighteen-bar introduction to any piece of music ever written. I heard a sleepy sigh from the bedroom, followed by a long yawn. I went through to greet her.

She smiled up at me. 'Good morning, lover,' she said. 'What time is it?' 'It's just after eleven,' I said, looking at my watch. 'I've booked a table for lunch at one thirty. There's plenty of time, but if you want to go home on the way and change, maybe we should be thinking of beginning to move. Only very gently, of course.' She laughed, and stretched. 'Anything you say, my darling,' she said. 'Would you like some tea or coffee?' I asked. 'Juice? Toast? Anything?' She thought for a moment, and then 'Coffee would be nice. If you go and put it on, you could come back and fuck me whilst it's brewing. How does that appeal?' she asked. 'That appeals more than anything I can think of at this moment in time,' I replied. 'In fact, the hell with the coffee. I'll see to that afterwards.'

I took off my robe, and got back into bed. I reached down to that adorable, shaven snatch between those creamy thighs, and felt how wet she was. 'Surprised?' she asked. 'Yes,' I had to admit. 'That was a very quick reaction.' She grinned. 'I was cheating,' she admitted. 'I woke up a while ago, and I started playing with myself, thinking about last night. And then, I thought, why play with myself, when the real thing is only in the other room? So I kept the engine running gently, as it were. And here we are. Wet and willing. At your service, sir.'

I laughed, kissed her fondly, and then settled down to some serious fucking. The energetic activities of the night had removed any need for urgency, so I think we both enjoyed the long, gentle, drawn-out, sensual fuck that followed. I know

I did, and Annabel made all the right noises as she reached her orgasms at the conclusion. It was certainly sexual, but I was conscious that there was also love and affection and, yes, even liking present too. We eventually dragged ourselves out of bed, and I got the coffee together whilst Annabel showered and dressed. My kitchen is far too small to sit in, so we sat next to each other in the dining room, drinking and talking, smiling at each other a lot, touching. You know the sort of thing. Annabel asked where we were going to lunch, and I told her. 'It sounds fun,' she said. 'I've not been there, although I've heard of it. What shall I wear?' 'Whatever you're comfortable in,' I told her. 'Anything from jeans to full evening dress is perfectly acceptable there for Sunday brunch. And if you think I'm kidding, just you wait and see!' It was true, actually. None of the White Elephant establishments were fussy about clothes. About who their members were, yes. About clothes, no. And brunch at the On-the-river, as we used to call it, was the most informal of gatherings.

We drove from Hampstead via Hyde Park Square, and I went up to the penthouse and sat and watched whilst Annabel changed. Off came the knickers, suspender belt and stockings that had served us both so well, to be replaced by plain black tights (passion killers, I always call them!), jeans, and a cashmere sweater. This girl didn't stint herself over anything, it would seem. But then, as I had discovered, she wasn't simply the night-club manageress that she had at first seemed to be. She was also a partner in what had to be a very successful business. Annabel checked her make-up, pulled down her sweater, took a last look in the mirror (don't they all?) and said 'Ready, sweetheart. That didn't take too long, did it?' 'No, my love,' I said. Nor had it. Perhaps fifteen minutes from the time we had entered the penthouse. It was one fifteen. We had all the time in the world.

I drove slowly through the park, turned down Sloane Street, and wiggled through Pimlico to the restaurant, where the doorman relieved me of the bother of finding a parking space.

Of such small pleasures is real life comprised. For me, anyway.

The restaurant was packed. It always was. The customers were a mixture of film and theatrical showbiz people, including a lot of those who were on the business side of cinema, theatre, or television, as opposed to being actors or actresses. Producers, directors. Music arrangers. Designers. There was a reasonable sprinkling of successful businessmen and their ladies. Usually, on Sundays, their wives. A few writers. Mostly – but not all – from television. And the inevitable hangers-on. Not at all a bad crowd, really.

Annabel was fascinated at seeing as successful a roomful of people as she superintended most evenings, but in an entirely different setting, and with, mostly, very different customers. We drank Buck's Fizz, and ate Eggs Benedict, and enjoyed each other's company. My prick twitched as I looked down, to see Annabel's nipples thrusting stiffly against the cashmere of her sweater.

I swear that the more you fuck, the more you want to. I remembered, thinking about it, that she hadn't got any knickers on. Just the tights. Well, they had a cotton crotch, didn't they? Who needed knickers with that sort of gear? I remembered, too, how her shaven cunt-lips looked through the black nylon of her tights, pressing against the fine mesh. I moved about until I got my stiffening cock into a slightly more comfortable position. Whatever else I was going to do that day, I made a mental note that my writing responsibilities – the letters – came first. They were due in with Carla the first thing the following morning. Annabel looked at me. 'Is there something wrong, darling?' she asked. 'You look a little – I don't know – upset? Cross? Preoccupied? Can I help?' I laughed, and leaned across to my left and whispered in her ear. 'I was just thinking how nice it would be to take you away from here, when we've finished lunch, and fuck you again,' I said. 'But I've got some work to do, and I have to go back to Hampstead and do it. Soon.' 'Oh, dear,' she sighed. 'And I was just thinking how I would like to be taken away from here and fucked stupid. It only goes to show, a girl can get too greedy.'

Of course, the inevitable happened. When we had finished our lunch, I drove Annabel back to Hampstead with me. But no! You're wrong there. We didn't fuck immediately. I got stuck into my work instead. Annabel read the Sunday papers, whilst I concentrated on my letter writing. We went to bed the moment I had finished, and stayed there until it was time for me to go to the office the following morning. We didn't even get up to eat that evening. As I remember, we didn't get a lot of sleep either. But during that time, we had the sense to discuss our rather different working hours, and we agreed that they didn't seriously allow an on-going relationship during the week. I was finishing work roughly about the time Annabel was starting, and when she was finishing, I should be in bed and fast asleep.

True love, if you believe in that, dictates that Annabel should have arrived at Hampstead direct from the Club at around three-thirty each morning, to wake me up and transport me instantly to sexual heaven. Reality said that, if I was to contribute what was expected of me at Tiptop Publications, I needed rather more sleep than that kind of schedule allowed. We agreed, albeit reluctantly, that we would, at least for the time being, run our love life from when Annabel left the club on Friday nights, to Sunday evening. It was, I still believe, the only reasonable decision. I was pleased too that, at that stage, Annabel didn't suggest that I gave my job up, since she could well afford to keep us both in a manner to which I would have loved to have become accustomed. I'm sure it was something that she thought about, and I like to believe that she knew that I would have found such a suggestion totally gratuitous. She was, amongst, many other lovely things, a very sensitive woman.

CHAPTER FIVE: ALL GIRLS TOGETHER

Carla gave me a Monday-morning kiss, together with a bit of an old-fashioned look, when I delivered the correspondence manuscript. 'And how is our deputy editor this flourishing Monday morning?' she asked. 'We look well. There's an air of … I'm not sure what. Something nice.' She looked at me again, rather more quizzically. 'Could it be …No …Are we …' 'Go on,' I said. 'For God's sake say it.' 'Oh, all right then,' she said. 'Are we in love?' 'In love?' I queried. 'Nonsense. You know me. Find 'em, fuck 'em, and forget 'em. In love! That's preposterous. Whatever gave you that idea?' 'I'm not sure, really,' said Carla. 'Just something about you this morning. Forget I said it.' She shrugged her shoulders, and, by way of dismissal, started working on the manuscript that I had just given her. What a very perceptive young lady she was.

I was due that morning to go up to the studio on the top floor to oversee a photographic shoot that Fred had set up before his departure. Somewhere he had discovered a woman who was adorned with more rings through more parts of her body than this world dreams of. (Don't ask me where he found her. There were lots of things we didn't ask Fred, and where he found certain things was one of them). I'd seen some rather bad, very amateur, nude photographs of her that Fred had brought into the office, simply to demonstrate why he thought she would make an interesting photographic set. She had more ear-rings than a punk rocker. On top of which she had a ring through one nostril. She had about five or six rings through each nipple. And then she had six rings – three each side – through her labia majora.

There are two main reasons for the sets of photographs that you find in the pages of men's magazines. The more usual one is to display, for your appreciation, full-colour photographs of young, pretty, unattainable girls, totally naked, or dressed (for dressed, read undressed) to raise your blood pressure, in sexy lingerie. Depending upon which country you are in, and which magazine you buy, you will be able to see their genitalia in any (and sometimes every) stage from totally closed outer labia, to totally open inner labia, revealing their pretty pink tunnels of love. There are those who find these latter erotic, and those who find them (or who at least *profess* to find them) offensive.

The other reason is to show something unusual in the field of feminine pulchritude. It may be someone's grandmother, cavorting with her daughter and her granddaughter, all suitably revealing everything in their birthday suits. At best, you may say, I suppose she doesn't look too bad for forty-five. It might be a girl who has a claim to having the largest breasts in the world. These claimants are usually American, and have usually had gigantic breast implants. They fill me with horror. I'm a small-tit man myself. Or it could be one of many variations on this particular theme. But we're basically talking about curiosities. Sexual curiosities. I arrived at the top-floor studio to find Roger Bates, one of *Tiptop*'s regular photographers, chatting with the piercing fan, who was still fully dressed. Fred had sent Roger copies of the original photographs, so he both knew what he was in for, and presumably had some idea of how he was going to shoot the woman. I introduced myself to her. Her name was Jane Powell. She seemed as normal and pleasant as any reasonably attractive woman you might meet anywhere. She looked much better live, as it were, than in those photographs, but she did, as I say, still have her clothes on. The only visible rings were in her ears and one nostril.

Roger and I were mates from way back. Fred had often called me in to provide the words to go with many of Roger's sets, and we got on well. He was a slightly strange man. I have no idea what his personal sexual proclivities were, but his photographic tastes were quite bizarre. If Fred ever wanted anything unusual, or kinky even, Roger was the photographer he would send for. Roger was photographically into S&M in a big way. He loved shooting women being dominated, preferably semi-dressed in rubber or leather, and almost always manacled, or tied down in some way. The scenes would be dressed with whips, Nazi flags and armbands, SS death's-head badges, cobwebs, ghosts, vampires, in fact, practically anything that any normal person *wouldn't* associate with sex.

The unfortunate girls were always being humiliated, tortured or tormented in some way before being raped or otherwise being forcibly subjected to sexual practices that they looked as if they would prefer not to perform. If you wanted a simulated photographic illustration of a pretty girl being forced to accept an enema, for example, Roger was your man.

John Stevens, *Tiptop's* art editor, was there too, and the three of us chatted amicably whilst Roger set up his lighting equipment. At that moment the studio door opened, and Charlie, Roger's assistant, came in, carrying one end of a large box, the other end being carried by a protesting cab driver. They put the box down, and Charlie quietened the cab driver with a handful of pound notes. 'Blimey,' said Charlie. 'Them chains weigh a bleedin' ton.' It transpired that Roger was going to photograph Jane with chains attached to each of her rings, and the other ends of the chains held by a selection of muscle-bound male models, dressed, inevitably, in leather posing pouches. Very bold. Very Roger. The models – six of them – were due to arrive a bit later, since they were hired by the hour, and there was no point in paying them to hang around whilst Roger set his shots up. I hoped Charlie was wrong about the weight of the chains. I didn't want Jane damaged, or *Tiptop* being sued for torn flesh.

I talked to Jane for long enough to get sufficient information to write the words that would accompany her pictures. She didn't seem particularly kinky. She'd started off with a pair of ear rings, as do millions of girls. And then the punk scene had come along, and she had been amused at the idea of having five or six rings in each ear. Then had come the nose-ring. After which she'd met a man who became – and still was – her lover. He was apparently turned on by the nipple and labial rings, and she had agreed to those for his pleasure with, she said, some trepidation. Now that they had been in place for some time, she said she actually enjoyed having them there. They made her feel different. More confident, somehow, she said. It wasn't her idea to be photographed for the magazine. It was her boyfriend who had sent the pictures in. 'Would you like to have a look at my piercings?' she asked, as naturally as if she had been asking me if I would like a cup of tea. I said that yes, if she didn't mind, it would help with what I had to write if I could see them close to, rather than rely simply on the photographs.

'I'll go and undress,' she said, 'and then I'll give you a shout, and you can come as close as you like.' She smiled at me as she disappeared behind the screen that stood in one corner of the studio. A few minutes later she called 'Tony,' and I grinned rather inanely at Roger, John, and Charlie, as I disappeared behind the screen. Charlie had put a Kinks tape on the studio machine, so at least I didn't have the embarrassment of knowing that they would be stretching their ears for every word that passed between Jane and me.

She was a tall, slim, beautifully proportioned girl, with long, blonde hair that she wore braided around her head. She had a good body, with firm breasts, and yes, there they were! Each nipple was triple pierced, with three matching gold rings of different patterns. I looked at them, feeling, I'm not sure why, rather foolish. I asked the obvious question. 'Do these piercings hurt?' I said, indicating the nipple rings. 'No, not really,' she said. 'The only ones that really hurt were the labial piercings.' Good God. I had, for the moment, quite forgotten about the labial rings. 'Why was that, do you suppose?' I asked. 'I don't really know,' she said. 'Except, of course, that piercers tend not to be qualified to give local anaesthetics, so that all they can use are sprays that aren't all that efficient. The sprays worked quite well on my nipples, but they simply didn't do a thing for my labia. But the pain went quite quickly. Don't be embarrassed. Look as closely as you like. You can touch if you want to. I don't mind. Here.'

She took my hand in hers, and placed it down between her legs. Her pudenda was bald. Shaven. I could feel it. I started to get a hard-on. I looked down. She was, of course, completely hairless. If you think about it, there wouldn't be much point in wearing labial rings if they were mostly hidden by a bushy growth of pubic hair. But I simply hadn't given it any thought, and for some reason I hadn't noticed it in the photographs. They were so badly lit, it probably didn't show anyway. Her labial lips were soft and smooth, and the rings were much larger than I had imagined them to be. As I tentatively touched them, Jane's outer labia parted, revealing a wetly pink slit.

I put a tentative finger over it, and she took my hand and pressed her groin against it. My finger slid inside her now well-lubricated cunt. 'That's nice,' she said. 'How does it feel to you?' She was moving her hips backwards and forwards slowly, finger-fucking herself on my finger. 'Mmmmm,' I said, somewhat lost for words. 'Er, it feels, er, good. Very good.' She leaned forward and put a hand on my fly, feeling my stiff prick through the material of my trousers. It jerked to attention under her hand. 'And that feels good too, darling,' she said. 'Shouldn't we introduce these two good feelings to each other?' She thrust her shaven pudenda harder against my finger as she spoke. She was so wet, the liquid was running down my wrist. 'Look, sweetheart,' I said, nervously. 'All we can do here, basically, is talk. If you'd like to take this part of the conversation any further, I'll give you my card. It's got both my home and my office telephone numbers on it. I'd love to hear from you, but right now, we should both be thinking of other things. You've got some photographs to pose for. And I've got to get back to my office.' She held my hand – the one with the finger deep inside her wet cunt – by the wrist, and fucked herself furiously with it, until she came, breathing hard. Then she let go of my hand and grinned at me, presumably amused by the expression on my face. 'I'll just have to make do with that for now then, won't I?' she said. 'It was good. As far as it went. I'll call you as soon as this is over. Then we'll go all the way. What do you say?'

'I say it sounds like a terrific idea,' I said. 'Now let me just tidy you up a little.' Her pussy glistened wetly from the love juice that was trickling out of it, and down her thighs. I found my handkerchief, and wiped her as dry as I could. I doubted that it would last, but provided that they started shooting fairly soon, they would probably put it down to the excitement of her being photographed naked.

Most girls get turned on by being photographed in the nude, particularly if their genitalia is a feature of the photography which, in magazines like *Tiptop*, inevitably it is. This makes them sexually excited, with the ineluctable result. Many are the photographs pinned to the picture editor's wall showing shots of pretty ladies with love-juice trickling out of their pussies. We never use them in the magazine. For legal, rather than aesthetic reasons. I finished my mopping-up operation, and tucked my handkerchief back into my pocket. 'Thanks, honey,' she said. 'If you miss me this afternoon, you're carrying my pussy scent around on your handkerchief. You can have a quick sniff and remind yourself of the pleasures to come.' I grinned, and kissed her firmly on the mouth. She slipped her tongue into my mouth, and began what would have been a long, erotic kiss if I hadn't pulled away. 'Naughty girl!' I said. 'Yes,' she said, smiling. 'It's nice, isn't it?'

Just then I heard the studio door open, and the six male models arrived. Jane and I emerged from behind the screen,

Jane wearing a robe. One or two of the models looked quite macho. I don't know why, but it used to be well-nigh impossible to find male models who looked really masculine. In the States, yes. Any time. (Think of all those butch cowboys in the cigarette ads.) In Britain, no. Or very seldom. So Richard had done a pretty good casting job. They wouldn't all be facing the camera at the same time, or at least, they wouldn't be if he shot the kind of photographs that I thought he had in mind.

I made my farewells and took the lift back down to the office. Looking at my watch, I saw that it was almost twelve-thirty. Lunchtime. I checked my messages, made a couple of quick telephone calls, and took off for Gerry's, where I found Tony Power, Paul Raymond's editor-in-chief. 'Hi, Tony,' I said. 'Hi Tony yourself,' he said. 'How's the new editor? What'll it be? The usual?' Dee was already getting me a large scotch, no ice, and some water. 'Cheers, Tony,' I said. 'What brings you to this side of the Atlantic? How's New York? How's your American magazine doing?' He grinned at me. 'I'm home for a spot of leave,' he said. 'Wendy hasn't seen her mum for a while, and I fancied some fish and chips, so here we are. As for the business, it's fine. But let's not talk business. How's your love life?' I laughed. Tony always had a gift for getting down to basics. Wendy was his wife, the mother of his two young daughters, Karen and Tiffany. He was a delightful man.

He it was who had persuaded Paul Raymond to buy up the old *Men Only* title when it was still a funny little digest-sized magazine, with pictures of young ladies with all their genitals air-brushed out. Tits were permissible. Pussies were not. Not in those early days, back in the late Fifties.

IPC, who owned the title at that time, put it up for sale. The price? One hundred pounds. Really. Tony went to Paul Raymond with a business plan which basically said here's this title, which every British male knows about, even if what they publish in it these days is pretty boring. You've got all those lovely girls who take off their clothes every night at the

Windmill Theatre. Pay them a bit extra, and get them to take their clothes off for the new *Men Only.* We'll go A4 in size, print in full colour, I'll be the editor, you be the publisher, and we'll make a fortune. Here's an editorial plan for the first three issues. After due consideration, Paul agreed, and the new *Men Only* was launched. It was an instant success, and neither Paul Raymond, nor Tony, ever really looked back. Paul was rich from his theatrical ventures (in those days, he was the biggest theatre-owner in London, owning either the freehold or long leases on five theatres, if you include the Revuebar). He became even richer from his magazines. *Men Only* sold in English-speaking countries all around the world: Canada, South Africa, Australia, New Zealand and America. Now Tony Power had launched Paul's new American magazine – *Club* – specifically put together for the American market. Not forgetting, of course, the British *Club International*, a completely different publication from *Club*, which did well here in the UK. Sales of *Club* itself were climbing in the States, which was the reason why Fred had gone out to launch a competitor. Fred and Tony were chums from way back. I asked how Fred's magazine was doing.

'Well, all right, I suppose,' Tony said. 'Of course, it will never do as well as *Club.* First of all we got in first. We were the first British girlie magazine to start up there, if you don't count *Penthouse*. And then it hasn't got me as editor.' Tony was never one to play himself down. And rightly so. I wasn't sure why he would want to dismiss *Penthouse*. Bob Guccione, its owner, publisher and editor (in those days) might be American, but he had in fact started *Penthouse* in Britain, and taken it over to America some years before any other British girlie magazine publisher even looked at that market. *Penthouse* sales had now, in fact, overtaken *Playboy* – the first, and for a long time the best – of all the girlie magazines, in sales in the States. Bob Guccione's claim to eternity was to be the first publisher to introduce pubic hair to the girl sets in his publication, something which had boosted its sales world-wide. His Penthouse Club in London's Shepherd's Market also competed with Heffner's Playboy Club in Park Lane, although the Penthouse Club never really recovered from the potential financial loss incurred by losing its gaming licence. The London Penthouse Club was the only one ever to open in Britain, although there was a casino and club being built, at that time, in Atlantic City, New Jersey. There had also been for a while a Penthouse casino and club on one of the off-shore Yugoslavian islands.

I told Tony that my love life was pretty fair. Thinking about it, I had no cause for complaint. We spoke about *Tiptop*, and my new job there, and I told Tony how helpful Allen Harbinson had been. Tony told me something that Allen hadn't mentioned to me: that Allen was shortly to give up his editorial job at Paul Raymond Publications in order to concentrate on his work as an author full-time. Allen had been writing books – and getting them published – since his national service with the RAF, out in Australia. I made a mental note to wish him well in his new venture. He would, I was confident, be eminently successful. I joined Tony for a plate of Dee's home-cooked delights, and then made my way back to the office.

I had a pile of manuscripts to read through, most of them left behind by Fred, who loathed reading manuscripts. Every magazine published gets unsolicited manuscripts: articles, fiction, humour, investigative pieces, you name it – particularly if your content, like *Tiptop*'s, covers most subjects – and you'll be inundated with them. But they're not really difficult to sort out. On average, about ninety per cent of them are unusable for one reason or another. Most of them are just plain badly written. I don't know why, but despite what he or she does to earn a living, be it dentistry or digging holes in roads, the world and his wife seem to think that they have a second, natural gift. That of being able to write. They don't seem to see it as a profession requiring, like any other profession, study and experience. They seem to see it as more of a hobby. Bad writing apart, the subject matter might simply be unsuitable. Other people have no concept of proper length for a particular kind of feature. No-one that I am aware of is going to use a three-thousand-word poem about the sex life of cats. Others pursue hackneyed themes covered too many times in the past. Some are simply obscene. Legally pornographic. Some are hand-written, and I have my own rule that I refuse to waste my time trying to decipher bad handwriting. That might sound brutal if you've spent six months producing your article, and you don't have access to a typewriter or a pc, but you wouldn't think so if twenty illegible handwritten manuscripts landed on your desk every day. I always send them back with a standard letter explaining my view. It is one held by most editors.

But amidst the dross, pure gold can occasionally be found. Enough to make the whole process worthwhile, at least for me. Over the years, it has been my privilege and my pleasure to help and encourage a fair number of young writers, whose first manuscripts, whilst being unpublishable in their original form, have been worth the effort of offering advice and encouragement.

One young girl I met in New York accepted my encouragement to turn what had really been little more than an ambition into manuscripts, which eventually I, then others, began to publish. She quickly became able to live on her writing skills, and eventually turned, as many writers do, from writing to editing. Today that editor is the managing editor, world-wide, of a famous monthly magazine. Make no mistake: it is all down to her talent. But she needed the encouragement from someone whose opinions she trusted. I worked my way steadily through the pile of manuscripts. I came across one piece of erotic fiction that was raunchy, original, reasonably well written, and which, with editing and a good illustration, would make an acceptable three pages for the magazine. I dictated a letter offering to buy the British serial rights. At least I'd make someone happy today.

Most of the material that appears in most of the magazines

published around the world is commissioned from writers who regularly produce material for the editors commissioning them. No editor wants to waste time undertaking the kind of editing that involves virtually rewriting a manuscript.

He would far rather use a writer whose work he knows, and who can be relied upon to turn in the manuscript on time, to length, and with the right content. Thus, at an editorial conference, where it might be agreed, for example, that an interview with a famous film star would be appropriate, either to coincide with the launch of a new film starring that person, or because the star themself is newsworthy for one reason or another, then one of the editors is likely to say 'Why don't we commission so-and-so to do that interview? He/she always turns in a good, solid, readable piece, and he/she's got all the contacts necessary to get directly to the subject.' The person's work will probably be known to all the people sitting around the editorial table, and the suggestion will be agreed, and the writer commissioned. So how do you achieve this eminent status? Well there, as they say, lies the rub. First, you need talent. If you can't write, you can't write. Experience teaches you tricks of the trade. Editors will explain house style. If you work on a tabloid newspaper, get all the news into the first paragraph. Short sentences. Short paragraphs. That ability won't get you a job on *The Observer*. But if you don't have any sort of gift in the first place, take my advice and forget it. Anyone who has the initial ability can learn the rules that apply to whichsoever part of the publishing world he/she writes for. What you can't do, for my money, is to learn to write from scratch. That's just my opinion. I can be wrong.

Assuming some initial talent, you can apply for jobs as a junior on suburban or weekly provincial newspapers. Great training grounds. You need a lot of luck to get one of those jobs, but if you persevere, you may get one. Eventually. The days when a first-class honours degree from Oxbridge would automatically get you into a national newspaper's training scheme are, sadly, long gone. But faint heart, as they say, never won fair lady. Keep trying.

Or you can start out as a freelance. This is called doing it the hard way. You need, at least initially, to specialize. You need a subject that you know backwards, that you are currently up-to date with, and for which you can think of and suggest angles that editors will want to accept when your special territory is in vogue. The basic problem is that, whatever you choose as your subject, every newspaper and magazine, every radio and television programme that you contact will already have someone on their books who specializes in your speciality. It's a hard life. And then, of course, there's influence. If mummy or daddy know the owner/ editor/ publisher of a newspaper/ magazine/ publication of any kind, a member of the BBC Board of Governors, or a director of a commercial television company, you're in there with a head start. Use all the influence you can wield, baby. You've got the competition by the short and curlies.

If I knew you better, I'd tell you how I started out. But I did start out as a freelance writer. And yes, in those days I was a fully paid-up member of the freelance branch of the NUJ. In those days, that meant that you had to prove that at least two thirds of your income came from freelance writing. That meant that you had to give them copies of published pieces to prove your claim. Don't think from that statement that I'm a fan of the NUJ. I'm not. They never did anything for me. Nor, to be fair, did I ever do anything for them.

I was reading a fascinating, but unusable piece written by (if one believed the contents of the accompanying letter) a husband who spent his evenings having happy threesomes with his wife and his wife's sister. It was patently a masturbatory fantasy, but it all sounded very jolly, and I was enjoying his description of him rogering his wife whilst he sucked her sister off, when my 'phone rang. It was Jane Powell, the piercing lady. 'Hi, sweetheart,' she said. 'Are you ready to ring my bell? I've been posing up here for what seems like all day with these raving queens, and what I need is a good fuck, to remind me that I'm a woman. Like I said, are you ready?' I looked at my watch. To my surprise, it was after six. 'I'm ready, honey,' I said. 'Where are you?' 'I'm upstairs in the studio, you great twit,' she said. 'Where did you think I was? Disneyland?' There's no answer to that really, is there? 'Hang on in there, darling,' I said. 'I'll be up there in about ten minutes.' I reluctantly abandoned the threesome manuscript onto the reject pile, and went through to say goodnight to Carla. 'Hello, darling,' she said. 'Where have you been all my life? Especially today?' 'Hiding,' I said. 'Oh, yeah,' she said. 'From whom?' That's what I like about Carla. She's always reliably grammatical. 'Well,' I said, 'you're going to find this hard to believe, but from a reader, whose boyfriend sent in pictures of her. She's pierced. Everywhere. I mean, you name it, she's got a hole in it, with a ring through it.' 'You don't mean...' said Carla, 'Yes, I do,' I said. 'I've seen them for myself. This morning.'

'This I have to see,' said Carla. 'Where is she right now?' 'She's upstairs in the studio,' I said, 'waiting for me to go up and collect her.' 'Collect her for what?' asked Carla, and then, without giving me time to reply, she said 'Sorry. Forget that I asked that. But why don't I come with you? It might be very amusing.' Why not? I thought. I wasn't mad crazy to get to fuck Jane Powell, although I was curious to know what the labial rings did for anyone who was fucking her. Patently her boyfriend thought they were good news. And who knew, with Carla? Anything could happen. And probably would. 'All right, sweetheart,' I said. 'Come join us. But don't blame me if it all ends in disaster. It was your idea. Remember?'

'Don't be nervous, honey,' said Carla. 'Trust me. OK?' We took the lift back up to the top floor. When I opened the studio doors, Jane was the only person there. The others had all gone. 'Hey,' she said. 'Who's this?' I was about to introduce Carla, but was forestalled by the fact that Carla went up to Jane, kissed her on the cheek, and said, 'Hi, baby. I'm Carla. I work with Tony. We do lots of things together.' She slipped an arm through Jane's, who looked at first startled, then pleased, and Carla said, 'Let's go find some supper. OK, Tony?' 'Sure,' I said. 'Where would you like to go?' 'Let's go to Alvaro's,' said Carla. 'I know Jane will like the food there. And it's a fun place to eat. And then, if we want to go on somewhere, the White Elephant on the River isn't a million miles away.'

'Oh, no,' I thought, selfishly. All I need is another late night. But girls will be girls, as all we boys know. 'Great,' I said. 'I can't think of anything nicer.' Alvaro was an ex-Trat waiter who, like all the original ex-Trat waiters, now owned his own restaurant. His was in the King's Road, Chelsea, and when he opened it, he immediately made it the only restaurant to be seen in, since he kept its telephone number ex-directory. Girls were reputed to give up their virginity, men to offer gifts of Ferraris, simply to be able to have the favoured number, and to be able to ring up and book a table. He didn't take in anyone off the street.

Alvaro was an old friend, from his Trat days, and I telephoned and made a reservation. 'For you, Mr Tony,' he said, 'I always have room. How many pretty girls are you bringing me?' 'Only two this evening, Alvaro,' I said. Bullshit, I thought. Of such insubstantial matters is the reality of life composed. Pretty philosophical stuff for early evening, don't you think? We got the Porsche out of the garage, and drove down to Chelsea. It was much too early to eat at Alvaro's, where I had booked a table for eight o'clock, so I took the girls to the Chelsea Potter, for a few drinks before dinner. I used to live in Chelsea, and I like the Chelsea Potter. It is an honest, down to-earth, efficient local pub. Other people might prefer the Admiral Codrington, or the Phene Arms, but I liked the Chelsea Potter. It was full, that evening, of people just like us, getting a few down before the serious business of the evening commenced. The men with fashionably long hair, wearing the shirt that this week's mode dictated, the flared trousers, and the black velvet jackets.

Men were allowed to dress prettily in those days, and I loved it. We could wear pretty scarves instead of ties, and our shirts, at least in the evening, could be as frilled and flounced as the most feminine of girl's blouses. The girls' outfits made for a slightly cleaner silhouette, with their Mary Quant haircuts, their copies of Chanel A-Line dresses (the skirts popularly – and accurately – described as pussy pelmets) and their white stockings and white lipstick.

Jane and Carla seemed to get on from the first minute together, and I was able to sit back and relax as they chattered away to each other about I know not what. I wasn't listening. I was thinking about Annabel. I hadn't telephoned her, and she hadn't telephoned me. I looked at my watch. It was only half past seven. Far too early, I would have thought, for her to have left for the club. I excused myself, and went over to the pub's telephone. She picked up on the first ring. 'Hello,' she said. 'Hello, my darling,' I said. 'Oh, Tony,' she said. 'Sweetheart. I thought I was never going to hear from you again.' I felt a serious lump in my throat. 'Darling,' I said. 'Whatever gave you that idea? I thought we had basically agreed that the weekends were our time together. You know. From Friday night, when you finish, to Monday morning, when I start?' She was crying now.

'Don't cry, my love,' I said. 'Please don't cry.' 'I'm sorry,' she said. 'I'm crying because I'm so happy. I know it's silly. I'll stop now.' She took a deep breath, and stopped crying. 'There,' she said. 'Nice to hear from you. What are you up to this evening? It sounds as if you're in a pub.' 'I am,' I said. I told her where I was, and said that I was taking the piercing woman out to dinner. Business, I said. I didn't mention Carla. We chattered on for a bit. I promised to 'phone again before the weekend, and said goodbye.

I was glad that I had telephoned. I went back to the others. They had their heads close together, and were laughing. Carla looked up as I got back. 'Oh, there you are,' she said. 'We were just talking girls' talk.' I'll bet, I thought, but I smiled at them and said, 'We've got time for one for the road before we're due at the restaurant. Is it the same again?' They said that yes, it was, and I went to the bar to get the order. I could see the barmaid's nipples showing erect through the thin, almost transparent material of her blouse. She saw me looking at them. 'Everything's standing up well, then,' I said, giving her my order. She giggled, bending low to reach beneath the counter, and showing me the separated globes of her luscious breasts. 'If you like to come back at closing time,' she said, 'I'll see if I can't do the same for you.' She smiled at me. 'That'll be one pound, four and sixpence, please.' 'I can't tonight, love,' I said. 'I'll try another evening if I may.' 'It's up to you, luv,' she said, mouthing a pouty kiss as she moved away.

I don't know what it was about the Sixties, but whatever it was I liked it. There were no longer any false pretences. If a girl fancied you, she more or less said so. Like the barmaid. The Pill, of course, had set girls free. They could fuck and get fucked to their hearts' content and have no fear of pregnancy. 'I never go to bed the first time out' had simply disappeared as a concept. If they didn't, you didn't take them out again. Simple as that. Back in the early Fifties, you practically had to marry them to get them to drop their drawers. In those days, a quick wank into your handkerchief was about the best you could hope for. If you were lucky. These days, they were all at it. Like little rabbits. It was marvellous.

We finished our drinks, and wandered along the King's Road towards Alvaro's, weaving our way in and out amongst the punks, the real Londoners (they were a bit thin on the ground: it was still a bit early) and the tourists. The latter mostly Americans. In those days, London was the centre of the universe. The one city in the world where it was all happening. There was full employment. Everyone had enough money to be able to enjoy themselves. Britain was the hub of men's and women's fashion, of newspaper and magazine journalism, of most kinds of design, and more importantly, or so it seemed to me then – of where and how to have a good time, with its plethora of fashionable and popular clubs, discos, and restaurants. Chelsea was the nucleus of that hub. I walked along with the girls on either side of me, our arms linked. Jane's appearance brought her interested glances, whilst the length of Carla's skirt (or, more accurately, the lack of length) almost brought the traffic to a stop. Alvaro welcomed us with the charm that had brought success to his restaurant. Not forgetting, of course, the excellent food.

The Sixties was the period which, originally through Mario and Franco, and then continuing through the abundant restaurants opened up by all of his original waiters, brought Italian food out of the greasy spoon era in Britain, and into the realms of *haute cuisine*. Sandro Tobi at the Chelsea Rendezvous, and Michael Chow – originally a hairdresser – did the same for Chinese food. Both the Chelsea Rendezvous and Mr Chow's, in Knightsbridge, had Italian waiters. Michael went on to open restaurants both in New York (with the most fabulous art deco glass entrance doors you will ever see anywhere) and Los Angeles. All three are still there.

I began to wonder what I was going to do with the two girls. I had a nasty feeling that I was going to get lumbered with taking them to a disco. Lumbered, because all I felt like was a pleasant, gentle fuck, and an early night. I didn't feel strongly about which of the two girls I spent the night with, but my curiosity leaned slightly towards Jane. She had, after all, propositioned me fairly strongly earlier in the day. But Carla was always a delightful companion, in and out of bed. Either way, it looked like a promising evening. If I could avoid the dancing. To my surprise, the girls had already resolved the problem for me. 'Are you thinking of going on anywhere?' asked Carla, all innocently. Oh, lord. Here we go, I thought. 'I'm easy, sweetheart,' I said. 'I thought perhaps Sybilla's might make a pleasant change.' Sybilla's was a small, newish, fashionable disco in Swallow Street, off the bottom end of Regent Street. It was reputedly owned by John Lennon, and I knew its secretary, Juliet Brightmore. She had been one of the witnesses at the marriage of an old friend of mine, David Jones, who had married his wife Betty, a travel writer, at Chelsea registrar's office recently. The club's membership card was exquisitely designed, and modestly difficult to obtain.

'Jane and I were talking earlier,' said Carla. 'And to cut a long story short, we both thought that it might be amusing for all three of us to go back to your place.' She paused, looking at me wickedly with those beautiful brown eyes. 'But, of course, if you'd rather go dancing ...' She fluttered her eyelids at me. 'It's up to you, love.' That was the second time that evening I'd had that said to me. But this proposition was very much out of the ordinary. I tried not to get too excited.

The first thing to do was to agree. So 'Oh, sure,' I said, as casually as I could manage. 'If Hampstead's where you'd like to be, that's fine with me.' I refused to meet either of their eyes. 'Good, then,' said Carla. 'That's settled then.' I ordered liqueurs and coffee, and asked for the bill. I was still thinking furiously when the waiter brought it. I signed it without looking at it, and added fifteen per cent. Those were the days before everyone had credit cards. Most people had accounts at restaurants, who sent them (or their companies) monthly bills. So, what exactly did these two girls have in mind? A threesome of some sort, presumably? Let's just see what we know about the people involved, I thought. Perhaps that will give me a clue. It would, I felt, be far too gauche to ask them what their intentions were directly.

I didn't know that much about Jane, other than that she was kinky about piercing, and wearing rings through intimate parts of her body. She was certainly into heterosexual sex, that was for certain. And she also had a live-in, male lover. As to any lesbian proclivities, I hadn't a clue. Carla I thought I knew much more about, but she had never, ever, raised the question of lesbian sex in my presence, nor had I heard any rumours in the office to that end. She was simply a young, pretty, sexy, and very available girl, as far as I knew.

But there are plenty of girls around who find three in a bed

– two girls and a man – tremendous fun, without any thought of lesbian interludes. They simply, basically, take it in turns to fuck – or get fucked by – the man. They usually add to the sexuality of the occasion by helping each other in such ways as holding each other's pussy lips open at the moment of insertion, stroking the man's cock manually whilst he fucks the other girl, letting the man suck one girl's pussy as he fucks the other's cunt, and similar, sociable, entirely jolly events. I felt my cock hardening at the thought.

And then, of course, all those things could happen, plus the added excitement of watching two girls make whatever kind of lesbian love turns them on. And finally, maybe they just wanted to make love with each other, and wanted somewhere to do it, and thought that my place was as convenient as anywhere else. Maybe they didn't plan that I should be part of the evening's continuing entertainment at all! As you can see, there was quite a range of possibilities.

We found the Porsche, still parked where I had left it, around the corner from the Chelsea Potter. And undamaged, too. Still wearing its radio. What more could a person ask? Three is as many as a Porsche 914 will take, and even then, it's not too comfortable for the third passenger. There is just the front bench seat, and nothing at the back. Bigger Porsches have what I call parcel shelves at the back, which they have the temerity to call 'occasional seats.' Only if you're an occasional dwarf. But the two girls didn't seem to have any problem squeezing up together on my right. Did I tell you that my 914 was left-hand drive? I think I did. I drove slowly and carefully. Not too slowly. At night, that's as suspicious as driving too fast. I drove at a steady thirty mph. Orange two-seater Porsches with three people in them tend to attract the attention of policemen who, if they're driving their own cars, are probably driving a five-year-old family Ford. Policemen are not pleasant people, not any more. They're ignorant, illiterate, fascist pigs, overwhelmed by what they believe to be their own superiority. I hate them. And jealous of anyone who can afford expensive motor cars that they themselves can't afford.

I drove gently up to Hampstead, avoiding – probably more by good luck than good judgement – any contact with the local *gendarmerie*. I parked in the driveway, and let the girls in. Carla led the way. She should know it by now, I thought. I didn't ask them what they wanted to drink, I simply opened a bottle of Louis Roederer Crystal, and poured three glasses. It was the '57. A bit young, but a good vintage for all that. We settled ourselves in the sitting room, and I put on a Jacques Loussier tape. Softly. Very seductive stuff, if you care for it. Carla took a long slug at her champagne, and then put it down carefully, and looked at me.

'Jane put a proposition to me earlier today which I found quite fascinating,' she said. 'I've never had any kind of a lesbian relationship, but, as far as I'm concerned, that's not because I have anything against that thought in principle, but simply, as far as I'm concerned, because I have never been in a situation where I have needed to give thought to that possibility. Jane has altered that, in that she has been telling me that she would like to make lesbian love to me. It is a thought which intrigues me, but I said that, if I was to partake in anything like that, I would have to ask for two concessions.'

She stopped for a moment, and smiled at me. 'One was that, if I agreed to enter into that kind of a situation, then if I should say "stop" at any time, then "stop" I would insist upon. The second was that I would want to enter into that situation only in certain circumstances, and one of those was that I entered into whatever it was in the presence of someone whom I trusted completely. That person is you. That means,' she continued, 'that you can watch Jane and me making love to each other – or perhaps that should be, you can watch Jane making love to me and you can feel free to join in at any time, in any way that you wish. Jane is entirely agreeable to that. So I have to ask you now if you have any objection, first of all, to Jane and me proceeding with our proposed love-making session, and secondly, whether or not you will wish to join in with us? In, as I said, any way that you wish. Nothing is barred.'

'My dear Carla,' I said. 'Such excitement. And Jane. How lovely. Of course I have no objection. Why should I? I shall be honoured – and excited – to be able to watch such an intimate occasion. As to whether or not I will want to join in, I think the answer almost certainly has to be a resounding "yes." But may I please leave my options open? In other words, if I want to join in, I may feel free so to do, but if I decide that I prefer to stay away from your amorous intimacies, then that I may also feel free to do, should that be the case?' The two girls looked at each other for but the briefest moment, before they both agreed, willingly, to my small fine-tuning requests. 'Terrific,' I said. 'Let's get on with it, then.' I got up, and led the way through into the bedroom.

I turned down the bed. I had, happily, made the bed up with fresh sheets that morning. The girls started to undress. I watched as Jane peeled off her blouse and skirt, revealing naked breasts. That she wore no bra wasn't a surprise, my having seen her splendid, firm breasts earlier that day. What was a surprise was to see the minuscule, totally transparent black knickers, through which her bald pussy and beringed labia were prominently displayed, and – but here comes the bigger surprise, simply because the two areas don't seem to have a lot in common – black fishnet stockings, held up by a sexy little black silk suspender belt. Every normal man's dream of erotic underwear. That, and a shaven pussy too. Suddenly I wasn't sure whether it was Christmas or Easter. Carla – unlike Carla, who was normally no slouch at getting her clothes off – was simply standing and staring. Whether at Jane's adorned piercings, or at her shaven cunt, I wasn't certain. Perhaps both. As I watched, she went over to Jane and touched one of her nipple rings. She then took it in her fingers and pulled it. Very gently. 'Does that hurt?' she asked. 'No, sweetheart,' said Jane. 'I like it. Do it some more. Please.'

Carla took two pairs of nipple rings, one pair in each hand,

and manipulated them, slowly. Carefully. Jane, standing there in her black knickers, stockings, and suspender belt, started to undress Carla, which prompted Carla to let go of the nipple rings, and divest herself of her clothes in a few, quick movements. As she took them off, I could see that she was wearing a saucy little pair of white knickers, and that her legs were bare.

Both now naked, Jane took Carla by the hand over to the bed, and then laid down on her back, pulling Carla gently down beside her. She then took Carla's face between her hands and kissed her, deeply. I could see Jane's tongue thrusting into Carla's mouth, and as that happened, Carla put her arms around Jane and pressed her body against her new-found friend. They continued like that for some time, exploring each other's mouths, their tongues busy, their arms around each other. After a while Jane slipped a searching hand between Carla's legs, and, parting her pubic bush, I could see her fingers feeling for, and finding, Carla's cunt lips. Carla gave a little gasp as she felt Jane's fingers inside her, and then she wriggled herself into a more comfortable position, the better to allow the other girl's fingers more thorough access. She followed that by then reaching her own hand down and finding Jane's bald honeypot. My prick was standing to attention at the sight of all this feminine love-play, and I had to resist the urge to pull it out and start wanking. I helped myself resist the urge by pondering on just how long I would have to wait before I was eventually able to plunge my weapon into one or other of these two ladies' wetly receptive pussies.

They continued frigging each other, their respective fingers moving slowly and indolently – none of your fast, frantic finger work here – and their ministrations to each other were accompanied by much sighing and gentle groaning, and whispering in each other's ears. Despite her earlier protestations, Carla looked as if to the lesbian manner born, and she seemed thoroughly at home both with what she was doing, and with what was being done to her. I could now see love-juice glistening on her pubic hair, little beads of it, looking like early morning dew drops on brown moss. Jane's bald cunt lips were, quite simply, running wet, there being no hair to soak up the moisture.

As I watched, Jane whispered something in Carla's ear, at which Carla withdrew her hand from the other girl's cunt, and lay down on her back, after which she first opened her legs, and then drew her knees up, offering her wetly open pussy to Jane, who now knelt down in front of it and, bending her head forward, started to lick and suck, whilst Carla oooh'd and aaah'd with pleasure. Carla then took Jane's head in her hands, and started moving her hips rhythmically up against Jane's face, whilst Jane performed her obviously well-practised cunnilingus, her fingers holding Carla's pussy lips apart as she thrust her tongue deeply down into her vaginal opening, undoubtedly searching for – and obviously, from Carla's ecstatic reaction, finding — her clitoris. It was an extremely erotic vision.

Carla started to writhe and sigh and moan, and soon she began to verbalize her pleasure, her voice gaining in volume, growing from a whisper to almost a shout as she approached the peak of her orgasms. 'Oh, yes, baby. Just there. Yes. Oh my God. I like it. Don't stop. Please don't stop. Ohhhhh, yes. You're fucking me with your mouth. Oh, darling, yes, there. Harder. Please. Harder. Oh, yes. That's lovely. Aaaaaaah. Oh, my God.' She flung her head rapidly from side to side and arched her back as she climaxed beneath Jane's mouth. Jane kept her mouth and tongue busy until the last paroxysms of slowly dying fervour had passed. She then lay beside Carla, her arm around Carla's shoulder. I wondered if either of them was conscious of my presence in the bedroom. I don't think that at that particular moment they were.

After a little while, Carla turned her head, and said, 'That was beautiful. Quite beautiful. Thank you. Would you like me to try and do it to you now? I'd love to try. But you'll probably have to tell me what to do. I mean, I've never even kissed a girl before. I know the theory, of course. But you'll have to help me. Shall I try?' Jane smiled at her. 'If you'd like to, baby. Thank you. That would be nice. But why don't you rest for a little while right now, and let Tony here fuck me? He'd like that. Wouldn't you, Tony darling? And then we can play little lezzy games again afterwards. He's been very well behaved up to now. Haven't you, sweetheart? What do you say?' she asked Carla, turning towards her and waiting for an answer. Carla grinned over at me. 'I must admit I'd rather forgotten about poor old Tony,' she said. 'I'm so sorry, darling. I just got rather carried away.' She turned back to Jane. 'And yes, of course. If that is what you would like to do.' She turned back to me. 'It's all nice and wet and ready for you, darling,' she said. 'Come and help yourself. Or even better, I'll help you.'

You could, as they say, have knocked me down with a feather. Both girls suddenly wanting to look after me. I tore my clothes off before they changed their minds, my prick standing out proudly in front of me as I walked over to the bed. Jane looked at me. 'Oh good,' she said. 'You're a Cavalier. I do so much prefer them to Roundheads.' I had to laugh. I don't believe I had heard anyone use that description to differentiate between circumcised and uncircumcised cocks since I was at school.

I hadn't been sure what Carla had meant when she said, just a moment ago, that she would help me, but I was to find out now. As I approached the bed, she took my tool in her hand, and masturbated it slowly for me for a few strokes, adding perhaps the odd centimetre or so to its swollen girth and length. 'I'll just lubricate it for you now, darling,' she said, and, leaning forward, she took it in her mouth, tonguing it and thoroughly wetting it with her saliva. She took it out of her mouth, and examined it slowly. 'That looks about right,' she said, and, letting go of it, she leaned back and pulled Jane's outer labia apart with her fingers. 'Here you are then, my darling,' she said to me. 'Your first fuck with a lady who wears rings in her labia. At least, I think it is. Is it?' I reassured her that it was, and she took my prick in one hand, using the fingers of the other to keep Jane's cunt lips spread, and helped me to feed it slowly into Jane's warm, slippery wet cunt. I looked down into a pair of the bluest eyes that I have seen for a very long time. They sparkled up at me as I thrust my cock deep into her.

'Ooh, that's good,' she said. 'I've been wanting that since I first saw you this morning. I just knew you'd have a nice, big cock. You can tell, you know. At least, I believe I can.' I could feel the labial rings rubbing on my cock as I fucked her. They didn't particularly add or detract from the act. They were just sort of there. I found her nose ring slightly distracting at such close quarters. I bent down and kissed her, and I could taste Carla's cunt on Jane's lips, which I found intensely erotic. I very nearly shot my load at the thought of what I was doing – licking one's girl's pussy juice off the lips of another girl. The one who had just been sucking Carla off.

She smiled up at me. 'You can taste Carla's cunt on my mouth, can't you?' she asked. 'Mmm,' I said. 'Sexy, isn't it?' she asked. 'Yes, it is,' I agreed. She stuck her tongue in my mouth, and an even fuller flavour of Carla's cunt permeated my taste-buds. 'Do you like the taste of that?' asked Jane. 'Yes,' I said. 'I do. I've always enjoyed the taste of cunt. Young, fresh, clean, beautiful cunt. Lovely.' 'Then just think what Carla will be able to taste when she sucks my cunt after you've fucked me,' said Jane. 'She'll be able to taste your spunk, after you've spurted it up me. If she sucks hard enough, she could get a mouthful of it, and swallow it. Does she like swallowing your spunk?' 'She always says she does,' I answered. 'She likes me to come in her mouth, and she always swallows it.' 'I like men coming in my mouth,' said Jane. 'I like them to come all over me. On my face, over my tits. In my mouth. Up my cunt. Everywhere. I love it up my arse. Do you like fucking girls up the arse? Would you like to fuck me up the arse?'

The excitement of her talking dirty to me, and the import of what she was saying got through to me right at that moment, despite my attempting to resist it, and I withheld my reply whilst I spurted hot come up her cunt. My resistance had already been considerably lowered by the sexual excitement of watching the two girls at their lesbian lovemaking. Then the sheer sensuality of tasting Carla's sexual effluent on Jane's lips, on top of which Jane was now asking me if I'd like to fuck her anally, was suddenly all too much. Well. I mean, what would you do? Exactly.

'Sorry about that, sweetheart,' I said. 'I usually last rather longer than that. It all too much excitement in one day for a young lad. But to answer your question, yes, I love fucking girls in the arse. And yes, thank you, I'd love to fuck you in the arse.' 'Then you shall, my love,' she said. 'It will be my pleasure.' I pulled out of her, and she reached down and squeezed the last few drops of semen out of my prick and onto her fingers. She then licked her fingers enthusiastically. 'Mmm,' she said. 'Lovely. Thank you.' I got off the bed and, satiated for the moment with matters sexual, I went and had a shower. When I got back to the bedroom, Carla was kneeling on the floor in front of the bed, on the edge of which sat Jane, her legs wide apart, exposing her open, thoroughly wet, bald pussy to Carla's tongue, which, as I watched, was lapping like that of a little cat. Jane was encouraging Carla in her duties. 'Yes, darling. Yes. That's exactly it. Right there. Can you feel it?' Carla made some kind of answering noise in her throat. She was too busy with her tongue to reply properly. 'Good,' said Jane. 'Yes. Very good. We can all find our own clitoris, but finding someone else's takes a little practice.'

Tell me about it, I thought to myself, remembering a delightful young girl called Ann, who had spent a great deal of time and trouble doing for me what Jane was now doing for Carla. Teaching me the way around a girl's pussy. With my fingers. With my tongue. With my cock. She made me practise and practise and practise, and I had loved every minute of it. She it was who gave me my constant desire to suck pussy. It had given us both a great deal of pleasure at the time, and I had learned an ability which had unfailingly stood me in good stead with every woman that I have ever met.

Suddenly Jane was saying something to Carla again. 'Oh, yes, darling. Now I'm going to come. Any moment now. I'm going to have a great big, lovely orgasm, and it's you who's making me have it. Oh, yes. Do it harder. If you can. Please. Oh, yes. There. Exactly there. Oh, I'm coming, I'm coming, I'm coming. Yes. Oh, God, yes.' She put her hands on each side of Carla's head, and began what would have been, were she a man, a fucking movement. She cried out noisily as she came, and I wondered if any of my neighbours could hear her. I doubted it. And then it was over, and Jane flopped back on the bed, giving every indication of exhaustion. I got a robe out of the wardrobe and put it on. Carla got up off her knees, and sat on the edge of the bed. 'Was I all right, darling?' she asked. 'Will I ever be any good at it? Did you enjoy it?' Jane smiled up at her. 'Sweetheart,' she said. 'You were magnificent. I hereby award you the lesbian cuntlappers award of merit.' Carla looked somewhat crestfallen. 'Oh, come on, darling,' said Jane. 'It was only a joke. A bad joke perhaps, but a joke for all that.' She put her arms around Carla and gave her a big hug. 'I'm a little crude sometimes. You must forgive me. What you did for me then was a perfect physical act, given with love, and accepted with love. Truly, dearest.' She suddenly looked at her watch.

'Christ, is that the time?' she said. I looked at my watch. It was nearly three in the morning. She looked at me. 'I'll have to go, I'm afraid. We'll have to save the arse fucking for another time. OK?' 'OK by me, love,' I said. 'Do you want a quick shower before you go? A drink? Anything?' 'I'll take the shower, if I may. And if you could give me five minutes, and then order me a cab. It's Tooting. Don't laugh.'

Carla showed her where the bathroom was while I telephoned for a cab. He'd be there in ten minutes, he said. I poured myself a scotch which I probably didn't need, but what do you do when someone's leaving? You can't say sod it, and get into bed. Not really. I was no television freak, but there certainly wouldn't be anything on at that time in the morning. I noticed that the tape deck still had its little red light on, and turned over the Jacques Loussier tape, which we'd all long since forgotten about. Jane and Carla passed through on their way back from the bathroom to the bedroom. As she went by, Jane asked me for a piece of paper, and a pen or pencil. When I got them together and went into the bedroom to give them to her, she was almost completely dressed, the shaven pudenda once more hidden by her skirt, the only rings visible the ear and nose adornments. 'Oh, thanks, honey,' she said, taking the pen and paper from me. She returned them after she had written something down. 'It's my telephone number,' she said. 'I can always get you at the office. This is my home number. Feel free to call me,' she said. 'Any time. I've already given it to Carla.'

She picked up her bag and looked around to see that she had everything. 'Thank you both,' she said. 'It was fun.' I looked out of the front window, to see that the cab was waiting outside, and I went down to see her off. She waved as the cab turned and headed south.

Carla was curled up in bed when I got back upstairs. It took just seconds to join her. She turned over and put her arms around me and gave me a sleepy kiss. 'Hello, darling,' she said. 'What do you want to do?' 'Sleep?' I said, hopefully. 'Oh, good,' she said. 'Me, too.' She gave me another kiss, and settled herself down again. In moments she was fast asleep, breathing deeply.

CHAPTER SIX: FORMAT FOR FUN

Carla was still asleep when the alarm woke me at nine the following morning. Work at Tiptop Publications – as with most magazine publishing companies – started at ten o'clock. You stayed until the day's work was finished, but you didn't start until ten, which I always think is very civilized. Let those people who manage to impress both themselves and others by their early starts stay happy with their choice of hours, and I'll stay happy with mine. I coaxed a still sleepy Carla out of bed, gave her some black coffee, and we were on our way by a quarter to ten. I drove down Haverstock Hill, turned right along England's Lane, then left and along over Primrose Hill, wiggled through into Regent's Park, turned left along Circle Road, and came out of the gate that leads across into Park Crescent, down Regent Street, and around Piccadilly Circus into Shaftesbury Avenue, where I turned left into Windmill Street, and let Carla out of the car, before I turned left again into the street where the garage was. I joined her in her little office ten minutes later. She was, as I had hoped, brewing up some coffee.

She looked up and smiled as I tapped on her door and went in. 'So,' she said. 'So, what?' I said. 'So, I'm not sure what,' she said. 'That was quite an evening.' 'Mmm,' I said, non-committally, wanting her to get to the point without any prompting from me. I was interested to see what she would say if anything at all – about her lesbian activities the previous evening with Jane. If she didn't want to discuss it, that was all right too, but I didn't want to raise it myself, and perhaps make her feel obliged to comment on something she would rather leave alone, at least for the time being.

She looked at me. 'I'd quite like to talk about it,' she said. 'But I don't want you to feel obliged to say anything. OK?' 'OK,' I said. 'Well,' she said, 'I don't know whether you realised it, but that was the first time I've ever made love of any kind with a girl. I didn't even indulge at boarding school, where it was rampant.' I didn't say anything. I didn't think she was expecting me to. Not right then. 'But the interesting thing is, I really enjoyed it. It felt good. Having Jane sucking my pussy, I mean. It was somehow different from when, say, you do it. Not better, not worse. But different. And very, *very* nice.' She grinned a positively salacious grin at me. 'Couldn't you tell?' she asked. 'I mean, well, you *were* watching us, weren't you?' 'Well, yes, since you ask me,' I said, 'it did look as if you were enjoying yourself. But why is that a problem?'

'I'm not sure,' she answered. 'You see, the whole thing is something of a surprise to me. I love men – as you know – and I've just never thought about making love with girls. And then, when Jane propositioned me yesterday, I simply thought, initially, what a gas. I thought, well, I can always stop, if I don't like it. And that was the condition under which I agreed to play what she calls lezzie games with her. But now I find that I've been introduced to something that I really like. Something that, if I'm honest, I'd like to do a lot more of. I'm not going to give men up, but I'd like to take this girls thing a bit further. You know, see what happens.'

'I don't see anything wrong with that,' I said. 'It's a free country. Well, reasonably so. If you like making love to girls, fine. I'm selfishly pleased to hear that you're not going to give men up. I don't see the girls as a problem.' Carla looked genuinely quite anguished. 'But you obviously don't understand,' she said, emotionally. 'The last thing I want in the world is to become a big, ugly butch dyke.' I had to laugh at the prospect. 'For God's sake, Carla,' I said. 'That's simply not possible. You couldn't become one of those if you tried. A little, pretty *feminine* dyke, maybe. The other kind, no chance.' Patently it was a bad joke, for the next thing I knew, Carla had her arms about my neck, and had burst into tears. 'B-b-b-but I d-don't want t-to b-b-become *any* k-k-kind of b-b-bl-bloody-d-d-dyke,' she sobbed. I hugged her to me, and stroked her hair, making that sort of shushing noise people make to other people who are crying, when they don't really know what else to do.

'Come on, sweetheart,' I said, after she had lapsed from big sobs into little sobs, interrupted by sniffs. 'There's nothing to cry about. And there's nothing to be afraid of. I can completely understand the emotional trauma of discovering that you do, after all, like a quite different kind of sex than the one you thought you were exclusively into. I would feel the same way. But at the end of the day, all you are feeling is guilt, which all the psychiatrists and psychologists tell us is the perfectly normal reaction.' She sniffed again, loudly this time, and I disengaged one hand to find a handkerchief, which I gave her. I let go of her so that she could have a good blow. She smiled her thanks, and sat down on her desk chair. She'd stopped crying now, apart from the occasional sniff.

I wasn't too sure what to say next. I wanted to reassure her, but I didn't want to persuade her. Either way. That had to be her decision. All I was trying to do really was to calm her down, and show her that, whatever she did, or decided to do, there was no real reason for guilt. 'I mean,' I said, 'look at Jane. She's a good example. She is completely bisexual, and obviously enjoys all of it. She seems a reasonably balanced person, all those piercings apart, and she has certainly managed to retain her sense of humour, along with her enthusiastic sexuality. I think what is worrying you is that you're conjuring up for yourself a future self-image that is totally out of context. You're never going to become one of those awful, overweight, short-haired, look-at-my-gross-tits-I'm-not-wearing-a bra, dyke feminists with halitosis, now are you?'

She had the grace to manage a small laugh. 'I do hope not,' she said. She sniffed a bit more, and blew her nose. She looked at my handkerchief. 'I'll give this back to you after I've laundered it,' she said. 'Thank you so much, Tony. You're very kind. Thank you.' She got up and came over and gave me a friendly hug. 'That was a great help. No, really. It just helps to talk to someone. You know, get it out in the open. Bless you.' She patted my arm, and I said 'Any time, darling,' and went back to my own office.

I wanted some peace and quiet to sit down and work out for myself exactly where I thought *Tiptop* ought to be going as a magazine. It would probably continue to sell profitably, simply by following the now well-established formula. But that wasn't how Fred had achieved his initial success, and I wanted very much to prove my ability by increasing sales whilst he was away. Just maintaining existing sales wasn't enough. Not for me. The rest of the editorial staff were not only nice people, they were entirely competent. But that was all. There weren't any innovators. No-one with serious creative flair. They followed in Fred's footsteps slavishly, and their worst criticism was to say 'Fred wouldn't like it.' Or 'I'm not sure that Fred would agree with you.' I picked up a copy of the current issue, and began to analyze it critically, making notes as I went along. I started, reasonably enough, with the cover. Attractive girl. Extremely erotic. The cover made you want to pick the magazine up and look for the rest of her pictures inside. That is what covers are supposed to do. And to look inside, you have to buy the magazine first. Excellent photograph. Good print and reproduction. Expensive cover paper. One could consider dropping the weight (and thus the cost) of the cover paper, without losing any noticeable quality. But basically, no problems whatsoever. I thought, subjectively, that the cover lines – those brief descriptions on the cover that are supposed to attract readers – were a bit thin, but since I would be writing them from here on in, I let that go.

Inside front cover. A black and white advertisement from a pipe tobacco manufacturer. A look farther inside showed colour ads running throughout the pages of the magazine. Something wrong here. The tobacco manufacturer was a household name, but the inside front cover ad position (followed immediately, in sequence, by the outside back cover and the inside back cover) is the premium position in any magazine. The inside front should be a full colour advertisement. If the ad team couldn't sell this premium spot, then they should be giving it away at black and white prices to a good advertising customer who was prepared to go to the expense of paying for the origination work; the four sheets of colour film from which colour pages are printed. Running a B&W ad there lost us prestige, and looked awful. I made a note to have a word with the ad director. Page three was split into two halves, vertically, between Fred's last editorial, illustrated by miniature pictures of what he was writing about, and the contents list and masthead (the publishing company's logo, address, and list of major staff.) It didn't look too bad, other than the fact that Fred had written so much that, in order to get all the words in to the space allowed for them, they had been set in far too small a type size. They were actually quite difficult to read. I guessed that the art director was nervous of telling Fred that he had written too much. I made a note to have a word with him too.

After that came what we call an up-front section. Most magazines have them, of one kind or another. They're usually an attempt to impress readers with the fact that *their* magazine gets out and about, and knows what is happening in the world. *Tiptop*'s left a lot to be desired. It had short columns on food and drink products which, to me, were patently the means whereby whoever wrote them received free food and drink from suppliers. They were badly written, and illustrated with the kind of publicity pack shot photographs that no magazine in its right mind should ever use.

There was a very over-written review of a new novel, in which both the novel and the review, in my opinion, were unlikely to interest many *Tiptop* readers. There were some insipid restaurant reviews of London restaurants, written by one of London's most infamous free-loaders, ignoring anyone who lives anywhere else. And so on. Three whole pages of boring rubbish. I decided there and then to replace them with a two-page spread, which would be, essentially, a diary of what was happening in the world of sex. And I did mean *world*. I would make it informative, visually exciting, verbally well put together and – where possible – amusing. I would write and edit it myself. I'd get a little bloody life into the editorial pages if I died in the attempt. The up-front section, thank God, was the worst. The rest wasn't too bad. All the girl sets were excellent. Pretty girls, good, imaginative photography. All well laid-out. I thought the fiction was weak, but that would be resolved from now on by the fact that I would approve all future material. I'd seen better cartoons, but cartoons are a very subjective – er – subject.

The sloppiness of the up-front section was repeated here and there. For example, in things like badly-written intros – the four or five lines of introduction beneath the title of an article, with which *Tiptop* told its readers what the feature about. There was some lazy picture captioning, and far too many typographical and literal errors. All those things came down to bad sub-editing, and I made a note to talk to the editorial department. And I noticed something that I hadn't noticed before: that an interview that I had written had obviously run about five or six lines over length, due to the number of photographs that had been used with it. It had been cut by cutting my final paragraph. Quick and easy, but an absolutely appalling thing to do. It ruined the readability of the end of the interview. I'd have somebody's guts for garters for that. That I had written it was completely immaterial. It was sheer, unadulterated laziness.

The pagination – the order in which the contents is arranged for the readers to read – was good. Design and lay-out weren't bad. But the typography was beginning to look a little old-fashioned. When *Tiptop* was launched, it was absolutely up to the minute in terms of design and typography. It still looked the same, but type and layout fashions had changed, and moved on. It was time for *Tiptop*'s to move with the times too. The only way to discover the future, as the old dictum goes, is to create it. I made another note.

There were some really exquisitely produced magazines about in Britain in those days. *Nova* was perhaps the best known. *About Town* was another. *Tiptop*, of course. *Men Only*. *Elephanta*. *Nova* sadly died eventually, and there were those at the time who attributed its failure to the fact that it became known as the magazine produced for people in the magazine business. There weren't enough of those to produce a big enough circulation to attract advertising or bring in sufficient revenue through copy sales.

Back in the Sixties, television hadn't achieved the gross viewing figures that we take for granted today, and newspapers and magazines all had much higher circulation figures than anyone currently achieves. People still read in those days to find out what was going on in the world. Their radios would give them the basic facts, but the detail came in their daily newspaper, and was analysed in depth in the weekly and monthly magazines. London in that era had three evening newspapers: *The Star*, *The Evening News*, and *The Standard*. That has to tell you something about falling contemporary circulations! And, most importantly to the publishers of newspapers and magazines, the advertising money goes where the circulation goes. In this case eventually to television, heralding the demise of dozens of famous publications.

A glance at my watch told me that it was lunch time. I went next door to Carla's office to see how she was recovering from her earlier depression. She still looked somewhat down, so I invited to join me for lunch at Gerry's, an invitation she accepted with a great big smile. Dee wasn't there when we arrived, but the bar was being looked after by Brian, her other half, and one of the regular girls was doing the cooking. Brian was a large, heavily bearded gentleman, who also acted as a film extra. You have almost certainly seen him in any historic British film made in the last twenty years. We ordered our drinks and lunch, and went and sat at one of the tables. Carla didn't raise the subject of the previous discussion, and I was happy to leave it be. She seemed reasonably back to her normal, sunny self.

'So how's the new job going, sweetheart?' she asked me, as we tucked into our steak and kidney pie. (There's no better food after a heavy night, in my opinion, than steak and kidney pie). I told her of my analysis of the current issue that morning, and was interested to hear her views. She basically agreed with me. She said that the problem, as she saw it, was that, having got the magazine off the ground successfully, Fred tended to lose interest in the detail. He probably wasn't aware that the design was becoming old hat, simply because he almost certainly hadn't looked at it in any detail for months. I agreed with Carla, but I also knew that if you sat down with Fred, and a copy of the current issue, and went through it with him, he would immediately see the problem. As for the people in the art department, starting off with the art editor, and including his assistants, they were pleasant people, but with little business sense, and not a lot of imagination, unless driven hard, as they had been in the past by Fred. There was safety, as far as they were concerned, in routine. There was also the added problem that the art editor and the picture editor had known Fred from his previous company, where they had all worked together, and they were small-minded enough to resent anyone other than their beloved Fred telling them what to do. That, I thought, was a bridge that I would cross when I came to it. Carla and I had one for the road, and took ourselves back to the office.

'By the way,' said Carla, as we walked back, 'I could use the copy for that Soho night club feature that you were going to put together. The photographs of the cabaret have been taken, and I've got stats of the ones that the art department are going to use, if they would be of any help. Would you like copies?' I said that yes, thank you, I would, and not to worry, I could knock out the required copy very quickly. 'How many words do you want?' I asked. 'Oh, about a thousand,' said Carla. 'Don't I remember that you were going to do a sort of road test on one of the tarts from there? That should be fun. Did you actually fuck one? Was she any good?'

'Er,' I said, wondering how to answer the questions. Near-honesty was probably the best policy. 'Er, yes, I did fuck one. And yes, she was good news. But I was talking to our lawyer about it the other day, and he said that it didn't really matter whether the club is running a disorderly house – in legal terms – or not. If we say that they are, they'll take us to court, and it will be up to us to prove it. At the end of the day, he says, it will be our word against theirs. Whichever way the decision went, it would cost us a fortune in legal costs. So I think, all in all, I'd do better to drop that particular idea.' Carla gave me a slightly old-fashioned look. 'Oh,' she said. 'That's a bit of a disappointment, isn't it? I thought I was going to find out some of the carefully-hidden secrets of your sex life. Tell Aunty Carla all about it. How old was she?' 'Oh, I'd guess about thirty,' I said. 'I don't know, really. It was fairly dark.' 'And where did you do it?' she asked. 'Did you take her back to Hampstead?' 'No,' I said. 'No, we went back to her place. Somewhere off the Bayswater Road.' Well, that was true, if you think about it.

'I don't know why you're being so unforthcoming,' said Carla. 'Anyone would think you had something to hide. We're simply talking about the intrepid editor of Britain's best girlie magazine doing some research on behalf of his readers. Aren't we? I mean, was she a good fuck, or wasn't she? How much did she charge? What particular kind of perversions was she willing to perform for money? Was she good value? I'm only asking out of interest. I'm not going to broadcast the answers around the office. This is me, Carla. Remember?'

Of course I remembered. That was the problem. I didn't want to tell the lovely Carla that I had actually fallen in love with the so-called 'tart' that I'd fucked that night. And nights since. And would be fucking on nights to come. Not for any other reason than that I didn't want to hurt her. Dear Carla. Everyone's delightful fuck when there wasn't anything else on offer. How could I possibly tell her about Annabel? I would have to lie. 'Well,' I said. 'Since you are so insistent, it was like this: the girl was recommended by the club's manageress. I told her that I wanted to buy one of her girls, and asked which one would she recommend as a good fuck. You know. Value for money. Everything. She made her recommendation, and that was the one that I went home with. Her home.

'To answer your questions in order, yes, she was a good fuck. In fact, she was a great fuck. How much did she charge? I have to tell you – take it or leave it – that when I left, she didn't charge me anything. The answer to your third question I'm not too sure about. What is a perversion? You tell me. But my understanding of this young lady is that, provided that it doesn't hurt, she will do anything sexual that a person might want to do. But then, I'm not perverted. At least, I don't think so. So there was no question of my beating her, or thrashing her, or doing anything nasty. The things that amuse and intrigue me sexually I do not see as perversions. But the Marquis de Sade probably felt the same way. You know me, sweetheart. Do you think I'm perverted?'

She looked at me, somewhat askance. 'No, baby,' she answered. 'I don't think you're perverted. But I know a man who might. You said it first. What *is* perversion? And, of course, I know the answer. Perversion is something sexual that your partner of the moment wants to do, that you don't want to do. Or that you don't want him to do. But then there are more extreme things. But they don't have anything to do with what we're talking about.' 'Oh,' I said. 'There are? Tell me about them.' 'Don't be so silly,' she said. 'You know exactly what I mean. Women getting fucked by donkeys. Or Alsatians. Serious S&M. People pissing all over each other. Drinking it. Enemas. All that sort of crap, if you'll forgive the expression.' 'Well, yes,' I said. 'I agree, of course. But to come back to your last question: was she good value? You remember? It's difficult to equate that with the fact that money didn't change hands. And while it is easy to say, remembering that I didn't have to put my money where my mouth was, if you'll forgive the pun, yes, she was.'

I tried not to show by my expression that my fucking with Annabel had probably been, by and large, the best in my life. Ever. I just didn't want to say that. Dear Carla was probably the nicest girl I have ever met, before or since. Amoral? Of course. An easy lay? Sure, if she wanted to be. But what's wrong with either of those descriptions? Nothing, in my book. Absolutely nothing at all. I'm an easy lay. (Chance would be a fine thing, as we used to say!). But I couldn't explain, either to you, or to Carla, my initially unexpected love for Annabel.

We had by this time of course long got back to the office, and we were sitting in Carla's little cupboard, drinking some of her excellent coffee. I stood up, putting down my coffee cup. 'Thank you, darling,' I said. 'I enjoyed that.' 'And thank you for lunch,' she said. 'that was nice too. We must do it again. My treat next time.' 'That would be nice,' I said. 'See you,' and I went back to my office. The red light on my telephone which told me that the switchboard had a message for me was glowing. 'Yes, darling,' I said to Joanne, the telephonist. 'Oh, there you are,' she said. 'Can you call Jane on this number,' she said, giving me the piercing lady's number. 'Oh, shit,' I thought. That's all I need. 'Thank you, darling,' I said. 'Any time Tony,' she said, in her sexiest voice. I hadn't yet met her, and I made a mental note to take the time out to do just that, knowing that sexy voices do not – really do not – necessarily mean sexy ladies. No, that's wrong. Sexy voices often do mean sexy ladies, but my limited experience tells me that they often mean ugly sexy ladies. Sad, but true. Pretty sexy ladies do not need to project themselves through sexy voices. Fact of life.

I didn't call Jane, I called Annabel. She answered the telephone with just her telephone number. 'Hello, darling heart,' I said. 'This is your favourite man. At least, I *hope* this is your favourite man. How are you? What are you doing? When am I going to see you? Why haven't you telephoned me? Do you still love me? Can I come round and fuck you? Now?' She started laughing half way through my appalling approach. By the time I got to the end, she was all sort of breathy and throaty. 'Do you mean it?' she asked. 'Now, I mean? Do you really mean now?' I looked at my watch. It was a little after three o'clock. 'Yes.' I said. 'Well, give me fifteen minutes to get there. OK?' 'Yes,' she said. 'Please. I'll be waiting.'

I must be honest and say that I have never really understood why I have been so lucky in my relationships with girls, leave aside two things. One, I was fortunate enough to be born with a large cock. But that is not a help in initial conversations. Think about it! Two, I genuinely like people. All kinds of people. And perhaps a third contributing factor: I was brought up to be polite. Pleasant, even. I find it easy to be those things. So many people these days, sadly, seem to find them difficult. But despite a reasonably high success rate, I have never taken it for granted. Really. Never. I am always surprised – and delighted – if a woman I fancy reacts to me in a similar fashion. I suppose some of it is in my genes. My father – whom I hated – could (and did) charm the birds out of the trees. Or, more accurately, out of their knickers. If it moved, he did his best to fuck it. And often succeeded. It was perhaps the fact that he was a Church of England clergyman that made this difficult for me to accept. But enough of that.

I told reception on the way out that I was off to research a story, and would be moving about a bit. If they wanted me, they could reach me in Hampstead later. I left the Porsche where it was, and took a cab to Annabel's penthouse. Annabel met me out of the lift, her arms around my neck, a big wet kiss on my mouth, a gentle hand caressing my prick. 'Hello, baby,' she said. 'Welcome home. I've got a small, tight, wet, throbbing cunt waiting for you. I've been tuning it up ever since you rang. Is there anything I can get you? A drink perhaps? Or would you rather fuck me now?'

What does any red-blooded white man do when asked a question like that? Exactly. That is what I did. I let her lead me into the bedroom, I tore off my clothes, watched her interestedly as she stripped down to lacy, all-white knickers, white suspender belt and white stockings, and then followed her into her over-size double bed. I pulled back the sheets and blankets, the better to see her revealed in her full beauty – her naked breasts, the tips hard and rigid, her thighs and legs embellished by the licentiousness of her lingerie and stockings. She lay there, a hand between her legs, slowly stroking herself through the lacy satin knickers. I could see that the crotch of the knickers was stained and wet from her juices. I spread her legs and put my head between them and started to kiss and suck her through the thin, wet material.

The feel of her sex under my mouth, lightly separated from my lips by the sensuous, damp satin fabric was exciting, and I felt Annabel's hand grasp my thickening tool as I continued my osculatory invasion of her private parts. I could taste the sweet, slightly bitter flavour of aroused woman, and feel the warmth emanating from her open orifice. As I slurped and sucked between her thighs, she began to masturbate me slowly, her hand feeling cool on my swollen prick as she pulled my foreskin up and down my shaft. She was wearing her knickers over the suspenders of her garter belt, and I started to ease them down her thighs. The waist came down easily, but the now thoroughly wet crotch clung between her cunt lips where my thrusting tongue had inserted it. As I eased the cotton-lined gusset from between those lips, I saw that it was stained the palest of yellow by her vaginal juices. As the puffy, enlarged lips of her pussy were exposed, the removal of her panties released the now much stronger scent of aroused female sex.

Her hand began to masturbate me faster, and she cried out 'Fuck me now, darling. Put it inside me. My cunt needs your stiff prick up inside it. Put it in me now. Please. Now, darling. Fuck me now.' Always ready to oblige a lady, I slipped her knickers right down her legs and off over her feet, pausing to inhale the delightful scent of cunt from the crotch before I dropped them on the floor beside the bed. She spread her legs wide and pulled her knees up, and I straddled her, my prick at the ready. She grasped it and guided it in as I lowered myself down on to her, and the feel of hot, wet cunt enveloping my rampant cock almost made me come before I even started to fuck her, but by a combination of iron self-control and holding my breath, I managed to overcome that almost instinctive reaction.

I began to ride her with long, deep strokes, and I could actually feel the nub of her erect clitoris against my thrusting prick as I delved in and out of her. I bent down and kissed her as we fucked, and she kissed me back, stopping for a moment to say 'I can taste my pussy on your lips,' before putting her mouth back on mine, her tongue in my mouth, kissing me wetly.

I tucked my hands under her buttocks, pulling her up to my body and, feeling them there, she took my buttocks in her hands. After a moment I felt one hand slip between my arse cheeks and start to massage my anus, then, moments later, she slipped a finger inside me, thrusting slowly in and out, finger-fucking my arsehole. I did the same for her, and, almost instantaneously, we both reached orgasm. My ejaculation exploded inside her, pumping my semen into her, and then, as she arched her hips up, I could feel her vaginal muscles contracting with the spasms of her own. 'Oooohhh, fuck, fuck, fuck,' she breathed, hoarsely. 'That was good. So good. Mmmmm. Fuck. Lovely. I like it. Thank you.' 'Thank *you*, my darling,' I said. I lay there for a while, breathing hard, and then, kissing her gently on the mouth, I slid carefully off her, my now limp cock making rude sucking noises as I withdrew it from her pussy, and I lay down beside her, an arm around her shoulders.

After a while she got up, saying nothing, and disappeared, returning moments later with a bottle of champagne and two pretty flute glasses. 'Will you do the honours, please, darling?' she asked, holding out the bottle. I took it from her and started to peel the foil. It was Louis Roederer Crystal. Seriously decent vintage champagne. And it was the 1949, one of the best years ever. And seriously expensive. I wondered if I had ever told her that it was my favourite champagne, and if she had bought it for that reason, or whether it was a brand that she kept about the place anyway. Whichever, it obviously needed some kind of appreciative comment. 'How lovely, darling,' I said. 'Not only my favourite champagne, but it's the 1949. Fantastic.' 'I know, sweetheart,' she said. 'You told me. So I got some. The partner who orders the drink for the club told me of the year. There's nothing like a decent glass of champagne after a good fuck. There's a case of it in the kitchen, so feel free to fuck me any time.' I laughed as I tried not to think of how much that would have cost. Mind you, we used to get a case for what you pay for a bottle these days. Seriously.

'I couldn't agree more,' I said. 'And thank you for the invitation. I'll bear it in mind.' I'd got the foil off, and I started to open the bottle. My father only ever taught me two things that I eventually appreciated as an adult. He taught me to cast a decent fly, forcing me to endure hours as a young boy in Wales casting a fly onto a saucer on the lawn, moving the saucer further and further away each time I got the measure of the distance. God, how I hated it. But I realised when I got older just how worthwhile those hours of practice had been. The other thing was that he taught me that the only proper way to open a bottle of champagne is to hold the cork and twist the bottle. It's surprising how much easier it is. If you're not already aware of that, try it the next time you open a bottle of bubbly. You'll find that you can ease the cork out without spilling a drop. I poured us each a glass. It was sheer nectar. 'That's beautiful, my darling,' I said. 'It really is the finest champagne in the world. I know that's subjective, but I really do believe that. You can have my share of Dom Perignon any day.'

I remember a time in my life when I thought I didn't like champagne. And then I had an affair with a delightful girl called Samantha. She was gorgeous. We actually lived together for quite a while. And she taught me that what I didn't like was *cheap* champagne. I'd never had any vintage champagne before that. It's a totally different drink, if you've never tried it. There simply isn't any comparison. It doesn't really matter which of the various brands you drink, if it's vintage, it's good. As you probably know, it is only pronounced a vintage year if it is up to a particularly high standard. If in any year it fails to reach that standard, it's still bottled, but it's pronounced non-vintage.

And Samantha was a vintage girl. She's the only woman I've had an affair with who wore wigs. They were really good wigs. I mean, you'd never know, if you didn't know. It was like having an affair with three different women. It used to excite the hell out of me. She was blonde herself, and she had a black wig, an auburn wig, and a sort of mid-brown wig. All three wigs were of different lengths and in different styles. Fantastic.

We drank the champagne. Slowly. It's the only way with decent champagne. As I poured the last of the bottle into Annabel's glass, she took it from me. 'Bottles are very phallic,' she said. 'Don't you think?' 'I've never really thought about it,' I said. 'I suppose they are. I mean, they're always listed amongst the objects that women fuck themselves with, aren't they? You know, candles, cucumbers, bottles. Isn't that so?' 'I guess it is,' she said, putting down her glass, and taking the bottle from my hand. She made sure that all the tinfoil was removed from the top, wiped the neck on a sheet, and, opening her legs, she slowly inserted the bottle. 'Mmmm,' she said. 'Feels interesting.' She started to move the bottle in and out, slowly at first, but gaining speed quite quickly, until she was seriously frigging herself with it. 'Mmmm,' she said again. 'It's nice. I like it.' She paused, still wanking away, and then, 'Does this turn you on?' she asked. 'Is it sexy to watch me fuck myself with a bottle?' She laughed. 'Does it make you jealous?'

I had to admit that the sight of her, still wearing her suspender belt and white stockings, her legs spread wide, wanking the bottle in and out of her bald, shaven cunt, the bottle now shining wetly for the length that was inserted so enthusiastically into her, was highly erotic. 'Yes,' I said, 'it does turn me on.' And I went over to the bed, knelt down in front of her and, taking the bottle from her hand, I started fucking her with it myself. The bottle made squelchy, slurping noises as I thrust it in and out of her. Annabel put her hands down on the bed each side of herself, and used them to raise her hips up off the bed, and she then started a fucking movement, thrusting her hairless pussy towards the bottle as I pushed it up her, pulling back as I partially withdrew it. I was fascinated, watching the neck of the bottle penetrate her labia, then reappear, wet and slippery, whilst Annabel got more and more turned on by the friction and the passage of the bottle, presumably, against her clitoris.

Remembering her questions, I continued answering them, but not slackening my manual efforts with the bottle. My prick, I suddenly realized, was now solidly stiff again. 'And, yes,' I said. 'It was very sexy to watch you fuck yourself with this bottle. But it's a damn sight sexier doing it for you. But not as sexy as watching a girl masturbate herself with her fingers. For me, that is one of the sexiest of all sights.' Unbidden, Annabel lowered herself down, thus releasing her hands which had been supporting her hips in her fucking motions, and slid a finger down to her fanny. She wiggled it into her cunt, avoiding the bottle as much as possible, and pushed it down and around, feeling for her clit, and when she found it, she started to rub it. She looked at me salaciously. 'Like this, you mean?' she asked, all innocently. Butter wouldn't have melted in her mouth. She withdrew her finger and, looking directly at me, she put it in her mouth and sucked it slowly. 'Mmmm,' she said, for the third time that afternoon. 'Nice. Would you like some?' I nodded. She reinserted her finger, making sure that it was copiously covered with her pussy juice, and then held it out to me. I leaned forward and sucked it clean. My favourite flavour. Wet cunt. 'More,' I said. 'Please.' She dipped deeply into her honeypot again, and offered me her finger. This she continued to do, and I continued to enjoy, until the bottle produced the inevitable result, and she came, gripping my arms as she did so, pressing the bottle into herself, relishing the spasms of a whole series of orgasms, until, finally, both her body and her hands relaxed, and she was quiet again.

I got up off my knees and sat beside her, my erect cock a minor embarrassment, in that I wasn't sure what to do with it. And then, suddenly, Annabel saw it. 'Oh, my poor darling,' she said. 'Here am I all happy, and sexually satisfied, and replete, and there are you with the mother and father of an erection, and nowhere to put it.' She got up off the bed, and knelt in front of me, just as I had been kneeling in front of her but minutes ago. She then took my swollen member in her hand and, pulling the foreskin down, she put her mouth around it. Her warm, wet, saliva-filled, cock-sucking mouth. She tongued my cock-head, encircling it with her soft lips, and then she started to bob her head up and down, oh, so slowly, until I felt as if I was fucking an angel.

I've no idea, of course, what fucking an angel feels like, except that it must feel exactly like the sensation she was producing in my penis as she sucked and slurped and sucked again, the suction drawing in her cheeks as I watched. And all the time she was sucking me, she kept her eyes on mine, sending me messages with them that said 'I love you, and I love doing this for you, and I hope it's giving you as much pleasure as it is giving me.' My ejaculation started deep down somewhere between my balls and my prostate, and as I felt it beginning she must have too, for she cupped my balls very, very gently, and squeezed them equally gently, and kept her head bobbing and her mouth sucking as I pumped my ejaculate down her throat, holding her head in my hands as I did so, and fucking her mouth until there was no spunk left.

She stayed with me until she was certain that there was no more come to extract from my still hard cock, and then she slowly took it out of her mouth and, smiling up at me, she said 'What can I do for you now, my darling?' What a girl. What an absolutely tremendous girl. I said, 'The only thing that I can think of, sweetheart, since you ask me so kindly, is that I wouldn't refuse a little more of that rather fantastic champagne that we had earlier on.' 'No sooner said than done,' she chuckled, taking herself off into the kitchen.

She came back moments later with another bottle of the Crystal, and we sat there beside each other on the bed, me totally naked, she still with the suspender belt and the white stockings on, and we drank the magical, pale yellow nectar slowly, enjoying each other's company. We didn't feel the need to speak a lot. Whatever we wanted to say, we said. There were long minutes of silence. Comfortable silence. I took Annabel's hand and held it in mine, enjoying the intimacy of just being together. I wondered again, as I had before, if this was love. Most of my relationships, up to now, had been more lust than love. Did I, I wondered, really want to spend the rest of my life with this gorgeous woman? Everything within me said yes. But why, I wondered, was I having these thoughts? Yes, Annabel was delightful. She was also truly beautiful. She loved sex, she was intelligent, and she appeared to be more than comfortably off. She owned a beautiful penthouse, and she said that she loved me. Not forgetting that shaven pudenda. What more could any reasonable person wish for? So OK, I thought. All that is true. But surely I'm adult enough to like her, and enjoy everything about her, without necessarily thinking about marriage? Am I not able to have a relationship without getting over-excited about it? Why would I get married now? I'm only 32. I'm too young. Why saddle myself with all that unnecessary responsibility?

But then the other half of me said, if you let this one go, buster, you must be out of your mind. You'll never find another girl that looks like this one. Importantly, you'll never find another one that is so sexually hungry, and so sexually compatible. Or one with whom you can relax, and talk about things as if you had known her all your life. And what about the money, anyway? You can't ignore money. Yes, you're making plenty. But how long will that last? If you don't take advantage of this young lady and all the lovely things that she's offering, including an unknown, but possibly impressive, amount of money, what will the girl you *do* eventually marry be earning?

She'll probably be a waitress, or a not too successful model. Money isn't what it is all about, but it is important. It's what people live on. Pay rent with. Buy houses – penthouses – with. I drained my glass, and helped myself to another, and then I looked at my watch. It was a quarter to eight. 'What about a spot of supper, sweetheart?' I asked, abandoning all thoughts of matrimony. 'We could get ourselves together, have a shower, and be on our way in half an hour. Are you hungry?' 'Starving,' she said. 'Where shall we go?' I thought for a moment. 'Is there anything that you fancy, especially?' I asked. She thought for a moment. 'Yes,' she said. 'Fish and chips.' 'Oh, terrific,' I said. 'So do I. That's no problem. We'll go to Geale's in Notting Hill Gate. Do you know it? I always think it's the best fish and chips in London. And they've got a decent wine list.' 'Yes, I do know it,' she said. 'It's my favourite fish and chip shop too.'

That decided, we showered with, inevitably, much fondling and kissing and feeling of each other, as new lovers do, but we made it down to the Bayswater Road by eight thirty, which wasn't bad considering, and got a cab to Geale's in Farmer Street, Notting Hill Gate. Old Mrs Geale, the grandmother of the present owners, was still there in those days. They used to fillet their own fish then, and Mrs Geale would deduct a penny from your bill for every bone you found in your fish. It was a very rare occurrence. I'd been going to it since I once lived in a furnished room in Notting Hill Gate, some years before, when Geale's was still just an ordinary take-away fish and chip shop.

There was a room upstairs then with long, plain wooden tables and benches where, if you wished, you could take your newspaper-wrapped order, and sit down and eat it, using the salt and vinegar supplied on the tables. That evening with Annabel Geale's had just begun to smarten itself up, with a proper little restaurant, with red-checked tablecloths, and waitresses, and a wine list. The take-away was still an integral part of the establishment in those days. Some years later it moved a couple of streets away, allowing for a much larger restaurant, so popular had the place become. And deservedly so. Today, in 1995, there are those who claim the Seashell, in Lisson Grove, provides better fish and chips. But I am not one of them. My money is still with Geale's.

Annabel and I both had haddock and chips, and of course two wallies, and I ordered a bottle of the Corvo. Or to give it its full title, Corvo Il Duca Di Salaparuta. It's an excellent dry white wine, and was remarkably cheap in those days. It's quite commonplace today, but to my knowledge, I was responsible for its introduction to London. I had discovered it on a visit to Sicily, where it was the product of a smallish wine co-operative. I liked it so much that I recommended it to every restaurant I went to, and young Mr Geale, one of Mrs Geale's sons, had kindly ordered it for his restaurant on my recommendation. There is a similarly named red, but it doesn't, in my opinion, compare. The other popular Italian white wine in those days was Frascati Fontana Candida. It came in a clear white bottle, with a gold coloured wire mesh covering. These days there is a lot of quite inferior Frascati about.

I asked Annabel if she would care to go on somewhere to dance, but she laughed, and said that if it was all right with me, she'd rather go home and indulge in some horizontal folk dancing, to which I was more than happy to agree. As I settled the bill, she leaned over and whispered 'And you can suck my pussy if you feel like it.' I felt like it, as you can probably imagine. I agreed with Annabel in the cab on the way back that I'd drop her off at her penthouse, and take the cab on back to the office car park, to pick up the Porsche, in order that I could go home later on for the necessary change of clothes. I collected my car and drove it back to Annabel's, parking it in her underground garage and taking the lift up to the top floor.

She opened the door with a big, welcoming kiss. She was naked under a silk dressing gown. 'Hurry up, sweetheart,' she said. 'I've only got about an hour before I ought to leave for the club.' To be honest, I'd been enjoying myself so much with Annabel that I had forgotten that she was working that evening. I undressed in record time, looking at Annabel as I did, lying naked on the bed, her legs apart, playing with her pussy while she waited for me. Knicker fetishist though I am, it was a delight to see her nude body in its entirety, her beautifully proportioned breasts, her hips and thighs, that entrancing, naked pussy, and her lovely long, slim legs.

I made love to her with my mouth slowly and attentively. I wanted her to relax and enjoy it. An hour is quite a long time for lovemaking. I licked her enthusiastically, feeling the softness of her hairless mound, the fleshiness of her engorged, swollen cunt lips, and the warm wetness of her love-hole. She played with her nipples as I sucked her, twisting and twirling them in her long fingers until they stood up to attention. Her pussy was oozing her juices, a sure sign that she was appreciating my attentions, and I began to concentrate on her clitoris, tonguing it with an increasingly rapid rhythm, until she came with a great shout, pressing my head down onto her pubis, keeping my tongue and lips in place until the last of her spasms had died away. When she was finished, I turned her over onto her flat stomach, raised her bottom up in the air, thrust my stiff prick deep into her well lubricated cunt, and fucked her doggy fashion, quite roughly. I came fairly quickly, a reaction due to the excitement of the time I had spent sucking her pussy. ‘Ooh, that was fun, darling,’ she said, as I withdrew. ‘What brought that on?’ I grinned at her. ‘You did, my sweetheart,’ I said. ‘I just wanted to fuck you doggy fashion. I love watching my prick going in and out of your cunt, all wet with your love juice, and that’s probably the best viewing angle.’ ‘We must do it again,’ she said. ‘I like it. Now, if you’ll forgive me, I must go, my darling.’ I dropped Annabel off at the club, and drove back to Hampstead, where I watched a bit of television, and took advantage of an early night.

CHAPTER SEVEN: TWO'S A CROWD

Next morning at the office, Freda the receptionist told me when I arrived that Wally Singleton, the publisher, wanted to see me. I went up and greeted the lovely Anthea, giving her a kiss on the cheek at the same time. 'How's my favourite young lady?' I asked. She slapped my wrist playfully. 'Now then, Tony,' she said. 'I'm not one of those naughty young models, you know.' She smiled up at me. 'Chance would be a fine thing. He's waiting for you. Do go in.' I knocked and entered. 'Good morning, Wally,' I said. 'Hello, Tony,' he said. 'Come and sit down.' I made myself comfortable.

'How's it all going?' he asked. 'I know it's early days, but are there any problems?' 'Not that I'm aware of,' I replied. 'But what does your jungle telegraph tell you?' He smiled. 'It tells me that all is well,' he said, 'and that everyone is very happy, both with you and with what you are doing.' 'Thank you,' I said. 'That's always nice to know. Now, what can I do for you?' 'I had dinner last night with a friend of mine, Tony,' he said. 'Bill Foster. I don't know if you know him. His company's into all sorts of things. Property. Importing from the Far East. He's got a largish share of one of the cross-channel ferry companies, and he's recently put some capital into one of those ailing Caribbean airlines. He's had a good look at the books, and he reckons that he can turn it around.

'One of the things he wants to do is advertise, and I've worked out a deal in which, if we want to, he'll sell us flights to, say, Jamaica, and we'll sell him advertisements. Both will of course be discounted, but I'm told it's perfectly legal, within certain parameters, provided that we invoice him and he invoices us. He's got one of those small, trendy, creative advertising agencies that he reckons will put him together a decent colour campaign, which will look good on whole pages in *Tiptop*. I've seen some of the agency's work, and it's good.

'But let me come to the point. My thought is – if you agree that it's a good idea – we could take a photographer and a number of models out there, and stay there for two or three weeks, and shoot, oh, I don't know. You tell me. Three or four really exotic girl sets. All at minimal cost. You know Jamaica, don't you? What do you think?' I thought for a moment. And yes, if Wally was happy about the cost of the flight tickets/advertising pages contra deal, then the rest, bar the actual model fees, would be reasonably cheap. 'It sounds good to me, Wally,' I said. 'The only thing that wouldn't be that cheap would be the model fees, but if we ask around, I'm sure we can do a deal with some of the girls. Who wouldn't drop their fees for two or three weeks in Jamaica?' Or their knickers, I thought to myself, thinking of the lovely Fran. Maybe I should call her. But then, variety is the spice of life. Or so they say.

'And, yes,' I said to Wally, 'I do know Jamaica reasonably well. I've got friends living there. I was out there over Christmas.' 'Terrific,' said Wally. 'Let's do it, then. You'll be in charge.' I gave him a bit of an old-fashioned look. 'And leave Harry Warner looking after things here?' I asked. I didn't want to put Harry, the associate editor, into Wally's bad books, if he wasn't there already, but I wondered at the thought of leaving him in charge. He'd probably sell the goddamned magazine, given half a chance. Or swop it for something. 'Oh, don't worry about him,' said Wally. 'I'll keep a careful eye on him. I'll have him report to me here at the end of every day, and I'll get accounts to watch his expenses. I know all about him, don't you worry. Fred's told me all about the problems.' Thank the Lord for that, I thought.

'It would probably make sense, if you know people out there, for you to go ahead of the main party and search out some good locations, wouldn't it?' asked Wally. 'Particularly if you've got friends there. Take a few days' holiday while you're there. Enjoy yourself. Just tell me when you've organized the models and the photographer, let me know your and their dates, and I'll arrange the flight tickets. You can arrange accommodation and so on when you're out there. OK?' 'Very much OK, Wally,' I said. 'Thanks very much.' 'My pleasure,' he said. He grinned at me as I took my leave. I kissed Anthea on the way out.

The next few weeks passed quickly, and then, suddenly, everything fell into place. The picture editor had selected three terrific models, whom I had seen and agreed, and all three girls had dropped their hourly rates for an agreed three-week fee. There was a naughty-looking little blonde, with an almost elfin face and a fabulous body, called Jean Bonnington, a black-haired girl called Annie Walters, again with a great body, and an equally well set up redhead called June Graham. The different hair colourings were intentional, because with three models we would naturally enough shoot two- and three-girl sets, as well as individual ones. Three blondes, for example, wouldn't have looked natural. I made certain that all three had done full frontal modelling before. I didn't want any of them refusing to drop their drawers, photographically speaking, that far from home. And I agreed to pay for them to have sufficient sun bed sessions to give them a basic tan, so as not to either waste time on location, or risk sunburn. I decided to take Phil Gordon, he of the cocaine habit, as the photographer. We would pick up a lighting assistant locally, once we got to Jamaica. Phil also met the models before everything was signed up. It didn't seem worth risking anyone not wanting to work with someone. It does happen, and the result is always bad pictures.

Annabel didn't ask me not to fuck anyone else whilst I was away, and I didn't ask her. But we spent every available minute (some of it stolen, by me, from *Tiptop*) fucking each other before I left. I also managed to spend a night with Carla, to her delight, bless her, and I telephoned Jane Powell, the bisexual piercing lady. I hadn't taken up her arse-fucking offer yet, and selfishly I didn't want her to think I wasn't interested. Frankly, I was. I didn't, of course, refer to that on the 'phone, and nor did she, but I think she knew why I had called. 'I'll see you when I get back, love,' she said. 'And I'll keep an eye on Carla for you.' She chuckled as she put the 'phone down. I didn't 'phone Judy. I didn't want her to know about the trip to Jamaica, if possible, since I hadn't booked her for it. I suspected that was probably the end of a beautiful relationship. Nor did I telephone Fran, in the end. For the same reason. And then, finally, I was on my way.

I had considered going via New York, since it didn't cost any extra. It's my favourite city, and I thought it might be fun to do some shopping, and look up Fred, but then I thought of Jamaica's fabulous beaches, and that wonderful climate, and I'd only got a week of actual holiday, and suddenly there was no contest. I have to tell you that I was greatly impressed to be flying first class. I'd lashed out on club class a number of times on long flights, but I'd never flown first before. By the time we were dropping down to Kingston airport, alongside that enormous harbour, I had made up my mind never to fly anything else, if I could possibly arrange it.

The stewardesses were all Jamaican, naturally enough, and Jamaican girls are almost all not just beautiful, but come equipped with natural charm and wonderful, genuine smiles. It was rather like flying in the Playboy Club. The London one, in its early days. Do you remember? And the seats were roomy and comfortable, the airline food was excellent, the drink flowed, and any and every whim was seemingly these lovely ladies' command. A truly great experience.

My friend John Lane met me at the airport. I was going to stay with him, at least for a day or two. On my last visit he had been living in a delightful house on Stony Hill Road, looking down over Kingston. By the time I arrived this time, he had separated from his wife Ann, and was living in a top-floor apartment in an elegant block nearer to the centre of Kingston, called Manor Court. It was the first time that I met his beautiful new Jamaican girlfriend Joan, who was to become his second wife.

That evening over dinner at the Blue Mountain Inn, a charming restaurant built over a stream in the lower region of Jamaica's Blue Mountains, behind Kingston, we spoke of the forthcoming model trip, and the question of locations. John knew Jamaica well, and was accustomed to finding locations for the television commercials produced by his advertising agency. It was his opinion that we couldn't do better than base ourselves in Port Antonio. The north coast of Jamaica, around Montego Bay and Ocho Rios, the two resorts where most tourists go, was not, he thought, as beautiful. Negril, in those days, had not yet been developed as a tourist centre.

This was excellent news for me, for I loved Port Antonio. The following morning John telephoned the agent through whom he had rented the beach house for me the last time I was there with Fran, to find – to my delight – that it would be available for the three weeks of the forthcoming trip. It had four double bedrooms and three bathrooms, so we would all be able to fit in. I booked it there and then, happy in the knowledge that not only would we have all the gorgeous Jamaican scenery that we needed for the shoot, but that we would also be staying in a place that everyone would enjoy, and which held particularly happy memories for me.

Later that evening, back in his apartment, John told me of what he described as a fabulous house at Port Antonio called

Dragon Point, out on a small rock peninsula called Dragon Bay. He suggested that we drive over to have a look at it the following day. It was a unique, architect-designed house standing on the headland overlooking a rocky promontory that ran into the sea. The rock had blowholes through which the sea was forced by the waves, resulting in spumes of spray that looked like dragon's breath.

It had been built by an American millionaire for his wife. Sadly, she had left him before it was completed. He remarried quite soon afterwards, but his second wife refused to live in it, simply because it had been built specifically for the first wife. It was one of the most beautiful houses that I have ever seen. Being built for the tropics, all four walls on the ground floor opened up completely to the open air, should you so wish, and it had an all-around veranda, with three sides overlooking the Caribbean Sea. There was a large swimming pool, and numerous individual guest cottages. It would, as John had suggested, make a perfect location for photography. The house was rented then by a charming Jamaican called Winston Stoner, who lived there with his wife Candice. Candice was a Canadian girl who had been employed as a Bunny at the Jamaican Playboy Club, until she was enticed away by Winston. She was as least as pretty, and possibly prettier, than the three model girls I was shortly to import. We had been shown around the house by Winston's helper (the word servant is no longer socially acceptable in Jamaica) and when I agreed that it would be an ideal location, John telephoned Winston at his office, and arranged to meet him in the rooftop Polo Lounge at the Pegasus Hotel, the place where Kingston's successful businessmen meet for a drink at the end of the working day.

When I met Winston that evening, it was the beginning of a friendship that still continues over the years. Winston was one of a number of kind Jamaican people – including my friend John Lane, who is now a Jamaican national – who had the patience to teach me backgammon, the game that is almost a

Jamaican national sport. If you ever have the good fortune to meet Winston, do not play him backgammon for money, unless you are a good loser.

That evening John took me to see some of the sights of Kingston. It is still one of the friendliest cities in the world, although in those days the blood-red-painted government building in the centre of Kingston, known locally as the Gun Court, was a reminder that it can also be a violent city. The Gun Court is long gone now. Most of the crime was, and still is, concerned with Jamaica's flourishing drug industry. We moved from the Polo Lounge to the Jamaica Club, a haven for male chauvinists, which does not admit lady members. It was delightfully old-fashioned, with ceiling fans and a unique atmosphere. We moved on from there to a place called Madam Georgina's, a small but pleasant bar, where there were a number of attractive young Jamaican ladies sitting about the place. John was telling me in the car on the way there that the Jamaica Club still has its original Complaints Book in use, from over a hundred years ago. The first complaint apparently recorded the details of a member taking exception to the lack of manners of a surly waiter, and he complains that the Club did not stock his favourite brand of Scotch whisky. Entirely reminiscent of the complaints book of any London gentlemen's club.

We had a few rum and sodas at Madam Georgina's, and I chatted with one of the girls, who was charming and amusing, as well as pretty. I was considerably taken aback after we left, when John told me that the young ladies were available for hire, and that the bar was also a brothel. Madam Georgina's, sadly, is no more. It had a certain attractively seedy Jamaican elegance.

We dined at the Terra Nova Hotel on Waterloo Road, an old Great House, as they are known, belonging originally to one of the wealthy sugar cane plantation owners in the bad old days of slavery and piracy. It is an elegant place, with excellent food and service, and it still retains an air of how one can imagine it used to be in its heyday. Over whiskies and water back at John Lane's apartment, sitting out on the verandah overlooking the twinkling lights of Kingston at night, John suggested that I add a little local colour by adding a black Jamaican model to the three English girls coming out. I thought that was a terrific idea, and I couldn't think why it hadn't occurred to me before. I explained to John the vital difference between nude models and any other kind. It is the simple fact that their bodies have to be perfect. No blemishes, no stretch marks, no cellulite, no drooping tits. It is a fact that a number of what are regarded as the top international fashion models couldn't earn a cent posing nude, for one reason or another. They look magnificent in clothes but not so magnificent out of them. Sad, really. But then, they make so much more money than nude models, who – quite wrongly, I believe – are at the more poorly paid end of the model business.

John put me in touch with a number of agencies, and I spent a happy couple of days looking at beautiful Jamaican girls wearing nothing but lovely smiles. It was difficult to make a decision, if only because they were all so exquisite. And all with perfect bodies. In the end, I picked one called Cindy, simply because she combined perfect beauty with an overtly outgoing sexy character. It's called different things by different people in different circumstances. Charisma. Personality. Star quality. In my book, it's the one you seriously want to fuck, and who seriously wants to fuck you.

Cindy was nineteen, dark brown, and just perfect. There is no other way to describe her body. Long, long legs. Flat stomach. Tiny waist. Small, but flawless breasts, tipped by over-size areolae and nipples, in a deep shade of black. I was to discover later that her vaginal lips were the same blue-black colour. She came to me by personal recommendation, not from an agency. She was wearing a white cotton Mexicana dress that set off her dark brown beauty to perfection. As she came through the door of the office that John Lane had lent me, she must have seen the expression on my face. She smiled, and did a model's twirl entirely for my benefit. 'It suits me, doesn't it?' she said. 'I bought it at Mexicana in Lower Sloane Street last year. I expect they're out of fashion in London now, but I like it. And it likes me.' She laughed, and came towards me with her hand out, giving mine a firm, warm shake. 'Cindy Johnson,' she said. 'I'm a friend of Marlene's.' Marlene was a girl I had met at one of Kingston's prolific parties. 'I'm used to posing for girlie magazines,' she said. 'I worked for a number of them whilst I was in London. And I really enjoyed it. I just love taking my clothes off. Shall I take them off now?' she asked.

'Please,' I said. 'I'm afraid I can't offer you a changing room.' 'No problem,' she said. 'It's much more fun taking them off in front of an appreciative audience.' She stripped off slowly, first taking off the dress over her head, revealing that she wasn't wearing a bra. Nor did she need one. And also that she was wearing the tiniest, flimsiest transparent white lace knickers that I had ever seen. Her black, curly pubic hair showed plainly through the thin material. I don't know if I imagined it, but I fancied, just for a moment, that the crotch of her tiny knickers was wet.

She simply dropped the dress on the floor, and then, bending down gracefully, she slipped the knickers down her long, firm thighs, and stepped out of them. 'Here,' she said, and threw them to me. 'Keep those as a souvenir. They'll bring you luck. I promise.' She laughed, showing her perfect, immaculate white teeth. I caught them, and put them in my pocket. 'Thank you, darling,' I said. 'They will be a perfect reminder of you.' She was now completely naked. 'What would you like me to do now?' she asked, arching her eyebrows, a delightful smile on her face, her eyes sparkling. She stood about five eight, her small but perfectly shaped breasts thrust pertly out towards me. I wanted to take hold of one and suck it, and play with her pussy beneath that curly, black-haired pudenda. Gently, Andrews, I said to myself. Don't spoil everything by rushing it. 'What I would really like you to do,' I said, arching my own eyebrows, and laughing at the extent to which she was making me react, 'is to come and have lunch with me. So that we can talk a little more about this modelling job. How does that grab you?'

'It grabs me,' she said. 'Thank you. I'd like that.' She picked up the Mexicana dress and put it on. She didn't ask for her knickers back, and I didn't offer them. I got John Lane's switchboard to order me a cab, and we took off. 'I thought we'd go to Heather's,' I said to Cindy. 'Is that OK?' 'Perfect,' she said. 'I love Heather's.' Heather's is a terrific restaurant in Haining Road, just behind the Pegasus Hotel, on Knutsford Boulevard. It is unique, even in Kingston, in that roughly a third of it is in the open air, well shaded of course by lush palm trees. It is run by the owner's wife, Heather, who is young, pretty, pleasant, and an excellent restaurateur. It has an extensive menu, which ranges from burgers to Jamaican specialities. The waitresses are all charming, and extremely efficient. It is popular at lunchtime during the week with Kingston's less pompous businessmen.

Cindy chose a burger, and I had the lamb curry. We both drank rum and mixers. Not too many Jamaicans drink wine with meals. I finished with an ice-cream, being an ice-cream freak, and we both had coffee. 'What now?' I said to Cindy. We had discussed the photographic shoot *ad nauseam* over lunch. 'Do you have any commitments?' 'No,' she said. 'I rather hoped that you would take me off somewhere and fuck me.' My dick began to swell. 'What a lovely idea, Cindy,' I said. 'But where would "somewhere" be? I don't really like to take advantage of John Lane's place without having asked him beforehand.' Cindy dug around in her large leather bag, and produced a cell-phone. 'So ask him,' she said. I called John at the office, and got through to him. He had literally just got back from lunch. Speaking quietly into the 'phone, I explained the situation, and asked whether he had any objection to my taking Cindy back to his apartment.

'None at all, old chap,' he said. 'No problem. Do you want

me to stay away all evening? That's not difficult, if that's what you'd like.' I looked at my watch. It was ten to three. 'Thanks, John,' I said, 'but that won't be necessary. If we go back there now, we should be finished long before you get home. But thanks, anyway.'

I gave Cindy her 'phone back. 'Thanks, darling,' I said. 'I'm ready for you now. Shall I ask for the bill?' 'Sure, honey,' said Cindy. 'I'm ready when you are. Let's go.' We ordered a cab back to John's apartment, and fifteen minutes later, I was watching Cindy get undressed again. It was just as exciting an occasion as the morning's display had been. I stripped off as enthusiastically as Cindy seemed to have done, and then, suddenly, there we were, lying on the bed in my bedroom, vying with each other to see who could get to whose private parts and engage them first! Cindy took hold of my cock, and pulled me gently towards her. 'Come here, lover,' she said. 'I've got just the place to take care of that for you.' So saying, she pushed me down onto my back, and straddled me, spreading her legs across me, and, lowering herself down, she began to feed my rampant prick up into her juicy, hot cunt. She was very wet, and very tight. A remarkable combination. 'Now, just lie back there,' she commanded, 'and let me show you how well trained we Jamaican girls are. Jamaican men are so damn lazy, we have to do the fucking ourselves. Otherwise we just don't get fucked.'

If you believe that, I thought, you'll believe anything. But perhaps Jamaican men in Jamaica are less athletic than their brothers in London. I've never heard London girls complain about the sexual energy of Jamaican men. Whatever the truth – or not – of Cindy's statement, she proceeded to give me the serious fucking of a lifetime. Over the course of the next couple of hours, she fucked me, sucked me off, masturbated me, and then fucked me again. I didn't believe that she could make me ejaculate so many times over such a comparatively short period of time. She did things with her cunt, her mouth, and her hands, that I wouldn't have believed possible, had I not been at the sharp end of those activities. Certainly no-one else had done some of those things to me.

It was the most marvellous experience, and I made no sexual efforts whatsoever. Cindy seemed totally happy administering to what started out as my needs, and ended up as some kind of one-woman sexual orgy. I loved every moment of it. She too gave ample evidence of enjoying what she was doing, orgasming regularly as she fucked me, shouting aloud to the world what was happening to her. 'Oh, my God, I'm coming again,' she said at one stage. 'Oh, yes. I love it. I'm fucking you, and I'm making myself come. Now. Can you feel me coming?' she asked.

I most certainly could. Cindy having an orgasm left you in no doubt at all as to what was happening. Her vaginal muscles contracted and expanded, squeezing your prick for its full length, until you too came with her. Her cunt was the equivalent of one of those milking machines you see farmers attaching to cows' udders. I was being milked. Regularly, and efficiently, until there was nothing left to milk any more. Finally, she slid off me. 'Was that your first Jamaican fuck?' she asked after a little while. 'You know. The first time you've been fucked by a Jamaican girl?' 'Yes,' I had to admit, 'it is. But I hope it's not my last.' I put a hand out, found her wet pussy, and started to finger fuck her. 'Give me five minutes, and then I'll fuck you. OK?' 'My pleasure,' she said. 'I'm ready when you are, baby. That's good.' 'What's good?' I asked. She turned over on her side and looked at me, her deep brown eyes alight with … what? Passion? Desire? Humour? Amusement? Probably a little of all four. 'I like a man with stamina,' she said. 'That's what keeps a girl happy.'

I gave it another ten minutes, frigging her quietly whilst I lay there, and then I took my hand away from her cunt and sucked her juices off my finger. She tasted strongly of aroused female. A soft but stringent combination. The scent of her on my fingers completed the erection that my frigging her had started, and I reached down and spread her legs. I then climbed onto her, and thrust my now seriously stiff prick into her wetness. She closed her pussy around me like a soft, warm clam, and I started to fuck her, my rhythm increasing as I felt her opening up to me. She was warm and wet, and her cunt muscles were doing their thing again. It made for a fabulous fuck. I held her hard little nipples in my hands and squeezed and pulled them until they were like small, elongated thimbles. Her mouth was open as she lay beneath me, and I leaned down and started to kiss her, putting my tongue into her mouth, and I took my fingers away from her nipples and slipped my hands underneath her slim buttocks, kneading and squeezing them whilst I pumped away at her cunt.

Her tongue responded to mine in her mouth, and we kissed wetly, enjoying the sensation of each other's warm saliva. One moment her tongue wrapped itself around mine, the next it was sensually exploring the rest of my mouth. I felt her hand reach down between her legs and find the base of my cock, and then she started to squeeze it in time with the tempo of my strokes. The result of that was that I came much more quickly than I would have done without the extra titillation, my semen spurting into her vagina in long, hot, thick, creamy spurts. 'Oh, yes,' she breathed in my ear. 'I can feel your come spurting up me. That's lovely. It's fantastic. All your lovely come.' And she squeezed her cunt muscles yet again, milking me of that which I did not believe I still was able to produce, so much had she extracted from me during the course of the afternoon.

'That was great, lover,' she said, when finally it was all over. 'You can fuck me any time. OK?' 'OK, sweetheart,' I said. 'And thank you. That's quite a compliment.' I looked at my watch. It was after six. John Lane might well be home soon. We took a shower together and, much as I enjoyed the proximity of her lithe, wet, black body, I was all fucked out. Friendly it was. Sexy, it wasn't. We dressed lazily, and were sitting out on John's veranda with our drinks by the time he got home. He poured himself a drink and joined us. He knew Cindy from way back, since she had modelled for his advertising agency. Not nude of course.

After a while, having swapped news of each other's day's events, John announced that he was taking us to the Wyndham Hotel for dinner. It too is on Knutsford Boulevard, close by the Pegasus Hotel. We were to meet his girlfriend Joan in the hotel's bar at eight-thirty. He invited Cindy to join us, who seemed pleased to accept. I looked at my watch. That gave us plenty of time for another drink. I helped myself.

The following morning I went off to see a lighting equipment company that John had recommended. They had everything that Phil Gordon could possibly need, and were happy to hire it out at a very reasonable rate, by London standards, and to deliver it to anywhere on the island that we wished. They could also supply a lighting assistant. I thought that I would leave that to Phil. He was, after all, the person who was going to have to work with the assistant. It made sense to me that he should select that person himself. Everything seemed to be pretty much set up. The beach house at Port Antonio as accommodation for everyone, and also as a location. Dragon Point as a second location, with a plethora of other suitable locations within easy reach. I would hire a Land Rover as transport, and drive it up to Port Antonio with the crew myself. We would send it back to Kingston, with a driver, to bring the luggage. The models were coming from London, and additionally I had hired the lovely Cindy. Lighting equipment was arranged, and assistants were there for Phil to choose from. Lingerie, bikinis, props, etc., were coming from London. Ah, yes. Hairdresser. The harsh sun, and the salt sea air on the coast would make a professional hairdresser essential. A quick call to John at his office, and that was arranged. And that was it. I had three days to relax and enjoy myself before the rest of the crew would arrive, and two of those days were a Saturday and Sunday, which meant that John would also be free.

I had arranged to meet him for lunch at Heather's, and he and I and some business friends of John's to whom he introduced me played a few games of backgammon before we ordered lunch. It demonstrated to me just how out of practice at the game I was. Over lunch, I asked John what he was planning at the weekend, and was delighted to hear that, subject to suitable weather – that meant sufficient wind, not fine weather as such, which is virtually guaranteed – he was intending to go sailing. The following morning he pronounced it a likely day, and we took off for The Royal Kingston Yacht Club, where John keeps his trimaran. The car was loaded with food, booze, clothing for every eventuality, a radio, and a large cooler full of ice.

Kingston Harbour is enormous, and the yacht club is right at the far eastern end, whilst the exit from the harbour out to the Caribbean is at the far western end. It is a fascinating sail, sailing parallel to the airport runway, past huge tankers and freighters moored in the harbour, and sailing by what is left of Port Royal, the original harbour, much used by pirates in the late seventeenth century, the greater part of which you sail over, since it disappeared beneath the water when a volcanic eruption occurred at the end of that century.

John had invited a couple of young Jamaican girls along for the ride, 'to act as crew,' he said. If you'll believe that, you'll believe anything, I thought to myself, but the sight of these two nubile young women in their minuscule bikinis added considerably to the enjoyment of the day. And to be fair, they scurried about the deck at John's command, trimmimg sheets, or whatever it is you do with the ropes that control the sails. One of the amazing features of Kingston Harbour – at least to anyone who doesn't live there – is the myriad fat brown pelicans who festoon every buoy you pass, and who fly in formation low over the water, suddenly dropping straight down in spectacular nosedives into it to catch the fish upon which they feed.

Outside the confines of the harbour, the wind freshens, and sailing proper begins. At this point, to add to my pleasure, the two girls abandoned their bikini tops, revealing breasts that certainly didn't need that support. There is a long line of small quays (pronounced cays) stretching out into the Caribbean from the harbour entrance, all of which are unoccupied, most of which have beautiful sandy beaches, and they are the places where the inhabitants of Kingston do their swimming and sunbathing, if they have – and can afford – the means of getting there. You can get there via a longish journey by, first, ferry across the harbour itself, taking a north to south direction, and then picking up a motorised canoe, which will take you out to the cay of your choice, and will return to collect you again at an agreed time. The sea outside the harbour is entirely unpolluted and crystal clear. John having selected the cay of his choice – simply a sand bar of pure, almost white sand, surrounded by gently sloping beaches – he and the girls negotiated the reefs which almost surround all the cays, making sailing right in to the shore a hazardous event, best tackled only by those who are extremely competent at their handling of sailing boats.

We dropped anchor in about four feet of the clearest water I had seen since my previous visit, and for the rest of the day we swam, lazed in the sun, drank, ate the food that John had prepared the evening before, chattered idly, and generally enjoyed ourselves. The two girls seemed more interested in each other than in either John or me, and I was happy to accept that possibility, relaxing in the hot sun, lying in the shade of the boat, swimming, gathering shells, and generally charging my batteries after the sheer physical efforts of the previous afternoon.

Towards the end of the day the wind freshened, and John judged it time to return to the yacht club. The girls leapt to, and they and John upped anchor, and manoeuvred the boat through the reef, after which we sailed back to Kingston at a rapid speed of knots. An absolutely exhilarating day. That evening John took me on a tour of the discos that in those days used to play real, old-fashioned, Jamaican reggae at ear-splitting volume. We were the only white people in most of them, and it says much for the friendliness of the Jamaican people that we were welcomed by everyone, without exception. In one of them I was picked up (it is the only accurate description) by two Jamaican sisters of, I would guess, about eighteen or nineteen. After a while, John indicated that he thought that it was time to move on, and I said thank you, but I'd find my own way home. He grinned at me, and nodded, and left. 'See you later, Tony,' he said. The girls were educated girls. One was a teller at one of Kingston's larger banks, the other ran an arts and crafts shop in one of the bigger shopping malls. They were out for some fun on their Saturday night out, and they thought that I might just be the fun they were looking for. They were drinking Gold Label rum and coke, and I was happy to join them.

They took it in turns to dance with me, but the actual dancing, due to the close press of the disco, consisted really of holding each other and rubbing one's genital area against that of the girl one was dancing with. Nothing wrong with that at all. Not in my book. There wasn't anything to choose between them. They were both beautiful. They were more of a pale brown than black, and their short skirts and low-cut blouses revealed gorgeous figures. They both seemed to get fired up as the evening wore on, and it wasn't too long before first one, then the other, reached down in the crowded dance floor and felt for, and found, my slightly swollen cock.

'Mmmm,' said the first one to do it, whose name was Marlene. 'That feels good, man. Do you like to fuck?' 'Er, yes,' I said, slightly nervously, still not accustomed to this direct approach, even after my experience with Cindy. 'Maybe we should go home soon,' said Marlene. 'Me sister and me share an apartment not too far from here. The car outside. What you think?' 'Sounds good,' I said, wondering how I would chose one of these delightful ladies, or if I could manage two. I took Marlene back to the corner where her sister was, and took the sister out onto the floor. Her name was Ann. We stood close, more or less stationary, rubbing our groins together. Down came Ann's hand, and stroked my now much more swollen prick. 'Mmm hmm,' she said. 'Marlene said you got a good-size cock, and that you like to fuck. What we waitin' for?' There's no answer to a question like that, is there? Other than to say you're ready, willing, and able, which is more or less what I said. We finished our drinks, and left the disco. The girls' car was a Honda which had seen better days, but in the economic climate of Jamaica back in those days, they were doing very well – especially at their age – to have any kind of car at all.

I didn't know Kingston well enough then (or now) to know where we went, but it was only about ten minutes' drive. It was a small, pleasant suburban-type cul-de-sac, with small, well-kept houses, and small apartment blocks. It was outside one of these apartment blocks that we drew up and parked. It was a two-storey building, and we walked up some outside stone stairs to the upper floor. Once inside, it was a simple, but pleasantly furnished three-room apartment, with a lounge, off which was the kitchen, two bedrooms, and a bathroom. There was no air conditioning, but the girls switched on the ceiling fans, and the place soon became cooler than at our first entrance.

Ann put a reggae tape on, while Marlene poured us all large rum and cokes, with plenty of ice from the large fridge which was a feature of the kitchen. I raised my glass, and the girls raised theirs. We drank. 'Who you goin' to fuck first, then?' asked Marlene. I took another swig of my rum. 'I don't think that's up to me,' I said. 'I think you two should decide that.' Frankly, I didn't care. They were both beautiful, desirable, and very, very fuckable. But I didn't want to be seen to prefer one over the other. Understandably, I think. The girls looked blank. There was a silence for a few moments. 'I know,' I said. 'Why don't you play the best of three games of backgammon? At the end, the winner can chose either to go first, or to give that to the other. What do you think?'

'Excellent,' said Ann, and went over to a cupboard in the

corner, from which she produced a well-worn backgammon board. 'No doubling dice,' said Marlene, as they sat down at the table and set the board up. 'Since we're not playing for money, there's no point.' 'Agreed,' said Ann. Ann won the first game, Marlene the second. They were patently experienced players. The third game was an interesting one, which lasted longer than the other two.

At first it looked as if it was Ann all the way. She was so far ahead, mathematically, that it looked as if she must win. But Marlene concentrated on closing up her home board, and caught one of Ann's pieces just as it looked as if it was all over. A classic end game. Which Marlene won.

She smiled at her sister, and got up and kissed her on the cheek. 'You take him first, darling,' she said. 'Warm him up for me.' Ann giggled, and came over and took me by the hand and led me into her bedroom. She shut the door. There were speakers in the bedroom, softly relaying the music from the tape machine. Ann undid the zipper at the side of her skirt, and stepped out of it, and followed that by taking off her blouse. This confirmed my earlier thought that she wasn't wearing a bra, but also revealed that she was wearing transparent, black lacy knickers. She wasn't wearing stocking or tights, which are more or less unnecessary in the tropics. She bent down and pulled the knickers down slowly, looking at me as she did so. She pulled them right down to her ankles, and then stepped out of them. She stood up, and faced me. 'Will I do?' she asked.

'Do, darling?' I repeated. 'My God. Yes. You'll most certainly do. Come over here!' She came over to me, and I took her in my arms and kissed her, slowly and carefully. I didn't want to rush anything. I wanted to take my time, enjoying every moment of this fantastic young Jamaican girl and her wondrous body. I wanted to imprint her on my memory. Burn her into my experience of life. Girls who looked like this simply didn't happen very often, not even in my business. She could have put Cindy out of the model business any day she wanted. She was about five eight in her bare feet. Slim and muscular. Totally fit. But with full, firm breasts, lovely long legs, and a beautiful, well-shaped arse, with firm, full buttocks that you wanted to take hold of and squeeze, the very first moment you saw them.

Her lips were soft and warm, and she kissed me wetly. I could feel her nipples hardening against my chest, and I reached a hand down and found her pubic mound. The black hair surmounting it was tight and curly, and I reached a finger into its centre, and found the wet slit that I was looking for. She groaned, and spread her legs. 'Oh, yes, baby,' she murmured. 'That's the place. Pussy wants you. Now. Please.' I picked her up and carried her over to the bed, placing her down upon it. Her nipples and areolae were quite black by comparison with her brown flesh, and now, looking down at the source of pleasure soon to come, I saw that the folds of her outer labia were the same black, but with a pink gash shining wetly down their centre. She was lying on her back, and I knelt in front of her and spread her legs to allow access to my mouth and tongue. I looked up at her and she smiled back at me. 'So you're goin' to suck my pussy,' she said. 'That's nice. I like that.'

Her pudendum was thickly covered with tightly curled, thick black hair, at the centre of which were the puffy lips of her outer labia, swollen with lust. I spread them with my fingers, the scent of aroused cunt reaching my nostrils as I touched her. I pulled the lips wider apart, examining her inner labia with interest. She was so wet that her juices were trickling down and overflowing her outer lips, the miniature rivulet making its way down the crack between her buttocks and disappearing from sight beneath her. I slid my forefinger into her, and she closed her cunt around it like a pink sea anemone. I pushed and pulled it in and out, gently, and watched as her vaginal muscles took hold of my finger as it entered her, and then clung to it, loath to let go of the object that was giving her pleasure.

I took my finger out and, using both hands, I peeled her

inner lips right back until I could see her clitoris shining up at me wetly from her innermost depth. I stroked and rubbed it, softly, and watched as it burgeoned, becoming engorged with blood until it was quite stiff, like an erect miniature penis. 'Oh, honey,' she whispered, her voice thick with passion, 'that's the place. Don't stop doing that. That's good. That's lovely. Oooh, Ann likes that.' I continued my massage of her clit, and she began to move her hips, her rhythm slowly increasing as she approached orgasm. 'Oh, baby,' she said. 'Now suck it. Please. Now suck my cunt. Suck my clitty. I'm ready for you. Suck me. Make me come.'

She was almost bouncing on the bed with her mounting desire, and I took my finger out and applied my mouth to her wetness, my tongue thrusting deeply in and finding her erect clit. She tasted of sex, a combination of honey-sweet nectar and slightly acrid, exotic tropical fruit. Over-ripe mango, perhaps. I liked the taste of her, and sucked and then swallowed a mouthful of the liquid that now flowed so copiously from her. I got back to her clitoris, working hard now to bring about her orgasm, so that I might (selfishly, perhaps) soon get my own end away.

My prick was throbbing with the need for release, and just as Ann started to shout her pleasure, as her orgasm started to cause her hips and belly to shudder in its all-consuming spasm, I felt a hand on my grateful cock. I looked around to see Marlene behind me. 'It looked so much fun, I thought I'd join in,' she said. 'Do you mind?' I lifted my mouth from Ann's pussy just long enough to say 'No, sweetheart,' and as I went back to keeping Ann's orgasms coming, Marlene wriggled herself underneath me in some way, and pulled my throbbing cock into her warm, wet pussy. She then started to fuck me, as I continued to suck Ann, and as Ann's orgasms at last died gently away, I let go of her and, turning around, I positioned myself properly over Marlene's now recumbent body, and began to fuck her enthusiastically. I bent my head, and began to kiss her. She tongued me immediately, sucking and slurping at my mouth. 'I can taste Ann's pussy juice on your tongue,' she said, 'That's sexy, isn't it?' 'Yes,' I said. 'It's a taste I know well,' she said. 'I often suck Ann's little black pussy, and she sucks mine. That's naughty, isn't it? Does that shock you?' I felt my cock swelling even as I fucked her, at the thought of these two girls sucking each other off, totally abandoned in their enjoyment of sex with each other, small pink tongues thrusting into fleshy back labia.

'Yes,' I said. 'Very naughty. And no, it doesn't shock me. Will you do it while I watch?' 'Sure, honey,' she said. 'Just finish this fuck, then we'll have another drink, and then we'll put on a little sex show for you. Would you like that?' Right at that moment, I ejaculated into her, my spunk jetting in hard spurts at the thought of watching these two physically perfect little black sisters at their sex games. 'I think that's your answer, darling,' I said. 'You've made me come just thinking about it.' 'That's lovely,' she said. 'It felt really good. It was quite hot. Next time, you can come in my mouth.'

I continued my fucking motions until the last of my sperm had been sucked out of me by this naughty young girl, and then I looked up to see what Ann was up to. She was lying back on the bed, seemingly in another world somewhere, frigging herself, her fingers a blur on her pussy as she wanked away, the wetness of her quim and the speed with which her fingers were moving making sort of little squishy noises as she worked away at herself. Marlene saw what I was looking at. 'Randy little cow,' she said. 'Can't wait even long enough for me to have a quick fuck. She's at it all the time. It's as much as I can do to stop her playing with herself in the car. I'll be driving along, you know, in the middle of Kingston in the rush hour. You must have seen what it's like. And there she is, her skirt up around her waist, her fingers inside her panties, wanking herself off whilst every driver on all sides is practically driving into us at the sight of what she's doing. I can't take her anywhere.'

As she spoke, Ann achieved the orgasm that she was

working so hard for, and when it was over, she lay back on the bed, apparently exhausted, at least for the moment. Marlene got herself up from the floor, and I did the same. She looked down at Ann. 'Drink, honey?' she asked. 'Mmmm,' said Ann. 'Yes, thank you.' She seemed suddenly to get herself together. I felt faintly foolish, standing there, naked. I'm not sure why, really. It was all my fantasies, rolled into one, coming true. Doing what I had been doing. Watching what I had been watching. Hearing what Marlene had been saying. It was obviously going to be a long night. Thank God it was Sunday tomorrow. I wondered what plans John Lane had for Sunday. Church wouldn't be amongst them, that was for sure. Possibly a late lunch somewhere, and a few games of backgammon. I could understand why he liked living in Jamaica.

Marlene came back with three fresh drinks, which she handed around. 'Cheers, sweetheart,' she said. I wasn't sure whether she meant Ann or me. I raised my glass. 'Cheers, girls,' I said. 'What a terrific evening. Thank you.' 'Don't thank us yet, Tony,' she said. 'We haven't started yet. Just pray for stamina.' She giggled, and then took a long draught of her rum and coke. 'I'm not serious,' she said. 'Just teasing. All we want to do is have fun. Any time you want to stop, just say so. We want you to have a good time too. OK?' 'Hey, listen,' I said. 'I'm having the greatest time of my life. No, seriously. I'm loving every minute of it.' It was true. Annabel might be in love with me. And even me with her. But this was raw sex. No one in their right mind would cop out on an opportunity like this. Would you? I wondered who would make the next move. Should it be me, I wondered? I didn't think so, somehow. If what Marlene had said earlier was going to happen, the next move was a lesbian exhibition by the two girls. I decided to hang in there, and wait and see what happened.

Marlene looked lazily at her sister Ann. 'I was tellin' Tony here that you and I enjoyed suckin' each other's pussies,' she said. Ann didn't move a hair. She just stood there, nude, looking slightly quizzical. 'Well, you were pretty preoccupied at the time, playin' with yourself,' said Marlene. 'Else you would have heard me. I promised him that we'd let him watch while we enjoyed ourselves. What do you say?'

Ann didn't reply for a moment. And then: 'I say OK. Great.' Marlene looked pleased, and I felt my cock rising to the occasion. 'But with one proviso,' said Ann. 'What's that?' asked Marlene. 'You've been fucked,' Ann replied. 'I've been sucked off. I enjoyed it, but now I'm goin' to get sucked off again. When am I going to get fucked, I ask myself? Seems to me that all the fuckin' that's going on, I ain't gettin' my share. So if Tony here wants to watch us suckin' each other's pussies, well and good. But at such time as he feels the need, or the urge, or even that he feels he can, then he can join in and fuck me whilst I go on suckin' you. Agreed?' She raised her eyebrows, and looked, not at me, but at her sister. 'Oh, hell, agreed. Sure,' said Marlene. 'I mean, I wouldn't want you to miss out on anything. Would you like me to get the dildo out, and use that on you, rather than my mouth?' Ann thought for a minute. 'No, sweetie, thank you. I'd rather wait for Tony, seein' as he's here. The dildo's OK when there's no man, but I'd rather have the real thing, if it's available.' I had to speak my piece. It was now or never.

'Oh, come on, Ann honey,' I pleaded. 'I've never seen a girl fucked with a dildo. It's something I've fantasized about all my life. Will you do it? Please? Just for me? Only for a little while, and then I'll take over and fuck you properly. I promise. Please?' Ann looked at me and smiled. 'That's the nicest way anyone has ever suggested that I get fucked with a dildo,' she said. 'For you, darling, anything.' She went over to a cupboard in the corner of the room and opened the door. She searched around for a moment, and then took hold of something and, shutting the door, came back to where Marlene and I were standing. She was holding an enormous pink rubber dildo in her hand. 'I understand that all the girls in London use big black ones,' she said. 'For the same reason, all us Jamaican girls use big white ones. Well, pink, anyway.' We all laughed.

Ann put the end of the dildo in her mouth and wet it. It stretched her cheeks alarmingly. She took it out and looked at the now wetly shining protuberance. 'That looks about right,' she said. 'Let's see how it feels.' She splayed her legs as she stood there, and began to feed the head of the giant dildo into her cunt. I noticed that its shape denoted that it had been circumcised. I wondered if purchasers had a choice. She groaned slightly. 'Hey, Tony,' she said. 'Make yourself useful. You put it in.' She stood there, waiting.

I knelt down on the floor and took hold of the dildo. It was as solid as a rock, but quite pliable. It was obscenely lifelike, apart from the colour, even down to the veins standing out down its shaft, and the frenum running down from its head. Ann bent down and, using her fingers, pulled her cunt-lips as far apart as they would go. 'Now just shove it in,' she commanded. 'But slowly. Yes, that's right. Oooh, it's lovely. Fuck me with it, somebody. Please. Fuck me quickly.' 'You see what I mean?' said Marlene. 'Dirty cow.' I pushed slowly and gently, and the dildo slid in to an alarming depth. Ann began to move her hips backwards and forwards in a fucking motion. Marlene got hold of her arm, and started to pull her over to the bed.

'Come on, baby,' she said. Marlene laid herself down backwards on the bed and spread her legs, pulling Ann's head down towards her glistening, half-open pussy. Ann knelt down in front of her and started sucking Marlene's cunt, while Marlene took hold of the protruding end of the dildo and started to fuck Ann with it. I sat on the bed beside them, my prick rigidly upright, and watched, fascinated. After a few moments, I'd have bet that they had forgotten I was there. Ann made little husky, animal noises in her throat as she sucked her sister's cunt, and Marlene gave soft moans of pleasure as she fucked Ann with the huge dildo. I got up off the bed and went and stood behind Ann, watching the dildo as it slid in and out of her cunt, glistening now not with her saliva, but with love-juices. As I watched, I became conscious of her tiny, puckered, black little anus, winking at me as she moved her hips to and fro, receiving the ministrations of the make-believe cock. It was small and tight and infinitely fuckable. I wondered if either of the girls' sexual tastes included anal sex, and my prick almost burst with the excitement of the visual image that thought conjured up. I had difficulty in keeping my hand off my cock and bringing relief to its engorged state of erection. It would have been a terrible waste.

I decided that faint heart never won fair lady, and that the chances were that both girls took it up their pretty little arses. There was only one way to find out, and I went into the bathroom to look for something to use as a suitable lubricant. I found a jar of some kind of face cream, which I decided would do the job, and took it back into the bedroom, where I unscrewed the top, and took a generous glob of it on my forefinger.

I went and stood behind Ann again. Marlene was wielding the dildo with great élan, and Ann was in the throes of a series of orgasms as I started to annoint her anal love-hole with the face cream. Her only reaction was to thrust her buttocks towards my finger, as if to encourage me to insert my finger into her anus, rather than simply playing around the outside. I took her gesture at face value, if you know what I mean, and, taking another dollop of the face cream, I thrust my finger in and began to lubricate her rectum as far as I could reach inside with my finger. Ann's series of orgasms seemed to have subsided, at least for the moment, and she turned and looked at me over her shoulder. 'Oooh,' she said. 'What a naughty boy. Are you goin' to fuck me up my arse?' I didn't know whether to make a statement (as in 'yes,') or ask a question. On brief reflection, it seemed more civilized to ask the question. 'Would you like that?' I asked. 'Oh, sure, honey,' was the answer. 'Jus' take it gently at first. OK?' 'OK,' I said.

I'd finished applying the face cream, and I took hold of Ann's slim buttocks, and guided my rampant prick slowly and carefully up against that little puckered hole. Taking one hand, I used it to hold my cock as I started to ease myself into her. I slid in quite easily, and then I started to press, gently, but firmly, and I slid all the way home without any trouble at all. Ann looked back over her shoulder again, her lips wet with Marlene's love juices. 'That's good, baby,' she said. 'Fuck me hard now.' I began to do exactly that, watching, fascinated, as my prick slid in and out of Ann's anus, stretching that little puckered hole into something the circumference of my swollen prick. It felt good. Really good. I took hold of Ann's pretty little tits, with their over-sized nipples, now hard and erect, and I kneaded them as she wriggled her arse, and thrust backwards against my strokes. Her arse was tight and hot, and well lubricated with the face cream, and it was rather like fucking the proverbial mouse's ear-hole.

Ann continued to suck Marlene, as Marlene went on fucking Ann with the giant dildo, and I concentrated on fucking Ann's arse. And then, almost as if by design, we all started to come at once. I groaned with pleasure as I spurted hot come up Ann's bottom. Ann shouted as she came, and writhed around like a demented dervish, and Marlene too shouted out her pleasure as she achieved the orgasms that Ann had produced for her so prettily. We all jerked and twisted and arched our backs and came, happily, in unison. And then we all lay on the bed in a heap, laughing, and groaning, and getting our breath back. After a while, Ann got up and brought us all fresh drinks, and I took off to the bathroom to wash my cock.

I was remembering that Marlene had said earlier that I could come in her mouth, and if she still had a feeling for it, well, who was I to refuse her? These two girls seemed to have the knack of stimulating me to the point where the thought of yet another ejaculation filled me with desire, without any hint of worrying whether or not I could manage it. I just knew I could. I went back to the bedroom, and we sat around on the bed, the three of us. No-one said anything about bed, or sleep, or going home, and I was beginning to get hard again, thinking about coming in Marlene's mouth. Ann's hand had wandered down between her legs, and she was idly playing with herself. Marlene looked at her, and then at me, and mouthed 'dirty little cow,' pointing at Ann as she did. I laughed.

Marlene then looked at my cock, which was now fully erect. 'Oh goodness, Tony,' she said, pointing a finger at my cock. 'Look at what's happened. It would be a shame to waste it, don' you think?' I said that yes, it probably would be a waste. Marlene got up off the bed and came around to my side, and knelt in front of me. She didn't say anything further, but she took my cock in her hand and put it in her mouth. I was glad that I had thought to wash it. Her lips were full and soft, and she pursed them prettily as she sucked me. Then she took my stiffened cock out of her mouth and, looking at me full in the eyes as she did so, she licked it thoroughly all over, pulling my foreskin down and spending time with her tongue giving my cock-head a loving tongue-bath. The sensations that this produced almost had me coming right then, but I managed to hold back.

She took her time licking all the way down the length of my shaft, and then all the way back up again. While she was down at the base of it, her saliva evaporated, causing my cock-head to get cold. The contrast when she then came back and enveloped it in her warm, wet mouth was just absolute heaven. She took me out of her mouth for a moment, and, masturbating me slowly with her hand while she spoke, she said: 'When you're ready to come, you'll need to decide whether you want me to finish suckin' you off – which will be my pleasure – or whether you then want to start fuckin' my mouth until you come. I'm sure you understand the difference. I'm happy either way. You don't have to say anything now, and when the time comes, I'll know by your actions which it is goin' to be. OK?' 'Thank you, darling,' I said. 'That's terrific. Thank you.'

In fact, although I knew the difference in theory, I had never experienced fucking any girl's mouth. It wasn't something one did to girls in London as a general rule. I'd heard of men doing it with prostitutes, but I'd never done it myself. And here was this lovely Jamaican girl asking me if I would like to! If she didn't mind, by God, this was going to be a new experience. I was sitting up, watching my cock slurping in and out of Marlene's mouth, when Ann, apparently tired of playing with herself, came over to my side of the bed, and gently pressed my shoulders back until I was lying back on the bed. She then knelt over my face, her back to Marlene, and lowered her wet pussy onto my mouth, leaving me enough room both to breathe and to manoeuvre. She put her fingers down and spread her fleshy, black outer labia, opening up her pink inner lips that I might immediately find her swollen clitoris. I wish I could have had a photograph of what must have been an amazingly erotic sight, these two beautiful black sisters, with their exquisite, naked bodies, the one sucking my cock with enthusiasm, whilst the other sat on my face as I sucked her pussy.

Ann's pussy was thoroughly wet, which was hardly surprising if you thought of the sexual activity in which she had been engaged almost non-stop now for some hours. She tasted gamey. Strongly sexually potent. I set to work to please her, sucking and slurping at her cunt, enjoying the taste and the scent of her well-used sex. I found her clitoris quickly, and she sighed as I began to massage it with my tongue. 'That's the spot, dear Tony,' she said. 'That is absolutely right on target. Now fuck me with your tongue.' I had no idea what the time was, but it had to be well into the early hours. I worked at her as hard as I could, for I was conscious of my own need to ejaculate pretty soon, with the delightful things that Marlene was doing with her lips and tongue, and I wanted to take her up on her invitation to fuck her mouth, just prior to my coming. To come in her mouth, as she had suggested much earlier. And patently I wasn't going to be able to do that with the lovely Ann basically sitting upon my chest. And then, happily, Ann started to move her pussy against my mouth. 'Oh, it's coming now. I can feel it coming,' she said. She moved even faster.

'Oh, yes. Here it comes. Oooooooh. Yes. Lovely. Nice. Yes. I like it. Oooooooh. I'm coming. Now.' She pressed hard against my mouth, and I kept my tongue working whilst her orgasms rose to a crescendo, then began to fade, and finally she was finished. She looked down at me. 'Nice,' she said. 'Very nice. Thank you.' I grinned up at her. 'My pleasure,' I said.

Ann got up, carefully, and took herself off. I could feel my own ejaculation beginning to stir, and I sat up again and took Marlene's head in my hands. She didn't stop sucking me, and as I held her head, she increased the suction and the pressure from her lips as I began to move my hips backwards and forwards, literally fucking her mouth. It was obscenely erotic, watching her face as I fucked her orally, and I came almost immediately, spurting my semen into her mouth, which she swallowed, slurping and gulping as my come filled her mouth. She kept on sucking until my orgasm was over, and she had milked me dry of come. I withdrew from her mouth, and she smiled up at me. 'I think you enjoyed that,' she said. 'I think I did, too,' I replied. 'It was tremendous. Thank you, darling.'

Thank God we all fell into bed then, me in the middle and one exquisitely beautiful Jamaican girl, still stark naked, each side of me. I fell asleep instantly, and slept the sleep of the completely sexually exhausted. When I awoke the following morning it was nearly midday. The sun was high in the sky, the temperature was pushing ninety, and the girls were fully dressed, as if for a garden party. They were wearing pretty, lightly starched cotton summer dresses, with elegant straw hats, and carrying white cotton gloves. The two of them were even wearing stockings, I noticed, with their court shoes.

'Oh, look, Marlene,' said Ann. 'He's woken up. Hello, darling,' she said. 'We didn't mean to wake you. We were going to leave you a note. We're just off to church, it being Sunday.' Of course, I thought. That explains the formal clothes. And then I saw that they were both also carrying prayer-books. I had to laugh to myself at the contrast between their activities of the long night just gone and their obviously genuine feeling for whatever their religion happened to be. I didn't, of course, let my amusement show.

'Help yourself to breakfast, Tony,' they said. 'There's juice and coffee, and bread for toast. The marmalade's in the fridge. There's bacon if you want it, and eggs. Whatever. But now, before we go, where can we get in touch with you? Don't think that we're goin' to let you get away, 'cos we're not.' I gave them John Lane's home telephone number, and explained that I would be up country in Port Antonio quite soon. I took their telephone number, and wondered if I would have time to enjoy their company again on this trip. It had been a tremendous experience, and one that I would happily repeat, circumstances permitting. Marlene looked at her watch. 'Come on, Ann, honey,' she said. 'Else we'll be late for church. Goodbye for now, Tony. That was all lovely. We hope you enjoyed it too.' They blew kisses as I reassured them that yes, I most certainly had enjoyed it, and then they were gone, and their little apartment was a less colourful place without them. I used their telephone to call John Lane. 'There you are, Tony,' he said. 'I was just thinking of sending out search parties. Did you have a good time?' 'I'll tell you all about it when I see you,' I said. 'But yes, I had a terrific time. I'm just going to get myself together, have a shower and drink some coffee, and then I'll call a cab, and I should be with you within the hour. OK?' 'Terrific,' said John. 'I thought we might go to the Liguanea Club for lunch. Why don't you meet me there at, say, one thirty? The cab driver will know where it is.' 'Great, John,' I said. 'I'll be there. Thank you.'

CHAPTER EIGHT: BEACH BUM

The Liguanea (pronounced Ligany) Club was once a bastion of Empire. Now that the Empire is no longer, this rather splendid relic is somewhat faded, but I was to discover that it is still a cool, pleasant place in which to eat a beautifully served, excellent lunch, in an elegant restaurant, surrounded by successful Jamaicans of every shade, from white, through many shades of brown, to blue-black. Jamaica is one of the least racially conscious places in the world, which is more than one can say, sadly, of the white colonialists who for so long raped the island of its bauxite and sugar, and cruelly enslaved its people, along with the African slaves imported via America.

One of Jamaica's most popular indigenous dishes – salt fish and ackee, made from salt cod and the fruit of the ackee tree originated because, all those years ago, salt cod was the cheapest food that could be imported in bulk from North America with which to feed slaves. That none of the slaves had probably ever eaten salt cod before was not considered at all important. Jamaicans have made it their own dish by the addition of ackee, a fruit which needs to be extremely carefully prepared, since integral parts of it are deadly poisonous.

The Liguanea Club occupies extensive acreage in what has become almost the centre of Kingston's thriving commercial area. Its tennis courts, swimming pool, and open-air dining area must, for the simplest of economic reasons, sooner or later fall victim to the developer's financial advances. It is prime commercial land, close by the Pegasus and Wyndham Hotels – two of Kingston's finest – on Knutsford Boulevard. John was amused by my adventures of the previous evening, and announced that, all things considered, I didn't look too bad. I felt – surprisingly – tremendous. It must have been the quantities of rum that I had been consuming. I've been a whisky and water (no ice) man since I first worked in West Africa, all those years ago. But I have a penchant for genuinely enjoying the local hooch wherever I happen to be, when abroad. Ouzo in Greece. Raki in Turkey. Slivovitz in what used to be Yugoslavia. Rum in the Caribbean. (The only exception is American whiskey in America. I can't stomach sourmash or bourbon.) Nor do I ever drink these drinks at home in England. But I love them in their appropriate places.

We moved on, after lunch, to what John described as one of the friendliest bars in Kingston: the Mayfair Hotel bar, which employs, reputedly, the two best barmen in the whole of Jamaica. Mr Royes, always known as Mr Royes, and Mervin, always known as Mervin. It is a small hotel, not advertised in the colourful brochures that flood the world markets. But the fact that it has the highest occupancy rate of any hotel in Kingston should tell you that it is a good place to stay. The hotel's rooms are in buildings around and about the central bar and swimming pool. It is a seriously friendly place, with much playing of darts and backgammon. It has an unusual menu, catering to a wide variety of tastes. You can, if you so wish, order egg and chips there.

John and I played a few games of backgammon, drank a few rum and cokes (for me) rum and sodas (for him), and chatted lazily for a while, until John judged that it was probably time to take a siesta. He drove us back to Manor Court, where we both collapsed for forty winks, which took us right through until eight that evening. The following day my colleagues from London were due. I decided that I needed an early night, with a full eight hours' sleep, and bid my friend John goodnight as

I took myself off to my bedroom. Frankly, I seriously needed the sleep.

Monday dawned bright and clear, and I took a cab to meet the London contingent's plane. They were due in at ten thirty Jamaican time, which, roughly, would have meant they'd have set off very early in the morning London time. Jean, June, Annie and Phil duly arrived, on time, but shattered. They looked the way I had felt the previous evening, but I suspected that their problem was simply a matter of lack of sleep and an excess of booze. I'd booked them in at the Pegasus, and once we'd cleared them and their considerable amount of luggage through customs, I organized a taxi to take us all to that hotel. I was pleased to see that the three models had done what they had been told to do, and had spent time and trouble getting themselves first class tans, prior to their journey out to Kingston. Jean Bonnington took my arm, and I escorted her to the cab rank, where we found two cabs to take us to the hotel. Jean, you may remember, was the little blonde that I had thought looked rather naughty when we had signed her up in London. She and I and June Graham, the redhead, took one cab. Phil Gordon and the other model, Annie Walters, followed us in the second.

'So this is Jamaica,' said Jean, looking out at the chaos which always typifies the forecourt of Kingston Airport after an international flight arrives. 'It doesn't look much right now.' I had to agree with her. 'No, it doesn't,' I said. 'But Kingston isn't famous for its beauty. Only for the friendliness of its people. You'll see when you've settled in. And the pretty part doesn't really begin until we get up country a bit from Kingston. We have to drive up over the Blue Mountains, where all the coffee grows, and down the other side into Port Antonio. Then you'll see all the travel brochure-style white beaches, palm trees, and so on. Just hang in there. You must be tired after your journey. May I suggest a quick shower, a change into something more suitable for this climate, and I'll buy you a very large, very cold, drink in the Pegasus Polo Lounge. The Pegasus is where we're staying until we leave for Port Antonio.' I looked at my watch. It was almost noon. 'Shall we say one thirty? June, does that suit you? And perhaps you'll tell Phil and Annie. OK?'

I remembered how shattered I had felt after the journey, and I hoped that my suggestion would cheer them up. When we got to the Pegasus, they took their bags up with them, and I arranged for the trunks and boxes of gear and props, costumes and equipment, to be stored until we asked for them. At one thirty promptly, the four of them trooped into the bar. They looked refreshed and happy after the long journey. They would look even better in a day or so. I sat them down, and waved a languid hand at a waiter. All of them ordered exotic rum cocktails, which is exactly what all first-time tourists to the Caribbean do. And why not? I had forgotten just how remarkably pretty the three girls were, and it was amusing to see the appreciative looks – and guess at the comments being made by – the other men in the Polo Lounge. The girls had all changed into tropical holiday clothes, and looked quite sensational. Even Phil had made an effort.

I took them off to Heather's for lunch, which I thought would be more fun for them than the semi-formality of the Pegasus's restaurant. I had arranged to meet John Lane there, and I had also invited Cindy, the Jamaican model, to join us, and meet the other people with whom she would be working. Happily, everyone got on well with everyone, and lunch was good, lengthy, and enjoyable. The presence of both John and Cindy was much appreciated by the new arrivals, since they felt that they were getting unprejudiced answers to their questions about life in Jamaica, as opposed to what they would have felt if I had been the only person they could question. Naturally enough, they didn't see me as an expert, which of course I'm not.

It eventually became time for John to get back to his office, and he asked me quietly what plans, if any, I had for the others that evening. I had none, and said so, and he suggested that we all meet after dinner at a disco called Epiphany, of which he was a member. It was, he said, the all-happening disco of the moment in Kingston, and he felt sure that we would all enjoy it. He would bring his girlfriend Joan, and the others would find dancing partners – if that was what they wanted – easily enough. 'Even you, Tony,' he said, grinning at me. 'Thank you very much, John,' I said. We agreed that I would take the party somewhere first to eat, and that we would all meet at Epiphany at ten. He went off, and the rest of us sat around in Heather's, drinking gently and chattering, until well into the afternoon. The London party were enthusiastic at the thought of Epiphany and eventually it was Phil who suggested that they all go back to the hotel for a siesta. 'I don't know about the rest of you,' he said 'but I'm knackered. What with jet lag, time lag, and whatever, my chances of staying awake this evening at a disco are absolutely nil, unless I go and get a bit of kip in now.' The others agreed, and I paid the bill and ordered us a cab. Cindy had come in her own car, but it was a little small to take five passengers. We bade her farewell, and said how much we looked forward to seeing her later on in the evening. The cab turned up, and I dropped the others back at the Pegasus and took it on to John's apartment at Manor Court. If anyone needed sleep, it was me. I went to bed, setting the alarm for six that evening.

When it went off I showered and dressed, and was just pouring myself the first of the evening when John arrived home. I poured one for him too. 'I tell you what, Tony,' he said. 'I'm going to cook supper for Joan here this evening. I'm going to do my wine merchant's fillet steak. Why don't you tell the others to eat at the hotel, and then you can telephone Cindy – or anyone else for that matter – and the four of us can eat here. I'd happily invite all of them, but I've only got enough steak for four. And frankly, I don't feel up to cooking for eight. Four's no problem. Eight's a hassle.' 'Terrific, John,' I said. 'That would be nice.' I called Phil, and then I found Cindy's number and telephoned to invite her, and she seemed pleased to accept. She and Joan arrived within a few minutes of each other and it transpired that they had met before, which made for a relaxed quartet. John performed his act with the steak, which really was very good. There had been a time, years ago, in London, when he'd run his own advertising consultancy during the day, and then acted as chef in his own restaurant, The Tun of Port, in Holland Street, off Kensington Church Street, in the evenings. For obvious reasons, he has had a particular interest in food ever since, and is an excellent cook. We all pronounced the Wine Merchant's steak superb, to John's obvious pleasure. It is an old English recipe that he discovered somewhere, which makes succulent and generous use of whole black peppercorns.

We met Phil, Jean, Annie and June at Epiphany around ten thirty, and the place was jam-packed. I knew my London disco scene pretty well in those days, but I have never seen so many beautiful women assembled in one place. Jamaican women are just made for dancing, and they have a grace that few of their European sisters can match. It was a joy just to sit and watch for a while. Epiphany's decor was made up of slides and moving film projected onto the walls, producing a constantly changing melange of Jamaican scenery, beautiful women, and abstract patterns. The sound was excellent, and the music was a mixture of London's and New York's top disco numbers. Sadly, it no longer exists.

Cindy soon had me dancing, and she worked me relentlessly, laughing off my pleas for mercy, until I was literally almost dropping. Eventually I had to cry enough, and I went to join the others at the table John had reserved for us. The girls all danced we men off our feet, but at about one o'clock, siesta or no siesta, the London crew began to feel the effects of their jet-lag, and we decided to call it a day. I said I'd be over at the hotel at about eleven, and we would start to get down to thinking about work and our trip to Port Antonio. I declined Cindy's invitation to join her at her place as politely as I could, for the previous night's delights and this evening's dancing had left me with no energy at all, sexual or otherwise. I think she understood.

I telephoned Phil at ten in the morning, and finding him up and about, I went over to the hotel to have a talk with him before the girls joined us. I asked him to sort out his props and equipment and get the hotel to arrange for their transport to the house at Port Antonio, and to get in touch with the lighting equipment company and select a lighting assistant.

When the girls joined us, I showed them photographs of the two houses, the one on the beach in which we were to stay, and the other one at Dragon Point. They made suitably agreeable noises, and I told them that they should be ready to leave at ten the following morning. There would be seven of us, including Cindy and the lighting assistant, and I suggested that the five of us present at the meeting should go in the Land Rover, with me driving, and the lighting person could follow us with Cindy in her car. All things being equal, I believed that we should get there by early evening, and I would telephone the house and get the servants there to arrange an early evening meal for us. I would order a packed lunch from the hotel to take with us.

The distance from Kingston to Port Antonio is not that far as the crow flies, but the road itself takes a very circuitous route across the Blue Mountains, and the surface, apart from the first few miles out of Kingston, is appalling, making it a much longer journey than you would expect, looking at the map. It seemed reasonable to allow the best part of the day, including the time taken up by stopping for lunch. That way, no-one would be disappointed if we got there sooner. Comfort aside, it is a delightful journey in scenic terms, offering an opportunity to see a great deal of the island's extremely varied countryside.

That evening I took my colleagues to The Trattoria, a restaurant on Munroe Road, in the Liguanea area, almost next door to CGR, John Lane's advertising agency. Strangely enough, the Liguanea Club is not situated in the area from which it takes its name. The Trattoria is an excellent restaurant which, as you would imagine, specializes in Italian food, but it is unique in my experience in that it has adapted the classic Italian recipes to include local Jamaican ingredients. Their Spaghetti Bolognese, for example, includes the famous (or, to the faint-hearted, the infamous) Jamaican Scotch Bonnet peppers, allegedly the world's hottest, adding a degree of warmth not present in the original Bolognese version. It is an attractive, intimate place of white walls, small alcoves and dark red hangings, and the mostly female staff are as delightful as they are pretty. The restaurant originated in an old Great House in the hills above Kingston. In those days it was both expensive and exclusive, and was called Temple Hall. Some years ago the restaurant's owners were attacked and robbed by gunmen, as a result of which they decided to move their operation down to Kingston itself, where it became The Trattoria. The chef (and present owner) is a member of the Confrerie de la Chaine des Rotisseurs, a society for gourmets which dates back to 1248.

We enjoyed an excellent meal. Despite an extensive and varied menu, on my recommendation we all had the Spaghetti Bolognese, after which everyone pronounced themselves both well-fed and happy. I noticed, with some amusement (thinking of London prices) that the most expensive item on the bill was the large espresso coffees with which we had all finished our meal. This perhaps has something to do with the fact that, whilst Jamaica is the home of the internationally famous Blue Mountain coffee, almost the entire annual crop is purchased these days by the Japanese, who have decided that it is their favourite coffee. As with everything that the Japanese decide they like, the price has gone through the roof, compelling even Jamaicans to pay through the nose for the local product – when they can get it.

We summoned a taxi, and I dropped the others off at the Pegasus before returning to Manor Court. I received delightful goodnight kisses from Jean, Jane, and Annie, and a grin from

Phil, whose offer of a kiss I refused. John Lane was still up when I got back, and we had a whisky or two and a few games of backgammon (which, for once, I am pleased to be able to say that I won: a rare occurrence for me in those days) before I went to bed, leaving John watching television. There are times when I wonder when he sleeps. He is always the last to bed and the first to rise in the morning. The new day started, as do almost all Jamaican days, with blue skies, soft, balmy winds, and strong sunshine. I picked up the rented Land Rover, and drove to the Pegasus, where Phil had got the hotel staff to assemble our luggage by the main entrance. The girls collected our packed lunch, and we got everything into the Land Rover. The lighting assistant arrived, a young man called Jim, whom Phil introduced to everybody, Cindy arrived with her car, and we were on our way.

We climbed slowly up the base of the Blue Mountains, passing first the Blue Mountain Inn, a popular restaurant in those days, and a little further on, an army post, and then there was nothing but road, winding ahead through the tropical vegetation. We drove at a gentle pace, trying to avoid the worst of the potholes, conscious that Cindy's rather battered little Simca didn't have quite the kind of suspension that the Land Rover boasted. A couple of hours later, just after twelve, I found a reasonable place to pull off the road, and we stopped for lunch.

The Pegasus had done us proud, with a simple chicken salad, fresh rolls and butter – the latter in a cooler – and bottles of red wine, together with a good supply of mineral water. Refreshed, we motored on, driving down the far side of the mountain range, with a spectacular view out over the northern coastline. After a while, we came to a spot called the Blue Hole, an inlet where the warm waters of the Caribbean mingled with icy cold water from an underground spring, which made for refreshing swimming. John Lane had appraised me of the existence of this delight, and I had warned the others to pack swimming gear and towels in easily accessible places if they wanted to swim. In no time at all we were all immersed, swimming in and out of the changing temperatures, enjoying the exercise and the freedom after the dusty confines of the vehicles. There was a small facility with simple changing rooms and offering cold drinks, both of which we used to advantage, and after changing back into our clothes, we were once more on our way again. We finally arrived at the beach house, just this side of Port Antonio, at six in the evening. We were greeted rapturously by the cook and houseboy, who turned out to be the same two who had looked after Fran and me on my previous visit. Phil and I took a double bedroom each, we gave one to the young lighting assistant, Jim, and the four girls happily doubled up in the remaining two. Should we need another room at any time, and for any reason, Jim and Phil could double up, freeing one double bedroom for anyone who might need it.

The entire party was enchanted by the house and its location, and the girls were soon in the sea, from whence they ran screaming hysterically – all except Cindy, that is – when they sighted their first sting-ray. It took quite some time for Cindy and Jim and me to reassure them that the rays were harmless. Phil wandered about, looking for places to set up his shoot the following day, and decided, reasonably enough, to start taking his pictures in and around the house, including, of course, the beach. He put his supply of film into the huge fridge in the kitchen. Film can deteriorate quickly in tropical temperatures.

He thought he would start by using all four girls, since the house provided a logical reason for having four girls in the shots who, for the purposes of the photography, would be staying in it. My activity was largely over now that the real work was starting, since, apart from actually being both responsible and in charge, my only real chore was to provide the words that would accompany the pictures when they appeared in *Tiptop*'s pages. Accustomed as I was to seeing naked women, I found the sight of the four pretty young models in their brief bikinis somehow strangely erotic. Their costumes were minimal, but, particularly when wet, they seemed to make the areas that they covered – the girls' breasts, nipples, pudenda, and bottom cheeks – all the more erogenous, and, perhaps for the first time, I really began to understand the term 'erogenous zones.'

All being models, the girls uniformly wore extremely high-cut bikini bottoms, and all had trimmed their pubic hair to make certain that none was apparent when photographed in these brief costumes. This made the small pubic triangles left seem almost obscenely attractive through the thin, wet material, and I found my eyes drawn as if by a magnet to all the girls' thinly-covered crotches in turn. On one occasion, later on that evening, when she was reclining on a sun-lounger out on the veranda, Jean Bonnington (the one I thought of as the naughty one) caught me staring at her crotch. She smiled at me, opened her legs, and pursed her pouty little mouth to blow me a big kiss, although she didn't actually say anything. I winked back at her, and thought to myself that her action bodied well for the future. I tried to ignore the hard-on that the sight of the shape of her cunt lips through the flimsy material of her bikini bottom gave me, and the salacious thoughts that this wonderful apparition brought on.

She was only sitting about four feet away, and she leaned forward and whispered to me quietly, 'Would you like some help with that stiff cock of yours? I can think of a number of ways to get rid of it for you if it's bothering you.' She remained leaning forward, and the angle of her body was causing her bikini top to pull downwards, revealing most of a pinkly brown aureola, together with its pertly erect, burgeoning nipple.

She followed my eyes again, and, looking down at her nipple, said, 'Oh, dear. Aren't I a naughty girl? Would you like to suck that?' She didn't make any attempt to cover it up. I still hadn't answered her first question, being somewhat taken aback by the directness of her proposition. Then I thought, the hell with it, and I said 'Yes. Please. I'd like you to help me with my cock, and I'd like to suck your tits. And your pussy. And I'd like to fuck you. If all or any of that appeals, follow me up to my room in five minutes. I'll be waiting for you.' And I got up and went back into the house, and up to my bedroom, which was on the top floor.

Minutes later the door opened and Jean came in, closing the door quietly behind her. She came over to me and, putting her arms around me, she kissed me, thrusting her tongue wetly into my welcoming mouth. She tasted of salt and sun oil. Then I felt a hand reach down and feel for my cock, which wasn't difficult to find, bearing in mind that it was almost fully erect. 'Don't lose that,' she said. 'I'll be right with you. I'll just take a quick shower. You can come and watch if you like.' I did like, and I followed her through into the bathroom, where I sat on the edge of the bath and watched happily as she peeled off her bikini top. Her nipples were erect and firm, and as she pulled down her bikini bottom she revealed that her blonde pubic hair was shaven into a little heart shape. She saw where I was looking once more, and smiled. 'Hence the expression "She took him to her heart,"' she said. She got into the shower and turned it on. That makes two of us, I thought. Turned on, I meant. She let the water run down her body, rinsing off much of the salt before she started to soap herself. She turned towards me and, smiling through the jets of water, she began soaping her breasts lasciviously, rubbing them first with the bar of soap, then with her fingers. She pulled and tweaked at her nipples until they stood out even more like hard little acorns.

I began to get seriously excited (for 'excited,' read 'erect') when she dropped her hands down to her cunt and started soaping down there. After thoroughly washing and rinsing her outer labia, she pushed first the soap inside herself, pushing and twisting, and making little grunting noises as she did so, and then she put down the soap and started thrusting her fingers in and out of herself in the same way. She watched me watching her, and then she suddenly said, 'Why don't you come and join me, Tony? Then we'll all start off nice and clean before we start getting ourselves dirty again.'

I didn't hesitate for a moment. Nor would you have done. I ripped off my short-sleeved shirt, shorts, and underpants and was in the shower alongside her before you could say knife. My prick stood out like some kind of obscene cucumber. Jean took hold of it positively joyfully, and, pulling my foreskin back, she began soaping me. It was a delightful sensation. Put simply, I was being masturbated, well-lubricated by soapy lather, by a beautiful, naked model, with whom I was sharing a shower, and who, from her dirty conversation, enjoyed sex in a healthy, uncomplicated, enthusiastic way. Could I wish for more? I didn't think so. I started to kiss her, but it wasn't actually that easy under the running water. It was difficult both to kiss and to breathe, and not being able to breathe tends to discourage one from kissing. 'Why don't we get out of here,' I suggested, 'and continue in the bedroom?' 'Sounds like a good idea,' she said. 'I was just getting a little carried away there. A cock in the hand, as they say, is better than no cock at all.' I laughed, even if it was an old joke.

We got out of the shower, and I turned it off. I looked at her whilst she was towelling herself dry. She really did have a fabulous figure. One forgets, sometimes, that being a model doesn't just mean a pretty face and good tits. It also means a good neck and good shoulders, a perfectly flat stomach, a proportionately small waist, long legs, good ankles, trim, shapely – which means the *right* shape, not just any shape – hips, good, firm, well-shaped buttocks, good, smallish hands with long fingers. And good bones beneath the good body.

Not too many people have that combination. On top of all that, you need personality, charisma, nerves of steel, the stamina of an ox, and a pleasant manner. Put that package together, and you still need luck. And whether you are a fashion model or a page three girl, you need editors to like you, so that they specifically ask for you. You need to be photogenic, an almost indefinable quality which, if you haven't got it, means that the finest, most famous photographers in the world won't be able to take great pictures of you. Good pictures, yes. *Great* pictures, no.

If you've got most, or indeed all, of the above, the best way in is probably to find yourself a good model agency. Don't waste your money on any of those advertisements you see offering to help you start your photographic portfolio. They're mostly expensive rip-off merchants. Go to one of the top agencies, make an appointment, listen to what they say, and do as they advise. They know their business. If they tell you, politely, that you're wasting your time, you probably are. If they say you're too short, too tall, too fat, too thin, you probably are. If they tell you to take a modelling course, and come back, take one, if you can afford it. If they send you to a photographer, you can be sure that he/she will take the kind of photographs that you really need. If they accept you, you're half-way there. Congratulations! That's when the really hard work begins.

We were both dry by now, and I took Jean's hand and led her through to the bedroom. Her short blonde hair was wet, but that didn't seem to bother her. My erection was still in good shape, and as Jean lay down on the bed and reached for it, I started the kisses that I had intended in the bathroom, and had to abandon. As her hand found my cock again, I reached down between her legs, which she obligingly spread for me, and I started to feel her warm, plump pussy.

The heart-shaped pubic growth felt stubbly around the edges, which reminded me of Annabel's shaven mound. I wondered what she was doing right now, and then I pushed that thought to the back of my mind. One woman at a time, Andrews, I thought. But I made a mental note to try to remember to telephone her. I found Jean's wet slit in the centre of her furry heart, and I slid my fingers into it, spreading her outer lips, and searching for her clitoris, which I quickly found. Her cunt closed tightly around my fingers as I rubbed her clit, and she started making little sounds in her throat as we kissed.

She soon pulled her head back and said 'Fuck me, darling. Please fuck me. I want your cock in me now. Pussy wants your cock. Please.' She let go of it as she spoke, and I raised up my hips, prior to inserting my cock into her, upon which she took hold of it again, and guided it herself into her secret place. It gripped my cock, just as it had gripped my fingers, and I started working it, revelling in the sensuous feel of her, the slick wetness of her, the feverish heat of her.

'Oh, yes,' she said. 'Oh, very yes. That feels good. That was what pussy wanted.' Her eyes were closed, her mouth half open. I leaned down and began to suck at one of those firm little breasts, the nipple erect in my mouth. 'Oooh,' she murmured. 'You're sucking my tits. I like that.' She brought up a hand and started to finger the other nipple, kneading it between her fingers until it too matched its sister. 'Do you like it when girls talk dirty to you, Tony?' she asked. I told her that, yes, I did. I found it a tremendous turn on. 'Oh, good,' she said. 'Because it turns me on to do it.' And she began.

'You're fucking my cunt, Tony. Your great, hot, steaming cock is fucking my poor, tiny, tight little cunt. You're stretching it. You're hurting me. Your cock is so big. I like it. My cunt is full of cock. Soon you'll make me come, and you'll spurt your hot spunk up into me. You'll fill my cunt up with your spunk.' I found that the naughty words, delivered in her soft, rather up-market, slightly prissy little voice, were a tremendous turn on, and it wasn't too long before her prophesy became a reality, and I did spurt my come up her, which started her off again.

'You're coming inside me,' she cried. 'I can feel you coming inside me. You're making me come. Your spunk is spurting up me, and I'm going to come too. I'm coming now. Arghaaaah. Oh, yes. I'm coming. Nowwwww. Oh, God. Oh, yes.' As she shouted her triumphal, orgasmic chant, she bucked and tossed and writhed beneath me, her cunt muscles working overtime, squeezing my cock. I was just about finishing as she began, but we came simultaneously for a short space of time. It was a great experience, and I enjoyed it enormously. She finally finished, and she lay there, looking up at me with the bluest eyes I can ever remember seeing. She smiled. 'Thank you,' she said. 'That was good.' 'Thank you, sweetheart,' I said. 'It was good for me, too. We must do it again.'

At that moment the houseboy sounded the gong with which he summoned the occupants of the house to meals, its deep, brass boom echoing up through the building. 'My God,' said Jean. 'What on earth is that?' I told her, and she laughed. 'Good Lord,' she said. 'I thought it was at least a fire warning, or an earthquake warning, or something like that. But it does remind me that I'm starving. I'll nip back to my room and slip into something more suitable.' She got up off the bed and quickly put her minuscule bikini back on. She stopped at the door and looked back, blowing me a kiss. 'Ciao, baby,' she said, and then she was gone.

Our first dinner at the house was fun. Everyone was relaxed and in holiday mood, despite having to start work the following morning. The seven of us seemed to get on well, and certainly James, the young Jamaican lighting assistant whom Phil had picked, fitted in happily. He was a good looking young man of, I guessed, about twenty-five or so, with short, frizzy hair, and a medium-brown complexion and a ready, attractive smile. We ate delicious, home-made pumpkin soup, with home-made bread, followed by soft-shelled crab, rice and salad. There was either ice-cream or cheese to finish with, and we drank an acceptable, if undistinguished white wine, imported from America, and doubtless purchased at the local Port Antonio supermarket. It is my understanding that Jamaica does not produce its own wine, at least commercially. Sadly, even Tia Maria, the famous rum-based, coffee-flavoured Jamaican liqueur, is no longer made on the island, but is produced, these days, in Mexico.

After dinner, James, Cindy and I were asked by the others to teach them the rudiments of backgammon, the boards for which the house came well supplied with. One can probably pick up the main rules of backgammon in an evening or two, but it takes quite a long time to become proficient enough to incorporate two of the vital elements of the game. One is the use of the doubling cube, which one player can offer to the other if he – the first player – thinks he is in an advantageous position. If accepted, it becomes the property of the second player, who can offer it back, if he believes that the odds have changed, and are now to his advantage. Thus the odds are doubled every time the cube changes hands. From evens, the odds move to 2, then 4, 8, 16, 32, 64, and so on. If the cube is not accepted, the game is won by the player offering the cube, at the odds currently standing. Since a game lasts, roughly, about ten minutes, and it is possible for the odds to change in favour first of one player, then the other, and back again, you will see that a lot of money can be won or lost in an evening. The odds of two to 64 are shown on a six sided cube, hence its name.

The second vital element is, of course, that of actually playing for money. My own opinion is that there is little point in playing backgammon other than for money, since either player can play as recklessly as he or she wishes if the discipline of the possibility of losing hard-earned cash does not apply. To learn to play proficiently, for money, and with a reasonable chance of winning, can take many years. And cost a great deal of money, since you have to buy the experience by challenging players whom you know are better than you are!

But it can be fun, especially with a group the size of ours, to explain the basic rules, and then play for matches or counters or pennies. The three English girls loved it, and there was much shrieking and giggling over the boards. When the novelty had somewhat worn off, I suggested a mini tournament for three to Cindy and James, both of whom, like all Jamaicans, grew up playing backgammon. We all played the other two, at the best of three games. I beat James, Cindy beat James, and then Cindy beat me, making her the evening's champion, a success much applauded by the other girls.

At midnight, the jolly, plump Jamaican cook, whom I had assumed was long abed, brought in, unasked, a huge pot of Blue Mountain coffee, and a plate of freshly baked, still hot banana bread. If you've never eaten home-made banana bread, it alone is worth the air fare to Kingston, just to try it. It was Phil's and the three English girls' first taste of this Jamaican delicacy, and Phil jumped up and gave the cook a huge hug and a big kiss, and told her that he was in love with her, which actions and announcement sent her off, laughing and quivering, and very happy, the tears of laughter running down her fat cheeks. We drank the coffee, bade each other goodnight, and took ourselves off to our rooms. If the others felt anything like me, then they felt happy, tired, relaxed, and ready for the arms of Morpheus, to whom I surrendered as soon as my head touched the pillow.

I awoke from a strongly sexual dream with an enormous erection, to feel a cool hand around my throbbing cock, and wet, hot lips on my mouth, a tongue probing between my lips. Whoever it was giggled. 'It's all right, darling. It's me,' said a woman's voice. With what was happening, it didn't really matter, but I thought I'd better ask. The moonlight coming through my open wooden window slats in bands didn't reach as far as the bed. 'Who's me?' I asked, politely enough, I thought. The hand on my cock was taken away, and the woman sat up, rather sharply, it seemed to me. 'Oh, for God's sake, Tony,' she said. 'Who do you think it is? Are you fucking everyone here? Really. It's Jean. Remember me? Perhaps you don't. I was here earlier today. You know. Jean. The blonde one. The one you fucked earlier. The one you said "We must do this again" to. I thought you actually meant it, or I wouldn't have come here.'

Oh shit, I thought. Some you win, some you lose. 'Of course I meant it, sweetheart,' I said, putting my arms around her. 'I'm delighted that you're here. It's just that I was fast asleep, and when you woke me up in that delightful way, I wasn't sure where I was, or what I was doing. Please forgive me. OK?' I kissed her long and hard, and gradually the stiffness left her body, and the anger evaporated, and she relaxed, and she began to kiss me back. We spent a long time making slow, gentle love, which culminated in a shared, intense orgasm, and then we slept in each other's arms, the cool breeze coming in from the sea caressing and cooling our sweating bodies.

CHAPTER NINE: PICTURE SHOW

I awoke at sun-up – just after six – feeling fit and refreshed, despite the shortness of real sleeping time, and at seven I gently awoke Jean, who sleepily made her way back to the bedroom she was sharing with Cindy. She gave me a big kiss when she left, and seemed to have overcome her anger of the night before. We all breakfasted on the veranda, where huge plates of grilled flying fish were carried to us by the houseboy, together with oodles of coffee and lashings of toast and delicious Jamaican marmalade. After breakfast, Phil started setting up his equipment on the same veranda, helped by Jim, and the four girls went off to undress. As they left, the hairdresser recommended by John Lane arrived in her car, and we introduced ourselves. She was a pretty little pale brown Jamaican girl called Wendy. I took her up to the girls' rooms, and introduced them all, leaving her up there to get on with her job. Back on the veranda, Phil was rummaging through a trunk full of lingerie, scarves, costume jewellery, hats, stockings and high-heeled shoes. The very essence of the things which dressed up the lovely girls who grace the pages of *Tiptop*.

I sat there idly on a sun lounger, watching Phil, and musing on the attractiveness of the new addition, Wendy. I'm sure I've said it before, but there is an essential *je ne sais quoi* about Jamaican women. Like the women from any other country, they can be divided into those who do, and those who don't. But there any similarity with other girls ends, for two admirable reasons. Far more Jamaican girls do than don't, and those who do, do it with style, charm, verve and enthusiasm.

I can't speak for Jamaican men, but for a lot of the girls from that island, lovemaking could aptly be described as the national sport. Kingston is noisy, hot, colourful, welcoming, and one of the easiest cities in the world in which to enjoy sex, with some of the most beautiful girls you are likely to see anywhere in the world. And be assured, I'm not talking about paying for it. There are no language barriers, for Jamaicans speak English, with a lilt which, to the English ear, sounds rather like a soft Welsh accent. Jamaican girls have been catering to the sexual requirements of foreigners since the seventeenth century, when Port Royal – the old capital, almost totally destroyed by earthquake in 1692 – was described by chroniclers of the day as 'the wickedest town on earth.' Henry Morgan, the most famous pirate of them all, knighted for his exploits against the Spanish, and later Port Royal's best known governor, made Jamaica his base, partially at least, one suspects, for the sexual pleasures available to him and his crews. It is a tradition that contemporary Kingston girls maintain, to the everlasting delight of sailors, tourists, businessmen, and anyone else who can find an excuse to visit this most beautiful of all the Caribbean islands.

Sex is available at a number of different levels. There is, of course, commercial sex, just as there is in every major city in the world. At night, the streets around Kingston's three major hotels are patrolled by what in any other country would be called prostitutes. Selling sex for money is certainly what they are about, but their motivation is rather different from the hardened prostitutes of the Western world. You really have to appreciate the desperately high level of unemployment – which runs as high as twenty-five per cent of the entire population – to understand that selling something that they would be just as happy to give away is simply one way of resolving the problem of keeping the family larder sufficiently well stocked.

If that's what you're after, be prepared to bargain. While the asking price might seem cheap by international standards, it is just that. An asking price. It is aimed at the American businessmen who make up most of the customers around the major hotels, and who are usually too lazy to look any further than their immediate surrounds, and who are accustomed to much higher prices in New York or Miami. But if that is the only kind of sex that you experience in Kingston, whilst you are unlikely to be disappointed, you will miss a lot of fun, both sexually and socially. Your best bet, failing friends or business acquaintances, is to enlist the services of one of Kingston's taxi drivers. They are the equivalent of London cabbies, but are often much friendlier, and they are always more than willing to help you if you tell them exactly what you want.

Taxis come with and without meters, but you won't get ripped off by the meterless ones, provided you establish the fare *before* you start your journey. If you don't know Kingston well enough to know whether the fare you are being quoted is realistic, simply tell your hotel porter that you want a cab with a meter. The taxis vary from air-conditioned Mercedes to beaten-up, twenty-five year-old Austin Cambridges. Whatever the style or condition of your cab, the fare remains the same – roughly equivalent to current London cab charges.

Nightclubs as such don't exist in Kingston, if you discount the cabaret rooms in the big hotels. Jamaicans relax of an evening in bars. They vary tremendously in ambience and character, but downtown Kingston bars have three things in common: non-stop music – usually tapes – played at ear-splitting level, pretty, available girls, and go-go dancers. Go-go dancing has been part of Kingston's night life for around forty-five or fifty years now. The non-Caribbean versions pale into insignificance beside that of the Kingston girls' sheer, totally uninhibited eroticism. Bars usually have at least three dancers, and often as many as nine or ten. The girls' costumes, invariably home made, reveal far more than they conceal, in an overtly sexy way. In all the bars, the girls dance on a raised dais. They twist and writhe, sweat-streaked bodies straining and quivering, breasts, bottoms and pudenda performing to the insistent reggae beat. Surprisingly, for a country with little or no false modesty, it is rare to see a topless go-go dancer. Rare, but not impossible.

Towards the end of the evening – and evenings in Kingston, where there are no licensing restrictions, end around dawn – you sometimes see a girl take off her bikini top, simply for the greater freedom of movement, and because of the heat, than from any thought of titillating the customers. But what you do see are go-go girls, lying on their backs, their raised legs apart in an upside-down version of the splits, the tiny join of their bikini bottom drawn so tightly into their crotch that you can see the outline of their outer vaginal lips, moving their whole genital area in rhythmic, copulatory motion to the music. If you're sitting three feet away from the girl at the time, as can often be the case, it's quite a sight to see.

Rather like some London clubs, you can negotiate at the end of the evening for the dancer of your choice, but you'll probably have a long wait. Most importantly, do remember one thing: these clubs do not exist primarily for the likes of you and me. No-one feels that the girls who come and chat to you in them are doing anything out of the ordinary. The girls genuinely enjoy fucking, and if you treat them like the ladies that they are, they will repay your courtesy a thousandfold. The average Jamaican man, according to the girls, is a chauvinist pig. So be it. I also strongly recommend that you keep your taxi driver with you for the evening. Take him into the bars he drives you to. You'll find out much more about Kingston, he'll enjoy showing it to you, and you'll probably end up with exactly what you're looking for. To help you with the local patois – although it's not necessary, English will do just as well – pussy is *pumpum*, and a fuck, in the vernacular, is *somtin' rude*. Conversely, if you're out of luck, and nothing's happening, the reverse applies – *nuttin' rude*. But that's unlikely.

If you want to see Jamaican night life with the certainty of being the only tourist in the area, get your taxi driver to take you to Red Hills Road. But take a girl with you. You're unlikely to pick up girls in the bars in Red Hills Road, simply because these are the places where Jamaican guys take their girls to dance to serious reggae, and girls who want to be picked up know that they're not going to find a partner there. Find yourself a girl in downtown Kingston and take her to one of the Red Hills Road clubs, and she probably won't charge you for her favours later on. Or take your own Jamaican girlfriend there. She'll love you for it.

If you're fortunate enough to make friends in Kingston, then you'll be invited to join the city's social whirl of lunch parties, dinner parties, drinks parties, backgammon parties, and you-name-it-and-they-have-a-party-for-it parties. And you'll meet Jamaican girls at their very best. They are an astonishing mixture. Beautiful, highly intelligent, highly sexed and – provided that they are not currently heavily involved – eager to make love. Perhaps I've just been lucky, but I don't think so. I've had only one serious disappointment in Kingston. I'll call her Jenny, to spare her blushes. And mine. Jenny was slim, ravishingly beautiful, exquisitely dressed and totally uninvolved. We dined. We danced. We whispered blandishments with heavily sexual overtones into each other's ears as we moved sensuously to the inevitable reggae music. She even came to bed with me. But not to fuck. Talk, yes. Cuddle, yes. Kiss, yes. Sleep, yes. Fuck, no. Nothing. I guess I simply didn't appeal to her, sexually.

Happily, the Jennies of Kingston are extremely rare. Take Beverly, for example, although that's not her real name either. She was one of the first Jamaican girls I ever fucked, all those years ago. Beverly was just eighteen. She was sweet and pretty and we met through friends, at about eight o'clock one evening, at a dinner party. By midnight we were dancing at Epiphany, and by two o'clock we were in bed. When she undressed, I was surprised to see that she wore the bikini marks of a European girl on her otherwise dark brown body. I didn't know then that brown girls, in the tropical sun, get even browner. If they wear bathing costumes, the bits the costumes cover are much paler. I found it somehow intensely sexual.

Beverly might have been only eighteen, but I soon discovered that this was no way her first – or even an early – encounter with a man. She had the body of a well-developed girl, the precocity of a teenager – and the sexual experience and expertise of a Parisian whore. Sex was a big thing with Beverly. There was no part of each other's bodies that we didn't explore throughout the warm Jamaican night. She was enthusiastic, energetic, original, tender, and loving. There was no question of a quick fuck as a 'thank you' for a lovely evening. She was patently looking forward to our sexual liaison as much as I was. We kissed, and she inserted a sweet-tasting young tongue hard into my mouth, while a soft brown hand encircled my cock, and a pair of breasts like little round apples, surmounted by peanuts, pressed against my chest. I slipped my hand between her legs and the feel of her wetness hardened my erection perceptibly, something I wouldn't have thought possible.

Then I went down on my first Jamaican pussy. It was sweet and clean, and tasted of mangoes and citrus. It seemed fully appreciative of the attention I was paying it, judging by the fact that its owner was squirming and moving herself against my mouth as I sucked and licked. I was in no hurry, and Beverly seemed happy, obviously enjoying my lip service from the little moans that she gave, and the increasing pressure of her cunt against my lips and tongue. After a while she came, making soft little noises, rather like a satisfied kitten. I didn't stop immediately, but suddenly my attention was distracted by the wet, soft warmth of Beverly's lips around my cock, sucking and tonguing enthusiastically.

I enjoyed a really affectionate mouth job for as long as I could, until I was forced to withdraw my cock from her mouth by the imminent danger of ejaculating, and thereby missing the immediate opportunity of thrusting into her wet little pussy, something I had been thinking about all evening. I had to hold her insistent, grasping hands away from my cock until I had regained the control over my ejaculation that I had been in danger of losing. Beverly whispered in my ear. 'When you goin' to fuck me, man?' she asked. 'Now, sweetheart,' I said. I mounted her, and she moaned and shuddered with pleasure as I thrust into her. She was tight and wet, and I could feel her elastic pussy muscles gripping me and working me towards a climax. I bent down and sucked a hardened nipple, standing out from her almost black, puckered aureola. I nuzzled the soft, warm flesh of her breasts, her warm skin smooth, like satin, a completely different texture from European skin. She moaned, and moved under me, then she clasped her legs together around my lower back and started to hump me energetically from below. That brought her rapidly to another orgasm, and the constrictions of her pussy in orgasm squeezed me to a climax too. I spurted into her, long and hard, groaning with lustful pleasure as I did.

I could almost feel myself ejaculating into Beverly as I lay there on the veranda, when I was brought back to earth by the arrival of the four model girls and Wendy, chattering away like a troop of little monkeys. The models' hair was exquisitely dressed in four completely different styles, and they were wearing lightweight robes. The moment they got down to the veranda, Cindy dropped hers and ran out onto the beach. Her brown body gleamed in the intense heat and sunlight, and the other three girls followed her lead, dropping their robes and running down to join her on the beach. Seeing Annie Walters and June Graham naked for the first time since auditioning them back in London, I was relieved to see that they had obeyed their instructions to get a good basic tan, so as not to waste time here in Jamaica, and also as a precaution against sunburn. I could see that June's pubic hair correctly matched her auburn crowning glory, and that Annie's was appropriately black. Phil had worked out his first shoot, and had arranged three cane chairs and a cane sofa on the veranda, draped here and there with pieces of exotic material, and small Indian cushions, gleaming with little pieces of mirror glass, which glittered and reflected brilliantly in the bright sunlight.

The lighting assistant, Jim, had got his equipment approximately in place, according to Phil's instructions, and Phil now called the girls to come and start work. He put them into the positions that he required, and explained to them the effects that he was trying to achieve. Jim made a few last-minute adjustments to the lighting, Phil took a number of Polaroids at different exposures, until he was satisfied with the result, and the shoot began. He started with them naked, for reasons that I have explained before. He arranged them in a wide variety of different poses and situations, reproducing what I can only describe as a heavily lesbian scene, the girls a tangle of bodies, spread legs, and wet, thrusting tongues poised within millimetres of each other's pussies. He had Cindy and Jean kissing each other, a situation which they appeared to thoroughly enjoy, holding the kisses long after Phil had said 'OK, girls. Thank you.'

He then slowly began adding, first of all, diaphanous knickers. These were followed by lacy bras. He got the girls to appear to be undressing each other, with the facial expressions and manual activity appropriate to this kind of sensually erotic performance. He had brought his ever-present tape deck, and Cindy had brought some Jamaican tapes, which were playing softly in the background. It was a delightful scene; the pretty girls, the sexy lingerie, the white, clapboard veranda, the cane chairs, and in the background, the white sand beach, and the sun, reflecting on the calm, aquamarine Caribbean sea. Cindy was wearing totally transparent white knickers and a similarly transparent white bra. Her clearly visible pubic hair transformed the white panties into an erotic, off-limits, sexual play area, whilst the diaphanous bra offered her black-tipped firm brown breasts for immediate violation. June, the redhead, was similarly clad, but in lavender-coloured undies, while blonde Jean's were black, and black-haired Annie's were of the palest green. As they played out the getting undressed role in reversal, Phil added exquisite garter belts, and black silk stockings for all the girls bar Cindy, who was given white ones.

Experienced as I was in the happy pastime of watching the photographing of two, three, four or even more girls in make-believe lesbian scenes (previously, usually in my capacity as the writer of the eventual copy) I always kept a weather eye open for the first sign of real enjoyment from any of the participants, that of a knicker crotch dampened by vaginal liquid flowing from an aroused pussy.

It does not – necessarily – mean anything other than the fact that the girl is turned on by displaying her naked and/or partially clad body for the camera. But, then again, it might well mean that the girl is aroused by the proximity of the other girl with whom she is supposed (for the purposes of the photography) to be having a sexual relationship with. The nice thing is that one can make up one's own mind up in the matter. I was not at all surprised to see the tell-tale little stain appear first on the white lacy cotton between Cindy's slim thighs, followed almost immediately by a similar dampness between Jean's black knicker-accoutered legs. It is only fair to say, of course, that such a stain is far harder to detect on black material than it is on white. I wasn't wrong about what was happening, but I may have been wrong about the timing. The next girl to expose her arousal was June, the redhead wearing the lavender panties, and the thoughts running through my mind at the idea of all those dampened knickers and wet pussies gave me an uncomfortable erection.

I tried to look as if I was feeling in my pocket for a handkerchief as I adjusted my hardening cock into a more comfortable and – I hoped – a less obvious position. But I didn't fool Jean for a moment, as her eagle eye closed in a theatrical wink, and she pursed her lips in a sexy, pouting kiss as she looked at *my* crotch. Being caught in the act, as it were, I could do little but mouth a kiss back.

As I watched, Phil was encouraging Annie, in the pale green ensemble, to kiss June (in the lavender) while sliding a hand up June's knickers. I wasn't more than about six feet away from the two of them, where June was draped on the cane sofa, and Annie was kneeling on the floor in front of her. I could see that Annie's fingers were slowly moving backwards and forwards beneath the lavender silk, in the minutest, but easily recognizable, strokes of one girl slowly and sensually frigging another girl. I sensed that I could smell the aroma of feminine cunt on heat, and as I watched, June moaned, and wriggled her body down, to be closer to the fingers that were so obviously giving her pleasure. I felt an almost irresistible urge to get up and say, 'Please girls, don't waste those adorable wet pussies, cop hold of my stiff prick, and let's fuck.' Right then Phil came to the end of a roll of film, and called halt, suggesting a break for lunch. I looked at my watch. It was just after twelve. It was an apposite moment for more than one reason, for the sighs of relief and the outbreak of conversation, with everyone talking at once, enabled June to achieve her orgasm without anyone else but me noticing what was happening. As far as I know, neither of the two girls involved realized that I was aware of what they had been doing together. And then the girls all looked at the cool Caribbean sea in sheer frustration, knowing, reluctantly, that they would not be allowed to bathe until their working day was finished, mainly because it would ruin their hair.

I announced that I would serve pre-lunch drinks here on the veranda in fifteen minutes, and everyone bar Phil and me disappeared, either to freshen up, or to change into a bikini or a robe for lunch. Phil, who had been very controlled up to now, got out his phial of coke, and his mirror and cutting blade, and cut us a couple of quick lines each before anyone else came back.

I didn't ask him where it came from, remembering my

instruction that he didn't come through Jamaican customs with any, but whatever drug anyone might want is available in Kingston, at a price, if you know where to go for it. Just then the houseboy arrived wheeling a wooden trolley bearing bottles, glasses, ice, and the wherewithal for mixing almost anything you might wish to drink. There was even champagne. Everything was supplied, he had told me, on a sale or return basis, by the local supermarket. Doubtless he got a cut. And so he should. The morning's shoot had gone well, and I felt extravagant. 'Champagne all round, please,' I said to the houseboy, who was sixty if he was a day, a charming, white-haired, grizzled gentleman, whose only wish was to please. He loved the pretty young girls who were surrounding him for the time that we were staying at the house, and I'm certain, from the way that he looked at them, that he would have given a good account of himself sexually, given half a chance. Maybe one of the girls would do him a favour.

He opened a bottle of Mercier non-vintage champagne with an agility that showed many years of practice. I'm not a great fan of non-vintage champagne, but this was Port Antonio, not London, and there *were* eight of us altogether. The girls suddenly arrived back in a giggling little flock, including Wendy, the hair stylist, and Jim appeared from somewhere moments later. The house boy coped with pouring us each a glass, handing them round, and opening another bottle in between, as if he had two pairs of hands. The champagne was well chilled, and I raised my glass in a toast to the others. 'To us,' I said. 'May we enjoy our time here together.' We all clinked glasses and drank to each other. Lunch arrived soon after, and we sat down at the long table that had been brought out for the purpose.

The cook kept our lunches to fairly basic salads, and let herself go in the evenings, which I think suited everybody admirably. Today's lunch was tuna salad and fresh mayonnaise, with cold boiled rice and freshly baked granary bread and butter. To my surprise, there were no protestations when Phil announced that it was time to get back to work. I had thought that perhaps the lethargy brought on by food and alcohol, combined with the heat of the early afternoon sun, might bring a few grumbles from the girls, but they all, bless them, got up without making a sound, and ten minutes later they were all back at work again.

The time passed slowly in languorous days of inspired photography by Phil. We sent the film daily to processors in Kingston by motorcycle messenger, and we viewed the developed transparencies after dinner on the evening of the day they came back. They were quite magical. He was shooting the girls singly, in pairs, in threes, and all four together, as he had begun. Yes, they were pretty. Phil made them *beautiful*. He made the Jamaican backgrounds look like paradise. His photographs made the scenery appear even better than it looked *in situ*.

Every day, after work, we all flung ourselves into the sea, and after a day or so we took to bathing naked. With the girls naked already for most of the day, it seemed natural enough for them to dispense with bikinis for swimming, and shortly after that, it seemed just as natural for Phil, Jim and me similarly to dispense with our costumes. We played backgammon at night, and then everybody fucked everybody else, until, by the end of our stay, we had all fucked each other – that is, all the men had fucked all the girls. Surprisingly, there were no tantrums, no broken hearts, no problems of any kind. We men, of course, had a better set-up than the girls, since there were five of them, and only three of us. Wendy joined in with us happily, as is the female Jamaican way. At the weekends we all piled into the Land Rover, and went off exploring Ocho Rios and Montego Bay, off to our north-west. We splashed about, as tourists do, in the Dunn River Falls, and went rafting in pairs down the river itself. Eventually we Europeans all ended up looking like native born Jamaicans, with deeply bronzed sun-tans. We radiated health, and we all lost weight, partly from the healthy diet of mostly fresh food, and partly from the daily swimming after work.

It came as something of a shock when we realised that our three weeks was up. Phil had taken enough photographs to fill the *Encyclopedia Britannica.* Our job was done. We swore undying love, and waved goodbye to Jim and Cindy, as they took off for Kingston in Cindy's car, and to Wendy, as she departed in hers. It was a Friday, and I decided that *Tiptop* could afford for us to stay for the weekend before we started back to Kingston ourselves the following Monday morning. I can only describe the Saturday and Sunday as a permanent orgy.

We were drunk for most of that time. Or at least, I was drunk for most of that time. There were just the five of us – Jean, June, Annie and Phil and me. We swam and sunbathed and played beach games and ate and drank all day, and we fucked and sucked and indulged in every kind of sexual excess all night. The cook and houseboy kept pretty much out of our way, simply appearing at meal times, or if we asked for drinks. I don't think they disapproved. They just felt that we would be happier left to our own devices. For all we knew, they were having their own orgy in the servants' quarters. I remember fucking Annie from behind while I sucked off little blonde Jean, with her heart-shaped pubic hair. And I remember June sucking my cock, while Annie sat on my face. I buggered all three of the girls one night over the weekend, for a bet. I think it was Jean who made a double bet with me that one, I wouldn't, and two, I couldn't. She didn't pay her losses, but it didn't seem very important at the time.

CHAPTER TEN: NEW YORK, NEW YORK

England and London seemed grey and cold after the tropical sunshine of Jamaica. There didn't seem to be any real problems at the office. I had kept Wally in touch with progress from Port Antonio, and I set up a special showing of Phil's photography for him, having done a basic edit with Phil, showing Wally just the material from which the final selection would be made. He was thrilled with it, and much taken with what could be seen of the Port Antonio beach house. I could see him taking one of his many girlfriends out there, courtesy of his discounted airline tickets. And good luck to him. At the end of the showing of Phil's photographs, having graciously thanked Phil for his work, he asked me to stay behind.

'Well done, Tony,' he said. 'Fantastic photographs. You and Phil have both done an excellent job. Thank you. I think you know how much I appreciate everything you've done here in Fred's absence. And that's really what I wanted to talk to you about. I want Fred to come back to London for a spot of leave. He's doing an excellent job out there, but I hear rumours that worry me slightly. You know Fred as well as I do. He never does things by half measures. I'm told that he's drinking too much, fucking too much, snorting cocaine too much, and generally letting other people do his job whilst he enjoys himself. I'm told he's up all night, and that he sleeps all day, and that he's hardly ever in the office.

'I think you know, too, that I don't give a damn, within reason, about what people do in their own time. But I pay Fred a great deal of money, and that is because he's the best in the business at doing what he does. But he ain't doing it right now. I want him back here for a while. A month or two. Maybe three. I want to make my own mind up about whether this is just a reaction to the excitement of New York that will eventually wear off, or whether he's got a serious problem.' 'I'm sorry to hear that, Wally,' I said. 'I was in touch with Fred before I went off to Jamaica, but I didn't call him from there. There wasn't any real reason for me to do that. But he sounded OK when we last spoke. And I haven't had a chance to call him from London as yet.'

'It does seem that he's keeping very strange hours,' said Wally. 'I have the greatest difficulty in getting hold of him, either at the office or at home. The time difference doesn't help, but it's not that difficult. But let me come to the point. I realize that you've been away from London for almost a month now, but how do you feel about going to New York to look after things while Fred comes over here for a while? Obviously, I would want you to go out initially while Fred was still there, and work with him until you knew what was what in the New York office. Once you felt relaxed about that, Fred could come home and get some real rest. Go off to Europe somewhere and relax. Go to a health farm. Anything. Would that cause you any problems? We'd obviously pick up any costs you incurred having your Hampstead place looked after, and we'd pick up your New York living expenses, and give you what? Say £500 a week extra while you were out there. New York's a very expensive city. What do you say?' He looked at me, his face quite expressionless.

I thought for a moment. Frankly, it was the opportunity of a lifetime. I'd only ever been to New York on business trips previously, for two or three days at a time, and the prospect of going there for a couple of months, maybe even longer – and at someone else's expense – fired me with a virtual frenzy of enthusiasm. On my brief business trips, I had found it the most exciting city in the world. It wasn't a problem finding someone to look after the Hampstead flat. Annabel had been doing that while I had been in Jamaica, and I felt certain that, whilst she wouldn't be happy at the prospect of my disappearing yet again to another country, she wouldn't mind going on looking after the flat. It would make her feel a little closer to me, being free to go to Hampstead whenever she felt like it, and looking after my post and bills and so on.

'Terrific, Wally,' I said. 'Thank you for your confidence in me. I'd love to. When do you want me to go?' He thought for a moment. 'I'll have a word with Fred first,' he said, 'and then I'll come back to you. I'll tell him what this is all about, naturally,' he continued. 'I know he and you are chums. But I don't have to say, do I, that this conversation is strictly between you and me? And, of course, Fred.' 'No, of course not, Wally,' I said. 'Understood.' 'By the way,' said Wally, 'have you got a US visa?' 'Yes, I have,' I replied. 'It's a multi-entry business visa, so there shouldn't be any problems.'

'Great,' he said. 'I'll get accounts to order you up some traveller's cheques and some American dollars, and I'll get Fred to find you somewhere to stay. Would you prefer a hotel or an apartment?' 'An apartment, please,' I said, without a moment's hesitation. Anyone can stay in a hotel. Not too many Englishmen that I know have stayed in their own New York apartment. Terrific. 'Good,' said Wally. 'I'll let you know how we're progressing. And thank you. If you need time off to catch up with things, make arrangements, you know, that sort of thing, just take it. You don't have to ask. Just let Anthea know where I can get hold of you if I need you.' He put out his hand to shake mine, briefly and firmly, and then I was on my way. Anthea looked up as I passed through her office. 'My God,' she said. 'What a tan. Why don't I get sent to Jamaica? Some people get all the luck. Come here and give me a kiss. That's if you can spare the time, of course.'

I gave her a big wet kiss and to my intense surprise, she slid her tongue into my mouth, explored it briefly, and then withdrew. I'd always fancied Anthea, from the very first time I saw her in *Tiptop*' s offices, but I'd always assumed that she was forbidden territory. I wasn't sure why, now, thinking about it. I was reasonably sure that Wally wasn't fucking her. His taste ran to little teenage trollops. The younger they were, the better he liked them. He didn't want them for conversation. Just to fuck. As many as possible. As often as possible.

But then, Anthea was certainly his guardian. The protector of his secrets. She probably knew enough about Wally to send him to prison, if she really wanted to. She laughed out loud at the expression on my face. 'Dear me,' she said. 'Have I shocked you? I thought you were the office stud these days. At least that's what I hear. Does that exclude the boss's secretary, then? What a shame.' She took my right hand and ran it over her breast, beneath her soft sweater. I could feel her nipple, firmly erect underneath her hand. 'Naughty, aren't I?' she said. 'It's been there for you for a long time now, but you've never shown any interest in it. And now you're off to New York. Whatever is a poor, sex-starved little girl like me going to do?'

I swallowed, uncertain of my next move. I didn't want to start something that I wouldn't be around to finish. If I was going to have some kind of an affair with Anthea, then I wanted it to be a serious one. Not a one-night stand. 'You can always pop over to New York for a couple of weeks,' I suggested, more in jest than anything else. 'Would you really like that?' she asked. 'Yes, I would, darling,' I said, trying to sound sincere. 'I'd like that very much indeed. And no-one here would know what we were doing,' I said. 'which has been the major reason for my staying away from you before now. Discretion, and all that.' 'Well, well,' said Anthea. 'And all along I thought you didn't fancy me.' 'Fancy you, sweetheart?' I said, bending down and kissing her on the cheek. 'I used to go home and wank just thinking about you. But I must go now. Please forgive me.' As I left, she was looking as if she was going to cry. Oh, God, I thought. What have I done now? And then I remembered that I hadn't actually done anything. Anthea was the one who had started it. I wondered if I had been foolish suggesting the two weeks in New York. Time would tell.

I'd seen Carla briefly earlier that morning from a distance, and had waved at her, but when I got back upstairs to my office she was sitting on my desk, waiting for me. 'So,' she said, slipping off the desk, and wrapping herself around me. 'The conquering hero returns. When are you going to fuck me?' 'Very soon darling,' I said, giving her a quick kiss. 'I'm glad to see you haven't given up men in favour of dykes.' She hit me, playfully, on the shoulder. It hurt. 'Oh, shut up,' she said. 'That's a closed episode in my life. I haven't seen Jane since about a week after you left to go to Jamaica. She became a damn nuisance. She simply wouldn't leave me alone. All those bloody rings and things. I think she's a man who's had the operation. Honestly I do. But you haven't answered my question.'

Nor had I. I decided that since the lovely Carla had always been totally up-front with me, the very least that I could do was to return the compliment. 'Of course I'm going to fuck you, sweetheart,' I said. 'But to do the job properly, may I please ask you to wait a day or two? I'm off shortly to see Annabel, and I don't want to be shagged out when I arrive. I'm sure you'll understand that. And I don't want one of your famous quickies, either. Not that there's anything wrong with them. But I want our first fuck for weeks to be an all-night, beautiful, romantic experience. You know, a decent dinner somewhere, a little bit of dancing, some romantic music, a leisurely bath, and then a whole night of beautiful fucking. Now, is that worth waiting for, or not?'

'Put like that, Tone,' she said, 'how could a girl possibly refuse? You've brought tears to my eyes. I'd wait until hell freezes over for an evening like that with you. Is that a promise?' 'Of course it's a promise, Carla my love,' I said.

'I just can't put a date on it at the moment. OK?' She grinned at me. 'Do you know something, darling?' she asked. 'What's that?' I asked. 'You're a real bastard,' she said. 'A real, one hundred and ten per cent, dyed in the wool bastard. It's just as well that I'm not in love with you, isn't it? You'd break my heart. You'll end up in the *News of the World*, that's where you'll end up, with some poor little girl who really *does* love you sticking a knife in you, because she's found you with your cock inside some other tart's knickers. Oh, you can laugh,' she said, looking at the expression on my face, 'but that's where you'll end up, you mark my words.' I patted her bottom as she turned to leave, and she turned back and slapped my face. Hard. I'd never known Carla take anyone or anything seriously before. Perhaps she meant what she said. She really seemed quite angry. So much for being up front, I thought.

I'd called Annabel from Port Antonio when we were leaving Jamaica, of course, and she had met me at Heathrow. It was a Tuesday, but she'd taken a night off work at the club, and we'd fallen into bed, and made love all night, and most of the following morning. When we finally emerged, she'd come back to Hampstead with me whilst I'd unpacked, checked the Porsche, looked at my mail, and generally got myself together. I hadn't gone into the office until today – Thursday – having called Wally at home on the Tuesday evening from Annabel's place.

I yearned for some Chinese food that evening, and a look at the London scene, so Annabel and I decided to go to the Chelsea Rendezvous, where Sandro greeted us as if we'd been out of town for six months. The restaurant was as crowded as ever, and I felt relaxed to be back in England once more. Jamaica – and particularly Kingston – had been a great experience, but it was good to be back. We went on from the Chelsea Rendezvous to the Scotch, in St James's, and boogied until the place closed at around three-thirty, after which we went back to Annabel's penthouse, and went to bed. We made gentle love, briefly, and I fell asleep, not waking until Annabel shook me on the Friday morning to tell me that it was time to get up and go to the office. I hadn't said anything to her about Wally's suggestion that I go to New York to look after the American office while Fred came home for some much-needed leave. I hadn't wanted to spoil what had been a very pleasant evening. What was so nice about Sandro's restaurant the Chelsea Rendezvous, I thought, on reflection, was that it wasn't just a restaurant. It was an entertainment. Sandro himself. The camp Italian waiters. The regular customers. The show business people. It all gelled, to make eating there an event.

Annabel made coffee and toast whilst I showered and dressed. I hoped that no-one would notice that I was wearing the same shirt as yesterday. There simply wasn't time to go back to Hampstead and get a fresh one. I decided to walk over to Jermyn Street when I'd parked the Porsche, and buy a new one. I could change into it when got to the office. In the end I went to Simpson's, where I chose a ready-made plain shirt in just a hint of palest pink, with a cut-away collar and double cuffs. I chose a tie that went with it, underpants and socks, and changed into them in the store's changing rooms. I put the cast-off clothes into the Simpson's bag, and made my way to the office, feeling better for my efforts.

Friday went by in a rush. I saw Carla, but simply on business, and she didn't refer to our exchange the previous day. I left early, and went back to Annabel's determined to tell her about the proposed New York trip. When it came to the crunch, she didn't seem at all distressed. 'That's all right, darling,' she said. 'It's a tremendous business opportunity. If you do well – and of course you will – then it must help your future in the magazine business. It'll look terrific on your CV. How many English editors get a chance to edit a large-circulation American magazine? It's not as if you're telling me that you're leaving me. That you've had enough. Or that you've found somebody else. You're telling me that you've been given an opportunity to go and look after the American end of the business whilst Fred comes home on holiday. How could I possibly be upset at that? And in any case, I can take some holiday and come and stay with you.' She looked at me archly from beneath raised eyebrows. 'That is, of course, only if you'd like me to?'

What a delightful girl. It was an open-ended arrangement, with no guaranteed return date. Fred might stay here in London for a month, or two months, who knows? Or he might miss New York, and go back there after a couple of weeks. But it wasn't, of course, quite the fantastic opportunity that Annabel was making it sound. Not really. Bearing in mind that monthly magazines work three months ahead of their publication date, what I would be doing in New York was basically two things: overseeing the illustration, layout, and production of issues actually conceived by Fred, and each month – together with the rest of the New York staff – putting together issues that would be printed and published after I left. In other words, if my issues had a good effect on sales, no-one would really connect that result with me, because I would be back in London by then. Except, of course, Fred and Wally. They would both know. Probably few of the other editorial people actually saw the full sales figures.

Beggars couldn't be choosers, I guess. At least I'd have some fun. I telephoned my friend John in Kingston, and told him what was happening. I was delighted to hear him offer to send me a list of friends of his to look up when I got there, which I instantly accepted. I asked him to telex it, to make sure I got it before I left. He had lived in New York for seven or eight years at one stage, working for one of the larger American advertising agencies, and still visited there on business from Jamaica on a regular basis. He also reminded me of something that I had forgotten: that it is both quicker and cheaper – much cheaper – to drop down to the Caribbean from New York than it is to get there from London. What fun!

Fred rang me at home from New York that evening. They

were five hours behind London, so it was early afternoon there. He sounded dreadful. 'Hi, Tony,' he said. 'How's it going?' We chattered on for a while, and then 'What are all these messages from Wally? I've just woken up, and my answering machine is choked with messages from both Wally and Anthea. He sounds as if he's got a wasp up his arse. What's his problem? They've called me from the office here too and woke me up to tell me that he's on the 'phone every half hour. What's it all about?'

I told Fred as best I could what the problem was. That rumours had reached Wally to the effect that he wasn't often seen in the office, and that the consumption of booze, birds, and nose candy was reputedly reaching record levels. 'Oh, shit,' said Fred. 'What the fuck does he want? The magazine's reached its highest sales ever, and they're still going up. We're turning ad sales away because we've reached the stage where, with nearly three hundred pages an issue, it costs more to print than we make from the extra advertising. The company here is netting around two million pounds – not dollars, pounds – a month. And that's after tax. And the stupid bastard's worried because I'm not in the office all day. Fuck him. What do you think I should do?'

I explained that Wally was going to ask him (tell him?) to come home for a rest, and that he had suggested that I go out there to look after things for a while, with a week or so with the two of us together in New York before Fred left for London, basically to show me the ropes. 'Well, at least that sounds fun,' said Fred. 'How does that grab you?' 'It grabs me just fine, Fred,' I said. 'I can't think of anything more exciting than some time in New York, looking after things while you take a break. But that's not really important. What I think *is* important is that, whatever else you do, first of all you call Wally soonest, and secondly, that you at least come over here for long enough to smooth his ruffled feathers. You know you've always been able to do exactly what you want with Wally. You can twist him round your little finger. But I think you need to come over here and do it. I don't know where the rumours are coming from, but someone out there patently doesn't like you.'

'Hell,' said Fred. 'What a pain. But if you think that's what I ought to do, then that's what I'll do. And I've just met the most terrific bird. You should see her. Say hello to Janice.' There was a moment's silence, and then a soft, sexy female voice said 'Hi, honey. Who are you? I'm Janice.' 'Hi, Janice,' I said. 'I'm Tony. I'm an old friend of Fred's.' 'You'd better be,' she said. I wasn't at all sure what she meant by that, but I didn't get a chance to ask her, for Fred was back on the line again. 'OK, Tony,' he said. 'I'll call Wally now, and we'll sort it all out. See you soon, I guess. Let me know your flight number, and I'll come out to Kennedy to meet you. Don't worry about a hotel or anything, you can stay with me while we're both here, and then you can have the run of the place while I'm in London. You'll like it. Cheers now.' And he put the 'phone down. Fred was a character, but he wasn't stupid. And I knew that he trusted me, and valued my advice. So I was glad that he had decided to come back to London and patch up his differences with Wally. The sooner, the better.

I'd gone back to Hampstead that evening to change into something more relaxing before going back to pick up Annabel and have an evening out on the town. She still had to report for duty at the club, but that gave us until about eleven, eleven-thirty. I parked the Porsche in her garage, and decided to take cabs for the rest of the evening. I'd booked a table at the White Elephant, and Nino, the barman, made his usual lascivious remarks to Annabel. He was a lovely man, who managed to be strongly suggestive without being in the least bit offensive.

Annabel was wearing a little Mary Quant A-line number in palest grey, the skirt of which just about covered her knickers, provided that she didn't bend over. The top was low-cut, and semi-transparent. If you were close enough – and at the other side of the bar, Nino was – you could see her nipples and the shape of her breasts quite clearly. 'What a pretty dress, Miss Annabel,' said Nino. 'Now you wouldn't get my wife to wear a dress like that.' 'Why not?' asked Annabel. 'Because her tits look more like spaniels' ears,' said Nino. 'She not-a have tits like yours, Miss Annabel, so she not wear-a the dress. Excuse me.' And, roaring with laughter, he went away to serve another customer. Nino probably knows more about the sexual circus prevalent amongst London's rich and famous than most. One of these days he'll retire and write a book, which will probably cause many a marital rift. Until that time, he remains London's best barman. No doubt about it.

We both had cold lobster, with new potatoes and salad, and with a decent Piesporter, followed by *frais du bois* and cream, and I had an august glass of vintage port with my coffee, whilst Annabel had *Strega*. Which, as everyone who speaks Italian knows, means witch. 'Your appearance this evening goes with your drink, my darling,' I said. 'I am bewitched. Totally bewitched.' She touched my glass with hers. 'Thank you, my love,' she said. She looked into my eyes. She was obviously going to say something that was important to her.

'Do you know, in a funny way, your being away in Jamaica didn't trouble me as much as I thought it would,' she said, eventually. I must have looked guilty, thinking of my active – and constant – unfaithfulness to her whilst away from her, because she put out a hand, and squeezed mine. 'No, don't be silly,' she said. 'I'm sure you weren't faithful to me. That doesn't matter. What matters is that you spoke to me whilst you were out there. You kept in touch. And that you came back to me. I was frightened that you would simply forget about me. That you would find someone else to take my place. You know. Out of sight, out of mind. I don't give a damn about what you got up to out there. I hope it was young and pretty, and fun, and that you enjoyed it. And that's how I feel about this trip to New York. Enjoy yourself. Have fun. But come back to me, when it's over. Please. OK?'

How could I possibly refuse? 'Of course, sweetheart,' I said.

'But don't forget that you said you'd take a couple of weeks off and come out and stay with me. We could spend a week in New York, and then go down to the Caribbean for a week, if you'd like that. We don't have to go to Jamaica. There's about three hundred other islands, if you'd rather somewhere else. Get some brochures from a travel agent, and see where you fancy. What do you say?' 'It all sounds too good to be true,' she said. 'But, to be honest, it's not the beaches and the sunshine that I'll be after when I come to New York. Which I will. That's a promise. It will be your bed and your cock I'll be wanting. And we may as well do that in New York as anywhere else. Unless you've got your heart set on Jamaica, or wherever.' I hadn't, and I said so. I expected that by the time Annabel came over, I would know some fun places to go in New York, and as she said, we could fuck anywhere.

We went on to Sybilla's for a while, and I couldn't help thinking of Epiphany. There was no way you could compare the two places, other than to say that Epiphany was indisputably the best disco in Kingston, and that Sybilla's was indisputably one of the three best discos in London. The ambience, the people, the music, the menus, everything was different. We danced ourselves to a standstill, and I had to plead for a rest, sitting down for a while with my drink, and watching the other couples, the girls in their see-through blouses and their little pussy pelmets, the guys in their flares and Chelsea boots, and with their long hair. I saw Gerrard Campbell and his wife Theodora, and Gaston de Chalus, who ran a public relations company, with one of the girls who worked for him. Sarah something, I think it was. I couldn't remember her name. It was a pleasurable, fun, and enjoyable place to be. After a final spell on the floor, we went back to Annabel's place by cab, and spent the rest of the weekend eating, drinking, and screwing.

On Monday morning, when I got to the office, there was a message in reception to ring Anthea. 'Hello, darling,' she said.

'Fred called Wally over the weekend, and everything is settled. Wally told me he'd spoken to you, so you'll know most of this already anyway. Wally says you can go as soon as you get yourself together. Have you any idea when that might be?' 'How about Wednesday?' I said. 'Not too early in the morning.' 'Oh, terrific,' she said. 'I thought you'd say give me a couple of weeks. Have you any preference as to which airline you fly? Wally says to book you business class.' 'Great,' I said. 'Pan-American, please.' I wouldn't have flown British Airways in those days if they'd paid me. I must admit, they're a little better today. In those days, they thought they were doing *you* a favour. 'Can you find me something leaving at a civilized hour in the morning? You know, like around ten?'

'I'll do my best,' she said. 'You can pick up American dollars and travellers cheques from accounts Tuesday after lunch. Don't forget to come and give me a goodbye kiss. Oh, and by the way, Fred says to stay in his apartment. Is that all right with you? If it's a problem, you can always move into an hotel, and we'll pick up the bill.' 'No, that's fine,' I said. 'It should be fun. I'll keep the bed warm for you.' She giggled as she put the 'phone down.

The next 48 hours were nothing more than a blur, really, and it was only when the Pan-Am flight took off on Wednesday morning that I looked down at Staines Reservoir, and then saw the dear old River Thames receding into the distance, that I realized that it was really happening. New York, I thought, excitedly, here I come.

ANONYMOUS

THE RUBY: VOLUME ONE

The dusty manuscripts of THE RUBY – the newly-discovered Victorian journal of erotica – recently came to light during preparations for the intended move of the British Library.

THE RUBY is even more revealing than its famously bawdy contemporaries, THE PEARL and THE OYSTER – matching if not outstripping anything previously published in this explicit field. Sexual excess follows on sexual excess, with the lusty enthusiasm for which our Victorian forefathers were famous. THE RUBY is a positive embarrassment of erotic riches: among other delights, we visit brothels, spy on servants' quarters, take lessons at a riding school, find out what a lady of leisure writes in her diary – and spend Christmas with some ladies of very easy virtue.

THE RUBY is Victorian sensuality at its most gloriousiy uninhibited.

A HODDER AND STOUGHTON PAPERBACK

RAY GORDON

THE UNINHIBITED

Attractive Donna Ryan works in a research laboratory where an explosion of lust is about to be triggered. For her boss has developed a new type of hormone treatment in the form of a skin patch, a treatment that has some astounding and unsuspected side effects. Any woman who comes into contact with a patch finds her sexual urges so dramatically increased that she loses all her inhibitions. And acts accordingly.

Donna accidentally picks up one of the patches, believing it to be an ordinary plaster. As a result, she becomes sexually alive as never before. She begins to explore amazing new realms of erotic experience, satisfying previously suppressed cravings and fantasies in an ecstatic orgy of liberated impulses. For Donna, a whole new world of sensual delights is opening up …

A HODDER AND STOUGHTON PAPERBACK

RAY GORDON

AROUSAL

Jackie is young and attractive – but her life is routine. Then, urged on by a colleague with a more highly developed lust for life, she decides to make some changes. Meeting David, an artist, in a bar, she is lured to his basement den where her sleeping sexual desires are dramatically, forcibly awakened.

This is just the start of the arousal of the stranger within Jackie. As she is drawn increasingly into a hitherto unsuspeced and darkly exciting world of sexual extremes, she finds her erotic cravings mounting to a burning fever pitch …

A HODDER AND STOUGHTON PAPERBACK